MP

By JOHN SCHEMBRA

Writers Exchange E-Publishing
http://www.writers-exchange.com

MP
Copyright 2002 JOHN SCHEMBRA
Writers Exchange E-Publishing
PO Box 372
ATHERTON QLD 4883

Published by Writers Exchange E-Publishing
http://www.writers-exchange.com

Electronic ISBN 1 920741 18 6
Print ISBN 1920741631

All characters in this book have no existence outside the imagination
of the author and have no relation to anyone bearing the same name
or names. Any resemblance to individuals known or unknown to the
author are purely coincidental.

This book began over thirty years ago, when I first

stepped foot in Vietnam as a Military Policeman.

Writing it has truly been a family project, from my wife, Charlene, with her support and encouragement providing the impetus to begin, continue, and finish the manuscript, to my daughter, Allie, who spent many hours transcribing my handwriting to the computer, to my son Scott, who provided the artwork for the cover.

To them, I dedicate this book.
John R. Schembra

PROLOGUE

3 June, 1968 2127 hrs.

The sprawling air base at Bien Hoa was lit only by the runway lights which the controllers turned off as soon as the plane came to a stop. The only other lights were evenly spaced along the perimeter wire a half mile away, and the lights from the terminal building south of the runways. The pilot shut down the plane's running lights as a jeep arrived at the boarding platform placed at the forward hatch by the air base personnel. The door opened, and Sgt. Vincent Torelli saw the interior lights had not been turned off again.

"Shit, Sarge, when are those idiots gonna learn?" Satler said, shaking his head.

"Maybe, Corporal, when the VC drops a mortar round in his cockpit."

"Never happen, Vince. Those gooks ain't no good with them mortars. Can't aim 'em for shit, then they only fire two or three rounds before they run off. Never hit anything but open space anyway."

"What's the matter, T.J.? You forget so soon what can happen?"

Vince shivered as the memory of the terrible night five months ago flooded back. He could once again hear the explosions and the gunfire, could feel the pain of his wounds, hear the cries of the dying. He closed his eyes, took a deep breath, and forced the memories from his mind.

"I don't want to be around if they get lucky, T.J. That open door is shining like a beacon, and maybe ol' Charlie will use it as an aiming point."

Torelli lit a cigarette, inhaling deeply as he watched the soldiers walking down the stairs from the plane. "Hey, T.J., how many of these guys you think will be getting back on a plane a year from now?"

"I dunno, Vince. I guess it depends how lucky they are."

"Yeah," Torelli said under his breath, "or maybe how smart they are." He turned to T.J. and said, "Let's get these newbies to the 90th before Charlie wakes up."

Phoung watched the soldiers walking across the tarmac with the binoculars he had stolen from the American deuce and a half parked in front of Three Doors earlier that evening. He could not see the unit patches on their shoulders from where he was, but he could at least count the number for his superiors.

He thought, *It does not matter how many come, we will prevail in the end. One year from now, maybe ten years from now, but we will prevail.* As the last of the Americans entered the terminal, he put the binoculars back in their case, and crawled through the brush down the low hummock he had been using as his observation point.

Sgt. Vincent Torelli stood on the table addressing the newly arrived troops. "Welcome to paradise, gentlemen. You're probably wondering what's going to happen to you now. Well, from here you will be bused to the 90th Replacement Battalion where you will spend a couple of days while your paperwork is processed and arrangements can be made to get you to your permanent units." As he looked out over the group, he could see fear and uncertainty in their faces. *Good*, he thought, *fear makes a man cautious, and a cautious man has a better chance of surviving here.*

"From here on out" he continued, "you touch nothing that isn't government issue. You do not leave the friendly confines of the 90th until ordered to do so, and starting right now, consider every gook your enemy. You will be right most of the time. Trust no one who doesn't have round eyes, and be careful of some of them. If you keep your head out of your ass, you just might survive long enough to get back here a year from now."

Torelli knew it wasn't his job to lecture these men, but he figured the more they heard it, the more likely they were to take it seriously. "I wish you all luck. Now, head out to the buses, out that door", he said, pointing to the exit behind him.

Watching them walk out the door, Torelli's mind drifted again, remembering when he had first arrived at Bien Hoa. He, too, had been a green 20 year old PFC, scared of the unknown, wondering what the next year would hold for him. He had stood at the top of the boarding platform, squinting in the bright sunlight. The heat and humidity were like a damp blanket, covering him and trying to pull him down. Now, here he was almost a year later, still alive, though somewhat worse for the wear. He was a short-timer now, with less than two weeks left until he rotated home. He thought of the last year and how it had changed his life. He was no longer the naive, sheltered, middle-class boy who had grown up in the San Francisco Bay Area. He had matured beyond his 21 years, and his eyes had been opened.

PART I
In Country

15 June, 1967 1145 hrs.

PFC Vincent Torelli couldn't believe how hot and sticky it was. When he left Travis Air Force Base in California 16 hours ago, it was 55 degrees out and foggy. As he walked across the runway to the terminal, he felt as if he was walking through a thick, hot fog. It was almost a struggle to breathe, and the smells in the air made his stomach queasy. "God damn, Sarge, what the hell is that smell?" he asked the MP sergeant leading them to the terminal.

"Garbage, private, tons of rotting garbage, plus the water buffalo shit the gooks use to fertilize their fields. Don't worry, after a couple of weeks, you won't even notice it any more."

After the short walk to the terminal, Torelli's uniform was damp with sweat. The hour he had spent waiting in the un-airconditioned building only made him hotter and more miserable. By the time the buses to the 90th Replacement Battalion arrived, he was wishing for a shower and a cold beer, neither of which he would get this day.

As he boarded his bus, he saw they were painted the usual O.D. green and had metal screens welded across the windows. He sat next to a buck sergeant and asked, "What's with the window screens?"

The sergeant looked at Vince and grinned, shaking his head. He pulled out a pack of cigarettes and offered one to Vince, saying, "Well, newbie, it's a favorite trick of the local VC to drive up alongside the buses on their motorbikes and toss a grenade or two in through the open windows. Those screens have saved a lot of GIs a lot of grief." *God*, thought Vince, *what have I gotten myself into now?* He looked out the window, nervously watching the motorbikes as they passed alongside the bus. He was quiet the rest of the trip to the replacement battalion, busily watching the people and countryside they passed along the way.

He saw that the buses were escorted by two MP gun jeeps, with three MPs in each jeep. An M-60 machine gun was on a pedestal mount welded to the floor behind the front seats. The sergeant saw him staring at the jeeps, and, nudging him with his elbow, said "That there is an M-60 machine gun. Perhaps the most effective weapon in use at this time. It fires a 7.62 mm bullet, and is effective up to 1100 yards. It can fire at a rate of 600 rounds per minute, and uses tracer, ball, armor piercing, and armor piercing incendiary ammunition. It weighs less than 25 pounds, is light enough to be hand-carried and fired, and can be set up on a bipod, and loaded in seconds. The barrel can be changed quickly, and it is the backbone of the grunts' arsenal."

"You sure know a lot about that gun," Torelli said, grinning at the sergeant. He remembered the range training at MP school at Fort Gordon, Georgia, and how much he liked shooting the M-60. He remembered the feel of the gun bucking in his hands, and the sense of power it gave him.

"Yeah, and so would you if your life depended on it", the Sergeant replied. He turned away, looking out across the fields on either side of the bus, forestalling any more conversation. Torelli settled back, and returned to watching the landscape as it passed by.

It took them about 30 minutes to get to the 90th Replacement. One gun jeep led the buses, and one followed. The machine gunners rode all the way standing up, manning their guns, as the VC liked to ambush the newly arrived troops on their way from the air base as they drove through the old plantation and marshlands east of the city. They would fire an RPG or two at the buses, then open up with small arms fire or a light machine gun, then break off and fade away into the brush before a response could be organized. The MPs would always return fire, but the effectiveness of this was never known. A sweep of the area would always be conducted afterwards, but usually nothing was found except some empty cartridge casings. This day, there was no ambush, and the buses made it safely through the main gate of the 90th.

The 90th Replacement Battalion was the processing point for all troops arriving and leaving from the huge air base at Bien Hoa. A miserable few days was spent there when arriving in country, and a joyful, though nervous, few days when processing out for the trip home. The base was relatively safe, the only problems being a few mortar rounds or rockets fired into it a couple of times a week. There was little damage in these attacks, as the base was spread out, and there were rarely any casualties. These attacks were mostly hit and run night time harassment by poorly trained local VC, pressed into service by the provincial VC commander through threats and intimidation. During the day, these local villagers tended their small vegetable gardens or rice paddies, using tools and seed provided by the U.S. and South Vietnamese governments. At night they fired mortars, rockets, or small arms at the American and South Vietnamese military bases, using weapons supplied by Hanoi. Most often, they only wished to be left alone by both governments, to live their lives simply. They held no real allegiance to either side, and did not care who was in control as long as they could live their lives in peace.

The 90th was always crowded with troops, the new arrivals trying not to stare at the old timers with their dirty, faded fatigues and dusty, cracked boots. The shoulder patches of the old timers were varied, from combat to support units from all over the country. Once processing at the 90th was completed, the old timers boarded buses for the air base and flights home, while the new arrivals were shipped to their duty stations by bus, jeep, truck, helicopter or plane.

Torelli handed his records and orders to the personnel sergeant, received his temporary billet assignment along with directions to his bunk area and the mess hall, and was told to check back in a few hours to see if transportation had been arranged to his new unit. He knew his orders assigned him to the 557th MP Company, Long Binh Post, but he had no idea where Long Binh was. He made his way to his billet, and saw it was an open-sided, canvas-covered area with rows of portable canvas bunks inside. About two thirds of the bunks were occupied. He dropped his duffle on an unoccupied bunk, took out some paper and a pencil, and began the first of many letters to his fiancee back home in San Lorenzo, California. Writing to her made the loneliness he felt all the harder to bear. They had planned to be married this year, but when he received his draft notice, they agreed to change their plans. Vince had resisted the temptation to have the wedding before he left for Nam, as he didn't know if he would ever return to her alive, and in one piece. He couldn't bear the thought of returning crippled, of being a burden to her the rest of their lives, so he convinced her to wait until he returned, giving her other reasons for the delay.

Their last night together was an awkward, difficult time for both of them. Each tried to be in good spirits for the benefit of the other, and each failed. There were many tears shed, and the sadness of parting was an awful burden to bear. Torelli still felt the weight of that burden, as he had only said goodbye four days earlier. He kept his letter lighthearted, not wanting her to know how miserable he really was.

Three hours later, he walked back to the processing point, and was told he would be picked up at 0630 hours the next day for transport to his new company. Torelli went back to his bunk to get his duffle together, and saw that the bunk next to him was now occupied.

"Theodore Josiah Satler, though nobody dares call me that. T.J. will do. So, who are you?"

"Vincent Torelli, lately of San Leandro, California. Call me Vince. Where you from, T.J.?"

"From a little town called Riggens, Idaho. Right along the Salmon River. Best steelhead fishin' anywhere."

Vince saw that T.J. was no more than 19 years old. He had a smooth, pinkish baby face, bright blue eyes, and a thin mustache. He was about 6 feet tall and thin, but looked wiry. Vince thought he would be stronger than he looked.

"So what brings you here, T.J.? You on vacation, or you planning to settle down."

"Just a little vacation, all expenses paid by the U.S. Government."

"Yeah, me too. Where're you stationed?"

"I'm being transferred to an MP company at Long Binh. Used to be with the 25th Infantry at Cu Chi northwest of here, but I got hit for the second time, so I'm gonna be an MP for the rest of my tour."

"Oh, yeah? I'm going to the 557th at Long Binh. Maybe we'll be in the same unit. You know where Long Binh is?"

"Yeah, you're next to it. I'm going to the 557th, too, so it looks like we'll be serving together. I heard this is a pretty secure area, not too much enemy activity."

"I guess if we have to be here, this isn't too bad a place. Sure glad I'm not going to be out pounding the bush somewhere."

"Yeah. Being a grunt is the shits. Humpin' the boonies all day, never knowin' what surprises Charlie has set for you, sittin' in a foxhole all night hopin' the sneaky little bastards don't shoot your ass or cut your throat, then back to humpin' the boonies again the next day, fightin' the heat, bugs, and snakes."

"Doesn't sound like my idea of fun," Vince said.

"Well, it certainly ain't been the highlight of my life! Actually, I'm glad I've been reassigned. Been wounded twice, now, and they say the third time's the charm. Sure don't want to press my luck."

"I don't blame you. If you don't mind me asking, what happened when you were wounded?"

"First time was about, oh, three and a half months ago. I'd only been in country a few weeks. We were on a two day sweep of an area south of Cu Chi. There'd been some minor contacts during the previous week, so our C.O. sent my platoon out on a recon. We was supposed to look for signs of enemy buildup or activity.

"We choppered in, and durin' the first day, we found lots of signs of enemy movement, like camp sites and stuff, though it didn't seem to be too large a force. Maybe company size or so. We struck a trail a couple a' hours later that showed signs of real recent use, and the L.T. decided we should follow it. We moved off the trail a couple a' meters and started forward. We hadn't gone too far, maybe a couple hundred meters, when Jennings, walkin' point, signaled a halt. He heard some voices up the trail, so we all hunkered down and waited. Sure enough, here comes these four VC walkin' down that trail like they was out for a Sunday stroll. The L.T. passed the word to let them get close, then to open up on his signal. Now, I didn't think that was such a good idea, 'cause we didn't know how many others were in the area, but the L.T. was a new guy, and kinda spoilin' for a fight, and he was the boss, so we open up and drop all four of 'em.

"Well, after the firin' stops, we wait a couple 'a minutes, then when nothin' happened, the L.T. tells me and four other guys to go out and check the bodies and take any papers and weapons. We went out onto the trail, and found those four gooks shot to shit, deader'n hell, so we start searchin' the bodies and collectin' their weapons. We're just startin' to move back into the bush when we start takin' fire from up the trail. I seen Johanson go down, shot through both legs. Smitty takes a round in the neck, but he makes it off the trail. I dive into the bush, and can hear the other guys movin' further off the trail. I can see six or seven gooks movin' down the trail towards me, so I figure it's about time to get my young ass outta there. I fired a burst from my 16, and started runnin' back toward the platoon. Johanson had crawled about three meters off the trail, and was layin' there, one leg broke and the other with a hole in it. He ain't movin', so I grab ahold of his collar, and start pullin' him along with me.

"Them gooks musta heard me 'cause they start layin' down some serious fire, shootin' up the jungle. Man, there was bullets flyin' all around me. All of a sudden, somethin' hits me in the back of my leg. Jesus, it felt like I'd been kicked by a mule. I went asshole over elbows onta my back. I can feel the blood pourin' outa my leg, but it didn't really hurt, at first. About this time, the rest 'a the guys came up, firin' at the gooks. Doc slapped a bandage on my leg, then went to check on Johanson and Smitty. The rest 'a the guys came back a few minutes later. They'd chased the gooks a couple hundred meters up the trail before losin' 'em. Killed two more in the process, but Youngblood took a round through his hand.

"The L.T. calls for a Medevac chopper, and we move to a clearing a little ways away. When the chopper arrived, me, Johanson, Youngblood, and Smitty are loaded up and flown to the 93rd Evac Hospital just a short ways from here. Me and Youngblood were the lucky ones. Neither of our wounds was very serious. The bullet that hit me went through the muscle 'a my leg a few inches above the knee, and come out the front. Didn't hit nothin' goin' through, so it's as good as new now, except for the scar. I spent four weeks on light duty with that one, working around the base camp, doin' all the shit details before I was sent back to the bush. Youngblood recovered o.k., too, but Johanson got a free ride home. I heard from one 'a the guys he's stationed at Fort Ord for the rest 'a his time. Smitty, well, he wasn't so lucky. Never made it outa the bush alive."

"Jesus, T.J., I'm really sorry about your friend. I didn't mean to stir up any bad memories."

"That's o.k., Vince. Smitty wasn't close to anyone in the company, kinda kept to himself. Still, it's tough to see someone you know get zapped. Kinda makes you feel real mortal, if you know what I mean."

"Yeah, I can understand that. Listen, you want to get something to eat? I'm kind of hungry."

"Yeah, that sounds good. All this talkin' has made me hungry, too."

Torelli and Satler found the mess hall, and after getting their food, made their way to an empty table. The food this day was basically the same as every day. There was some sort of meat, though most of the time it was hard to tell exactly what kind, and mashed potatoes, the dehydrated kind that is like wallpaper paste, along with a vegetable, and bread. There was always some sort of dessert, either a yellowish pudding of unknown origin, or what was supposed to be cake, and the ever-present Jell-O. The army liked to be creative with its jello, always putting something in it. If they were lucky, it would be fruit. If they weren't, it could be celery, carrots, or rice, which not only looked bad, but tasted as bad as it looked. The soldiers learned not to look too closely at their food, though, because it was that or nothing, and the discriminating eater often went hungry.

Torelli and Satler kept to themselves while they ate. When they were done, they bused their table and started to walk back to their bunks. Torelli lit a cigarette, offering one to Satler.

"No thanks, man, never use the stuff."

"T.J., I sure hope you don't mind me asking, but I don't

really know what to expect here. You've been in country for a while, so maybe you can help me out?"

"I know how you feel, Vince. I'll be happy to help, much as I can."

"You said you were wounded twice. What happened the second time?"

"That was no big deal. Just got a gash along my ribs from some shrapnel. It seems ol' Charlie didn't take to us settin' up camp in his territory, so one night he dropped a few mortar rounds on us. I was on watch along the perimeter when the first round hit. One 'a them was pretty close to our hole. My flak jacket kept it from bein' worse, but it took 9 stitches to fix me up. Just got 'em out a week ago."

"How long you been here, T.J.?"

"Almost six months now. Only six to go, then it's back to the world for me."

"I envy you, man," Torelli said. "I'm just starting my tour. Only been here about seven hours, but it seems like seven days."

"Yeah, I know, but the time will go fast enough. Let me give you a little advice my platoon leader gave me when I first arrived in country. You can never, ever let your guard down. If you want to survive this place, you always got to be ready for the worst. Never trust any gook, any time, anywhere, even our ARVN counterparts. You got to look out for yourself. Be smart, man, and the chances you will make it outta here in one piece are pretty good. Be dumb, and you'll still make it outta here, except you may be in a box when you go."

"Thanks, T.J. I appreciate you telling me this stuff," Torelli said, yawning. "I'm about ready to call it a day. It was a long plane ride, and I'm really beat."

"Yeah, me too. Let's go, Vince."

They walked back to their bunks, talking about their homes and lives back in the world. They realized they did not have a lot in common, coming from such different backgrounds. Each wondered why they liked the other, and felt they could trust each other, that he was someone who could be relied on.

When they got back to their bunks, Torelli grabbed his kit, and made his way to the latrine where he stripped to his shorts and washed as well as he could, since there weren't any showers for the new guys. He felt better afterwards, and put on clean undershorts and a t-shirt, though by the time he finished, he was sweating profusely, as he was not yet acclimated to the heat and humidity.

After he shaved and rinsed his face, he looked at himself in the mirror. He saw a good-looking, olive-skinned 20 year old with green eyes. His 175 pounds filled out his 5'10" frame, though he had very little body fat. His shoulders were broad, and his waist was slim, his chest and arms well muscled.

As he stared in the mirror, his thoughts turned back to the day he had gotten his draft notice. He was surprised when his mother handed him the brown envelope with tears in her eyes. He did not realize what it was until he opened it, and saw it actually did say "Greetings from the President of the United States." Vince couldn't believe he had been drafted. He thought he still was exempt with the student deferment he'd received a year and a half ago when he started college at San Francisco State University. He turned to his mother, and took her in his arms, hugging her tightly.

"It'll be OK, Ma. Don't worry, it'll be OK" he whispered to her as she sobbed softly into his shoulder. He dreaded having to tell his father when he came home from work. A World War Two veteran, he had been wounded in Sicily while a grunt with the Big Red One, and knew firsthand the terrors of war. Those were terrors he did not want his sons to experience, and had many times expressed his fears they would end up in "that funny sounding place, having to fight."

He arrived at Fort Lewis, Washington, one month later for basic training. After ten weeks, he received his orders to MP school at Fort Gordon, Georgia. Ten weeks later he graduated and caught a bus for Atlanta where he had a flight home for a two-week leave. He carried orders with him assigning him to the 557th MP Co., Long Binh, South Vietnam.

Sighing deeply, he pulled his thoughts back to the present and went back to his bunk. Covering himself only with the sheet, he lay on his back, staring at the canvas roof. He was very tired, but found it difficult to sleep.

"Still awake, Vince?" Satler asked.

"Yeah, can't seem to get to sleep."

"I know. I don't think I've had a decent night's sleep in the six months I've been here."

"You have much family in Idaho, T.J.?"

"Just my folks. Got one sister, but she moved to Boise 2 years ago, and got married. Don't hear from her much. Got an aunt and uncle and 3 cousins livin' outside St. Louis, but I haven't seen them for 10 years. One thing I know for sure is I won't be goin' back to Riggens to live when I get out. Town's too small. No work unless I wanna get into mining or be a hunting and fishing guide, and that ain't for me."

He was silent for so long that Vince thought he had fallen asleep.

"I miss my Ma mostly," T.J. said, quietly. "Never was too close to my Dad. He was always workin', never around much, and when he was, he was usually drunk. Used to get mean when he was drinkin'."

"Doesn't sound like he was much fun to be around when you were growing up."

"Naw, he wasn't, but we never wanted for anything. Just wish he treated Ma better."

14

Torelli and Satler talked long into the night, and by the time sleep overtook them, they knew all about each other, and had become firm friends.

16 June, 1967   557th MP Co., Long Binh Post

Torelli and Satler were picked up by an MP jeep at 0700 hrs. the next morning and driven to the 557th MP Company HQ. The ride took about 15 minutes, and their driver, a very large and very black Spec. 4 by the name of Sanders, drove in silence, refusing to respond to any of Satler's or Torelli's questions. The route took them down Hwy 316, past fields once cultivated but now abandoned and barren of trees and bushes to deny the VC the cover he needed to carry out his terrorist activities. There was an occasional rice paddy, but most of the area had been cleared as a security zone for Long Binh.

At the main gate of Long Binh, they were passed through by MPs from the 615th MP Co., whose main responsibility was not only gate security, but Long Binh patrol duties. They saw a row of trucks being searched by the MPs, just inside the gate in a holding area. Vince saw the MPs had all the civilians out of the trucks, and were searching their bags and clothing, as well as the trucks. He later found out it was standard procedure to search all vehicles carrying Vietnamese workers onto the base. The workers were always searched unless escorted by American MPs. Since there were several thousand civilians working on the base, it was a necessary precaution.

The number of VC and VC sympathizers on the base was not known, but there had to be a significant number who were spying and gathering information for later use. The searches were done to keep sabotage to a minimum, by denying the enemy access to information, weapons and explosives. It was not unusual to find crudely drawn though accurate maps of key areas of the post hidden in the clothing or belongings of a Vietnamese employee.

15

When the MPs found someone in possession of those items, they were taken away for interrogation by American and Vietnamese intelligence officers. Once the interrogation was over, they were turned over to the ARVN Military authorities for further "interrogation", and nobody seemed to know what became of them. Mostly, they were sent to a P.O.W. camp outside Bien Hoa, usually with no trial. Some simply disappeared, their fate never being known, and U.S. military authorities seldom asked.

Though Vietnamese applying for jobs on post were screened as well as possible, it was not known where their true allegiance lay. It was a common practice for the local VC command to infiltrate as many agents as they could into the big American base. Every opportunity for sabotage would be utilized to frustrate and impede the American war machine. If the Americans could be hurt at their largest, most secure bases, it would prove that the U.S. and its puppet, the Saigon regime, was not omnipotent, and was ineffective and incompetent in administering the country. The people would see the true face of the Saigon Government, and would join the freedom fighters from the North in a "General Uprising" to overthrow the current government, and reunite north and south once again under a communist rule.

As they drove to the 557th Company Area, Torelli was surprised at the size of Long Binh. He had heard there were 20,000 Americans there, and he could believe it. Sanders pulled into the gravel parking area next to the CQ office, and parked by the front entrance. As they got out of the vehicle, Satler said, "been a real pleasure, Bro" to the driver, at which Sanders slowly turned his head and stared at him. The look in Sanders eyes made Satler shiver involuntarily. Satler got the distinct impression it was better not to antagonize Sanders, and said, "Hey, man, no offense, OK? Just tryin' to be friendly." Without a word, Sanders backed up and drove off.

"Whoa, T.J., that's one scary guy!" Torelli said.

"Yeah, man. I get the feeling he don't care too much for new guys."

As Sanders drove off, a voice boomed from the open doorway of the CQ, "If you two are replacements, get your sorry asses in here." The voice belonged to Sergeant First Class Burton Polachowski, known as "Ski" to those who knew him well.

Ski was the kind of soldier referred to as a "lifer" by the troops, a career soldier who went by the book. Most lifers were not well liked because they tended to be too "regulation" to suit the draftees or four year enlistees. Even so, Sgt. Polachowski was respected and well liked by the men in the 557th.

He had grown up on a farm outside Sun Prairie, Wisconsin, and had enlisted in the army at the age of 17, shortly after Pearl Harbor. The Japanese sneak attack had so angered him and stirred his sense of patriotism that he, along with tens of thousands of other young Americans, had gone to the local recruitment office and signed up. He had lied about his age so he could join, against his mother's wishes. He told her he was determined to join, with or without her consent, and though she did not approve, she did not protest his decision.

Ski found he liked the strict regimentation of military life, and grew to enjoy the army, re-enlisting each time his commitment was up. Here he was, 26 years later, involved in his third war, and still the patriot, still serving his country.

He was a solidly built man, stocky and strong as an ox. Though he only stood 5'8" in his boots, no one challenged his authority. With his crew cut grey hair and deeply lined face, he had the look of an angry bulldog that caused others to believe it was not a good idea to piss him off. Those who really knew him had come to realize his true

17

nature was just the opposite. He was always willing to dispense advice, always good, and to lend a sympathetic ear to others' problems. To him, the men in his company were his family, and he took it upon himself to guide them along. Wounded twice in World War II, he had earned a Bronze Star on Guadalcanal, and a Silver Star on Okinawa. He received his second Silver Star in Korea, along with his third Purple Heart. He nearly died that day in Korea from shell fragments that severed an artery in his leg. It was his good fortune to have a medic in the foxhole next to him when he was hit. He ended up at Letterman General Hospital in San Francisco to recover, then was assigned to a recruitment office in Madison, Wisconsin, not far from his Sun Prairie home. Three years later, he was promoted to Sergeant First Class, and re-assigned as the First Sergeant at the MP school, Fort Gordon, Georgia. In 1966, he was assigned as Company Sergeant for the 557th MP Company when they were deployed to Vietnam. When his first tour of duty was over, he extended, opting to stay another six months.

He had never married, though he had come close once. His bride to be had begun to pressure him to leave the army life he loved and settle down in one place. Three weeks before the wedding, he told her he couldn't give up the army, that it was his life. She told him he had to choose, the army or her. Two days after that, he re-upped for the third time, and she said goodbye forever. Ski never regretted making that decision.

Torelli and Satler sat through the welcoming speech by the First Sergeant, which in reality was nothing more than a lesson in surviving the next year.

"Torelli, you're new in country, and don't know shit about this place. You got a rough education ahead of you, son, so pay attention. You understand me?"

"Yeah, Sarge, I understand."

"Good. First of all, this place ain't like nothing you ever

imagined. It's hot, it's dirty, it smells bad, it's filled with disease and death, and most of the gooks don't care if you live or die. Never, and I mean never, put your trust in any of them, even those supposedly on our side. Old men, women, kids, the whores, none of them can be trusted. You never know where their loyalty lies. And let me tell you, they can be real creative in ways to kill ya."

Turning to T.J, he said, "Now you, Satler, you been here awhile, so you got a pretty good idea of what's goin' on. Only thing is, you ain't in the jungle no more, boy. It's a different kinda war in the city. You ain't humpin' the boonies now, so you pay attention, too. This country is the anus of the world. It's worse here than any place I ever been, and this war is worse than the other two I been in put together. At least in those two, I knew who the enemy was, where the lines were drawn. Here, shit, anybody could be the enemy, and there ain't no lines. Let me tell you, boys, I got a bad feeling about this one. I got three more months here, and a year left in this enlistment. If I make it outa here, I think I'll be taking my pension then. I figure it's time for me to quit. War is a young man's game, now."

"C'mon, Sarge, you're startin' to depress me," Satler said, grinning uncomfortably.

"Sorry about that, but I get to talking, and sometimes don't know when to stop. You boys need to know what it's like around here. I'm going to have Corporal White take you to your hootch and get you settled. Your duffle bags should already be there. After you unpack your gear, go get some chow, then be back here at 1000 hours. Sgt. Anderson will get you going on some orientation. I'll be back later this afternoon, and check on you then."

Corporal Andrew White sat at his desk outside the First Sergeant's office listening to Ski brief the new guys. He had heard this speech, or rather several variations of it, many times in the eight months he had been serving as company clerk. Most of the time it was given to replacements for the guys that rotated home after their year's tour was up, but sometimes it was given to replacements for guys wounded or killed. When that happened, Cpl. White knew, the replacements heard Ski's "anus of the world" speech, as these two had. He entered Ski's office on cue, and led the two new guys to their hootch.

"Here's where you guys will be bunking," Corporal White said, pointing to two empty bunks. "Make yourselves comfortable. Get your gear stowed away, and get something to eat. Mess hall's out this door and three buildings down on the left. Just follow your noses. Meet me back at my office in an hour and a half."

"Hey, Corporal, where's the showers?" Torelli asked.

"Out that door and to the left. All the way down. It's the last building on the right. Don't expect any hot water, though. We're lucky to have showers. See you in 90 minutes," he said, leaving the building.

Torelli and Satler started unpacking their uniforms and gear, placing them in the footlockers by the end of the bed. Vince saw that about half of the bunks were occupied, most of the men sleeping, having worked the night shift. As Vince and T.J. unpacked, they saw that the last bunk by the door was occupied by the driver of the jeep that had brought them to the company area. He was reading a book, and seemed oblivious to them as they got settled. Torelli stripped to his shorts, grabbed a clean towel, a pair of undershorts, and his soap, and headed to the showers. As he passed Sanders bunk, Sanders lowered his book and watched him walk by, his face expressionless. Vince grinned at him, and said "How ya doing?" Sanders nodded, then raised his book and continued reading. Vince saw the title was "Journey to the Center of the Earth" by Jules Verne, which surprised him, as Sanders did not seem the type to be interested in that kind of novel. Vince walked to the showers, and found that the hootch maids were washing their laundry at the far end. Figuring it was no time to be modest, he stripped off his shorts, and took a quick, cold shower. Though the walk back to the hootch was short, he was sweating by the time he got back.

Satler came back from the mess hall while Vince was dressing.

"Food ain't too bad here, Vince. You hungry?"

"Nah. Besides, we gotta be back in a little while for orientation."

Orientation for the new guys usually lasted a week. The first day, they were issued their weapons, an M-16 rifle and Colt .45 pistol, along with their web gear, steel helmet and MP helmet liner and arm band. The helmet liner was fiberglass and painted black with a 1" white band and 1"red band around the bottom. MP was painted in white 3" letters on the front. On the right side was the double axe in gold with a green sword between them, the 18th MP Brigade insignia, and on the left side was the 8 point green and gold star insignia of the 95th MP Battalion. The arm band was black vinyl, and had the 18th MP Brigade patch sewed on it above the 3" white MP letters. It was worn on the left shoulder

They were given a tour of the company area and of Long Binh, then spent some time filling out pay forms, signing for their equipment, and picking up their bedding and other gear they would need during the next year. They were allowed to go to the PX to buy some essentials, then were assigned work details for the rest of the day.

During the rest of their orientation, Torelli and Satler were schooled in Vietnamese customs, the layout of Long Binh, the makeup of the surrounding countryside and Bien Hoa City, and the type of duties they would be doing. Often their time was spent learning the fine art of filling and stacking sandbags around the ammo bunker.

A couple of days later they spent the day at the firearms range, being checked out on the weapons they would be using. They fired their M-16 rifles, .45 pistols, M-60 machine gun, and M-79 grenade launcher. They were also instructed in the use of the .50 caliber machine gun. It was unlikely any of them would ever have the occasion to use one, but if one thing had been learned, it was that it paid to be prepared. Their instruction included the proper use of each weapon, how to field strip and clean them, how to clear malfunctions, how to maximize the firepower of each, and their limitations. Much time was spent on the importance of proper and continuous care. In a climate such as Southeast Asia's, rust and corrosion could start forming after only a few hours. Weapon failure was a real problem with a firearm that wasn't properly maintained. They were told that each weapon in their care would be inspected every time they turned it, and they were to strip, clean, and oil each weapon before turning it in to the arms room.

Their duty shift would start each day at either 0600 or 1800 hours by standing guard mount in the company area. The day would end twelve hours later.

There was plenty of time during their orientation when their "training" consisted of filling and stacking sandbags around bunkers and hooches, cleaning weapons from the arms room, loading magazines and ammo belts, and raking the gravel in the company area. Torelli and Satler's real orientation began after their duty hours, when they could talk to the others in the company. Their real school began then, and they learned what it took to survive in a war with a hidden enemy, where there seemed to be no rules, and the enemy was everywhere. They learned that death awaited them with open arms around every corner, just behind each door, in every bush, and along each stretch of road. No one could be trusted except the people they worked with. They listened carefully to the stories the others told of their day.

"Wild Bill" Hickok told of how he and his partner,

22

Jackson, had to stand by with two dead bodies found floating down the Dong Nai River. One of the PBR's found them and hauled them onto the bank, where an Army ambulance called the "meat wagon" would pick them up. During the three hours it took for the meat wagon to get there, he and Jackson had to stand guard over them. Hickok said the bodies were most likely peasants or village officials from up river, murdered by the VC as part of their terror campaign to keep the villagers in line.

"Chances are they'll never be identified," Hickok said. He described in detail how the bodies had been mutilated by the VC, and said they had been in the river for several days. The ambulance from Long Binh would take the bodies to the ARVN III Corps Compound in Bien Hoa, and turn them over to the Vietnamese Military Police, the Quan Canhs. Vince was surprised to learn that a dozen bodies a month were pulled from the river. Most were Vietnamese civilians, though sometimes they were NVA or VC soldiers. Occasionally ARVN soldiers floated down, and once in a great while the body of an American soldier, who had been murdered while on some "unofficial" business, like black marketeering, running prostitutes, or drug running was pulled from the river. These soldiers were always listed as killed in action to avoid any embarrassment to the military or the soldier's family.

Renfro told of sitting on a checkpoint in the city with the Quan Cahns and a Cahn Sat, a Vietnamese National Policeman, called "white mice" because of the white uniform shirts they wore. They had set up in a vacant lot along Hwy 1 just around a bend in the road. Renfro was the jeep driver, with "Andy" Anderson riding shotgun, and "Booger" Baines as machine gunner. They met their Vietnamese counterparts at 0800 hours, and began conducting random checks of people and vehicles traveling through the city, looking for contraband, weapons, and undocumented civilians. If a civilian was found without proper papers, it usually meant that they were draft dodgers, deserters, VC or NVA. Renfro told Vince and T.J. they sometimes would find weapons or explosives headed for the local VC cadre's use against the ARVNs or Americans. In particular, they concentrated on men and women 10 to 40 years old, as they were the most likely to fit one of the categories of people they were looking for. "Booger" Baines job, as the machine gunner, was to remain alert at the gun whenever a random check was being done on a vehicle or person. Renfro and Anderson provided cover with their M-16's for the QC's who did the actual inspections.

These checkpoints were somewhat effective in finding contraband of all types being transported to the Saigon area via Hwy 1 from enemy supply points northwest of Bien Hoa. This contraband, usually consisting of arms, ammunition, or explosives, was destined for the VC that operated in the Saigon-Bien Hoa area. Never were any hard core VC or NVA captured, as the drivers were only sympathizers recruited by the VC to make the deliveries. Though thoroughly interrogated by Vietnamese and American Intelligence officers, they never provided any useful information, simply because they were not told anything other than where to pick up their load, and where to drop it off.

Parker and Gilchrist told of a traffic accident between an ARVN deuce and a half and a civilian Lambretta taxi. Three people were killed when the Lambretta driver tried to turn left in front of the truck, and was struck broadside. Two women and an old man were killed, and the driver slightly injured when he was thrown clear by the collision. Parker said they waited over an hour for the Vietnamese Accident Investigation Team to arrive. In the meantime, they treated the injured and got them off to the dispensary at the III Corps Compound, cleared the roadway, and placed the three dead along the shoulder of the road, covering them with a poncho. Gilchrist couldn't get over the fact that no one seemed to care that three people had just been killed. They merely went about their business, walking around the bodies.

Later, after Gilchrist left, Parker told Vince and T.J. that Gilchrist was having a hard time adjusting to being out on the road. He was nervous all the time, jumping at shadows, and had begun talking to himself. He kept his M-16 locked and loaded all the time, set on full auto. More than once, for no apparent reason, he pointed it at groups of people as they drove. He wore his helmet and flak jacket all the time, and refused to allow Parker to drive off the main roads while on patrol. Parker said he was worried about how Gilchrist would react if they got in a dangerous situation. He doubted his stability, and planned to talk to SFC Polachowski again the next day and ask for another partner. Vince decided at that time to keep a close eye on Gilchrist, and avoid being teamed with him if at all possible.

That night Vince and T.J. were at the EM Club to celebrate the completion of their orientation. They were scheduled to begin training on town patrol the next day, and were looking forward to getting off post. Vince had been assigned to a gun jeep with Sanders and Hickok. Normally, being the junior man would mean he was the machine gunner, but for the next few days, he would be riding shotgun. T.J. was assigned a checkpoint with Jackson and Gilchrist, along with two Quan Cahns and a Cahn Sat.

Vince ordered a hamburger and fries from the EM Club's kitchen, and another round of beers for Parker, T.J., and Jackson. When he came back to the table, he saw the three of them talking quietly. As he approached, he heard Parker saying "... about to lose it, man. I mean he's

25

real shaky. He could go off any time now, and Ski won't take him off the road." Turning to T.J., he said, "You and Jackson got to work with him tomorrow. You guys better keep a close eye on him. He's ready to break, and when he does, there could be big trouble."

T.J. said, "You said Ski knows all about it, but won't take him off the road? Why not?"

"Well, actually it's not that he won't, it's that the LT won't let him," Jackson said, lowering his voice even further. "We're short handed, and activity seems to be picking up a bit lately. Until you new guys are trained, we need all the bodies we can get on duty. There's been a lot of talk lately about increased enemy activity around An Loc and Loc Ninh, too. Seems the VC are gettin' bolder. Even been some reports of NVA regulars showin' up in the area. I heard from some grunt friends from the 199th that they had some contact with a pretty good-sized enemy outfit north of us three days ago. They said they found NVA bodies after the firefight, and they all had new uniforms and equipment. He said it's a bad sign, and he thinks something big is comin' down."

Parker snorted, saying "I don't think so. I think the gooks are just sending replacements. They've been hit pretty hard over the last few months, and I'll bet they're just trying to replace their losses."

Vince sat down in the empty chair. "Of course, I don't know, being new here," Vince said, "but from everything I've been hearing lately, I would agree with those grunts from the 199th."

"O.K., newbie," Parker said, laughing, "now that you've graced us with your wisdom, you can pass out those beers."

Vince and T.J. had a couple more beers, then made their way back to their hootch. As Vince was sitting on his bunk writing a letter, Sanders walked over and said, "Listen, newbie, tomorrow we'll be workin' together, so you watch, you listen, you learn. You don't do nuthin' I don't tell you to do. You can ask questions all you want, but if and when I tell you to do somethin', you do it with no question or comment, and without hesitation. If I tell you to shut up, you shut up. You see anythin' that don't look right, you tell me. Understand?"

"Yeah, I understand."

"Good. I'm drivin' tomorrow, you ride shotgun, and Wild Bill's the gunner. Get some sleep."

As Sanders walked to his bunk, T.J. said in his best John Wayne voice, "Ya got that, Pilgrim?"

Vince laughed, then said, "You know, in spite of how he comes off, I think I'd rather be working with him than anyone else. He seems to really know what's going on, and how to handle himself. I think I got lucky being assigned a jeep with him. Anyway, I better get some rest. See you in the morning, and watch your ass tomorrow, T.J."

"For sure, GI. 'Nite, Vince."

23 June, 1967   0600 hours

Vince stood at attention at his first guard mount, wearing his web belt and MP helmet liner, holding his M-16 at port arms while the LT and Ski made their way through the ranks, inspecting uniforms and equipment. Once in awhile the LT would inspect a rifle or pistol, but mostly it was a routine performed each morning because of military regulations and procedures.

On the ground next to each MP was the rest of their gear. Their steel helmets, flak jackets, M-60 machine guns and ammo, M-79 grenade launcher, grenades, and extra M-16 ammo was all neatly stacked for inspection. Lt. Carlton finished the inspection, then dismissed the men, reminding them to be careful, as he did after every guard mount. As the formation broke up into groups, Sanders approached Vince and told him to collect his gear and follow him. "Wild Bill went to the motor pool to get our jeep," Sanders said. "We'll meet him out front."

The motor pool was located across the road that ran by the 557th. Sanders and Torelli walked through the company area to the road, arriving just as Wild Bill drove up. They loaded their gear while Hickok mounted the M-60 and loaded a belt of ammo in the gun. Sanders climbed in the driver's seat, and motioned Torelli to get in. When all was ready, he drove off, heading for the main gate. Sanders turned right outside the main gate onto Hwy 316. A few minutes later, he turned left onto Hwy 15, and headed south into Bien Hoa City. As they entered the city, Sanders pointed to the left, and said, "See that alley over there, just inside the city limits?"

"Yeah. What about it?"

"That's Death Alley. You don't go in there unless it is absolutely necessary, and never alone. It ain't called that without good reason."

Vince saw a narrow alley leading off the main road, lined on both sides by two story buildings. There was barely enough room for a jeep to drive down it, and after about 30 meters, the alley curved to the right. It was littered with trash and garbage, and several dogs roamed freely along its dusty length. There were several young men loitering at the entrance. They watched the MP jeep closely as it passed. Sanders said "We call those guys 'Cowboys'. They're youth gangs that are at the least VC sympathizers. Most are draft dodgers, some are VC agents, and all are dangerous. They are the main reason you don't go down there, day or night. There's been lots of GIs and ARVNs who got in big trouble goin' to the whorehouse in there. They've been beat up, robbed, and even killed. You ever have to go in there, you better take a couple'a guys with you. Best if you don't go in there at all. That's Indian country, man, and belongs to the bad guys."

"I'll remember that," Vince said.

As they continued into the city, Vince was surprised at

the number of people walking around. There was a constant stream of pedestrians on both sides of the road. The road itself was just wide enough for two vehicles to pass abreast. Though the roadway was asphalt, the shoulders were dirt, hard packed by the thousands of feet passing by each day. During the monsoon season, it would become a muddy quagmire, with small rivers of water running on both sides of the road.

Vince saw all the American products displayed in bins in front of every building. He asked Sanders about this, and Sanders told him, "That's the black market. The G.I's from Long Binh and the air base buy the stuff at the PX, and trade it to the Gooks for just about everything. They can get tailoring done, souvenirs, weapons, or one of the whores. The Gooks'll trade anything for PX stuff."

"Don't we ever do anything about it?" Vince asked.

Hickock said, "It ain't hardly worth the effort. As fast as we pick the stuff up, it's replaced. And we can't get the White Mice to do nuthin', since the local Police Chief is paid protection money from the sellers."

"We could spend all day confiscatin' stuff, and not make a dent. The word gets around too fast for us to get it all. Most 'a the stuff gets hidden before we really have an opportunity to seize it, and we can't go inside their buildings to search unless the White Mice let us, and that ain't going to happen" Sanders said. "So all we can do is try to get the GI's that sell or trade the stuff to them. Those guys got to know that some of this stuff, like food and medical supplies, goes directly to the VC. I guess all they're interested in is making a buck."

As they drove through the city, Vince asked lots of questions. Sanders and Hickock answered all of them, and told him many things about the city. He learned where the whorehouses and bars were, where they were most likely to find GI's off Post, since the whole city had been declared off limits. They pointed out the Combined Police

29

Station, known as the CPP, the main gate to the large American air base, and the Vietnamese Army III Corps Compound. Hickock pointed out a butcher shop with dog haunches and butchered monkeys hanging out front.

"You got to be kidding me," Vince exclaimed as he looked at the shop. "These people really eat dogs and monkeys?"

"Yeah," Sanders said. "And rats. Remember, these people don't raise cattle or sheep or any other meat animal, so they make do with what they have. Some people actually breed and raise dogs to sell to the butcher shops. Monkey is fairly rare, so most of the time what they call "monkey" is really rat. There are millions of 'em around. Wait until you get on nights. You'll see 'em then."

Hickock said, "We'll show you a couple 'a little cafes that are safe to eat at. They use black market Spam for their meat, and nobody's ever gotten sick from eatin' there. Stay away from any other places. They ain't safe, and you never know what you're eatin'."

Vince learned where Cambo Alley and Turkey Road were, and that Turkey Road was o.k. to travel at night since it followed along the air base south perimeter. They showed him Three Doors, a favorite whorehouse for both American and Vietnamese soldiers, and where the two most popular bars were, the Cherry Bar and Susie's. They drove to the PMO in Di An, a few miles south of the city, then went as far south along Hwy 316 as Newport, crossing the bridge over the Saigon river. They told Vince that Newport was where they usually escorted convoys, as a lot of cargo ships came and went there. On the way back, they stopped at a little cafe in Thu Duc, and had a bowl of soup similar to won ton soup. They bought fresh baked bread and Ba Mui Ba beer, which means 33 in Vietnamese. The M.P.'s called it "Tiger Piss."

The signs of war were all around. Blasted and burnt jungle along the roadway, bullet scarred buildings, large areas cleared of vegetation, barbed wire everywhere, helicopters of all types constantly passing overhead, jets en route to bombing or ground combat support missions, troops on the move. Every so often, a convoy passed loaded with soldiers or supplies, and weapons were everywhere. The smell of diesel was thick in the air, and the noise from the vehicles and aircraft was constant and loud.

Sanders drove back to the MP company area for chow a couple of hours later, parking the jeep by the mess hall. As they ate their lunch, he told Vince to stop waving back at all the Vietnamese people, because they were not waving to say hello. That was their way of saying "come here" when they wanted something. Sanders told Vince he usually ignored them, unless they appeared frightened or were upset.

"Hey, newbie," Sanders said, "did you see the PMO next to the security area? That's where the 615th MPs hold their prisoners until they can be picked up or transferred to LBJ."

"LBJ? What's LBJ?"

"Long Binh Jail. It's the main stockade for this area. You'll see it when we drive by later today."

"We going to take a look around it?"

"No. We are gonna go in that PMO, so you know what the place is like. There might be a time you need to leave a prisoner in one of the holding cells. Finish up, and we'll stop by there on the way out."

They finished their lunch, then drove to the main gate, parking by the PMO near the perimeter fence. Vince followed Sanders inside, and saw there were three holding cells about six feet wide by 5 feet deep, each in a row along the wall on the right side of the building. The back wall was composed of cement blocks, like one side wall of the first and third cells. The other walls dividing the cells and the doors were made of 1" steel bars from the floor to the ceiling. The doors had a slot in them at floor level so food

31

trays could be passed in. There was a wooden bench bolted to the floor of the cells along the back wall. There were no toilets in the cells, or sinks or running water. Everything was painted o.d. green, including the benches. "Looks like a real nice place," Torelli said.

"Yeah, real nice," Sanders replied, grinning. "Sometimes they get some really violent or obnoxious prisoners. There's one of them steel conexes outside next to the building. You know, those boxes about eight feet high and six feet wide, and maybe 15 feet long they use to ship supplies on those container ships."

"Yeah, I saw it. I wondered what that was for."

"Some smart MP got it from somewhere, blow torched a 6" by 12" window in the door, and put it by the PMO as an extra holding cell. They only put the meanest prisoners in there."

"Must get pretty hot in there during the day. Isn't there any other ventilation except for that little window in the door?"

"That's it. It's solid steel, and during the day, a prisoner in there can last only an hour or so before the sun beating down on the top has him begging to be brought inside the PMO, with promises to be on his best behavior. At night, it takes about two or three hours before the heat and mosquitos have the same result. To the 615th, this is the best attitude adjustment tool they have."

As they walked out to the jeep, Torelli grinned at Sanders, and said, "It must make model prisoners out of the worst of the lot."

"That it does, newbie," Sanders said.

As they drove out the main gate and turned toward town, Sanders explained their radio procedures to Vince. "Every day we get a new two word identifier and frequency to keep the enemy and other GI's from eaves-dropping. Today's code is "Sydney Oiler", frequency 63.40. It ain't unusual for the V.C. to use captured

32

or stolen American or ARVN radios, and listen in to find out troop or convoy movements. Sometimes they can get enough information to set up some pretty good ambushes. They've also used the radios to give fake orders and assignments to our units patrolling the city or providing convoy security. The new frequency and identifier each day makes it very hard for them to figure out what unit is on the frequency, since we only use our numbers, not our unit name."

The individual M.P. units, to further complicate matters, used different call signs each day. Vince's unit call sign today was 3 Bravo. Tomorrow, working the same detail and area, they could be 4 Delta or Tango 6. Each morning at guard mount they were given that day's identifier, frequency and call sign. A different set was given to the night shift at their guard mount.

Once they exited the gate, they were back on the main road, heading north on Hwy 1 to Ho Nai village to check out a report of a 2 ½ ton truck that had run off the road, and overturned down an embankment. The truck was an ARVN army cargo truck, and the driver could not be found. When they arrived, they found the truck on its side, about 25 feet down the embankment 150 meters from the village. Military clothing was scattered everywhere, and they could not see the driver anywhere around the truck.

"He may still be inside," Hickock said. "Somebody's gotta go check it out, Sanders."

"I'll go," Vince said, getting out of the jeep, and starting to walk toward the truck.

"Hold it, Newbie. Hickock, you see anything unusual about this?" Sanders asked.

"Yeah. How come the cargo's still laying around? It should've all disappeared by now."

"That's what I was wondering. Hey, Torelli, you want to go down there, you can, but you might want to take your

33

'16 with you. Me? I'm gonna take it a little slower, check things out a bit. Hey, Hickock, why you suppose the gooks ain't stolen everything they can from the wreck? Call in the numbers on that truck. We're all gonna take this one slow. Meanwhile, Torelli, you get that '16 of yours, and keep your eyes open."

Jackson, Gilchrist, and T.J. set up their checkpoint along Hwy 1 by a vacant lot across from the Bien Hung theater in the center of town. Gilchrist remained at the M-60 while Jackson and T.J. assisted the Quan Canhs and Canh Sat in stopping vehicles and people for searches and I.D. checks. T.J. found this duty very boring. All he did was stand guard while the Quan Canhs and Canh Sat questioned the Vietnamese Nationals, checked their I.D.'s, or searched vehicles. After a couple of hours in the sun, Jackson walked across the street to a small cafe and bought cokes for everyone. T.J. asked him if it was always this boring. Jackson said it was always this way. Everyone knows about the checkpoints shortly after they were set up, and anyone who didn't want to go through merely took a different route.

"Once in a while we get lucky and find some weapons or ammo or other stuff being delivered to the local V.C., but not very often. Relax and enjoy it. This is the easiest duty you can get."

During the next hour, T.J. noticed that Gilchrist had started muttering to himself. As each vehicle was waved over, he carefully followed its progress with the M-60 until it came to a stop. He then kept the gun trained on the occupants, seemingly oblivious to the fact that the Quan Canhs and Canh Sat were also in the line of fire. T.J. casually moved to the side, out of the way, and gradually moved closer to Gilchrist. As he neared the jeep, he could hear him saying, "Watch 'em now, careful, always careful. Are you the enemy? Are you? So careful. Can't let down, gotta watch 'em all the time."

After a few minutes, T.J. walked over to Jackson, and said, "Hey man, Gilchrist's talkin' to himself. He's got this look in his eyes like he's not with us. He doesn't seem to see or hear nuthin' else. He's scarin' me, man."

"Yeah, I've been watchin' him. I think we need to get him down off that gun, like, now."

"I agree. I'll take over if you can get him down."

"O.K. You watch him carefully, O.K.?"

Jackson called to Gilchrist, "Hey, Larry, come on down here and give us a hand. You're due for a break from that gun. T.J.'ll man the gun for a while."

"I'm o.k. Jackson. I gotta stay with it."

"No, man, come on down. Let T.J. do it for a bit."

"How am I going to watch 'em? I gotta be careful, gotta watch out."

"We'll watch 'em for you, Larry. Me and T.J. C'mon down now."

"You sure, Jackson? I mean, we gotta be careful."

"We will be, Larry, I promise."

"O.K., if you say so." Gilchrist jumped down, and as T.J. was climbing up, the radio crackled to life, ordering them to go assist Sanders with the overturned truck.

As they were driving to meet Sanders, T.J. told Jackson, "First chance we get, we gotta talk to Ski. This guy is scary. He's gonna break, Jackson. I've seen it before, with the 25th."

"I know T.J. I'll see Ski tonight. I'll take care of it."

Hickock called the PMO on the radio, and advised them of the situation. They advised that a second gun jeep was enroute to assist, and they were to secure the area and the truck, and wait until the other unit got there before doing anything. As they waited, they kept a close watch on the two dozen or so villagers milling about the area. They each kept an eye on a different group to ensure their safety. Sanders bad feelings about this was rubbing off on Vince. He felt uneasy, and remained alert to a possible trap. When the other gun jeep arrived, Sanders saw it was Jackson, Gilchrist and T.J.

"Jackson, you come with me and Torelli to check out the truck. Wild Bill, you and Satler look sharp on those 60s. Gilchrist, stay alert and cover us."

Sanders led them down the embankment, directing them to fan out as they approached the truck. Vince was nearest the cab, and could see the driver through the shattered windshield. He appeared to be an ARVN soldier, and was lying on his side. His head was covered with blood, and he was not moving. Vince signaled to Sanders, pointing in the cab and pantomiming driving. Sanders came over, and they approached the cab together. When they got closer, they could see there was a sizable chunk missing from the back of the driver's head. Sanders backed away and told Vince and Jackson to move back to the roadway. When they arrived at the jeeps, Sanders told Hickock to call the PMO. "Tell them we need the engineers to come out with a tractor or bulldozer with a couple hundred feet of steel cable to pull the truck back up to the roadway. The driver's had it. Looks like he was shot in the head. I'm gonna have the truck pulled up to the road. I think it may be booby trapped by the way the gooks are keeping their distance. I guess we'll find out soon enough."

The engineers arrived 40 minutes later with a heavy bulldozer. They carefully hooked the cable to the rear axle of the truck, ran it up the embankment, and attached it to the 'dozer blade, which the driver had raised as a shield, protecting him while he was in the 'dozer's cab. Vince and the others put on their flak jackets and steel helmets, and took cover on the other side of the roadway embankment. The driver began to back the 'dozer down the road, causing the cable to tighten. The 'dozer struggled against the weight of the truck as the driver slowly increased the power. The rear of the truck began to swing up the embankment, and after moving a couple of feet, the 2 pounds of C-4 explosive wired to the cab exploded with a tremendous roar, blowing the cab apart, and vaporizing most of the truck driver's body. The blast wave rolled through the embankment, lifting Vince off the ground. Debris from the truck and dirt clods rained down all around them as they lay flat on the ground. After a bit, Vince lifted his head and looked at Sanders.

"You remember this, newbie," Sanders said. "The next time you get careless, you might not be so lucky. Let's go clean up this mess."

They spent the rest of the afternoon securing the area while a detail from Long Binh arrived and cleaned up the debris. Sanders completed the reports while they were waiting.

When they arrived back at the company area, they were besieged by questions from the other guys, who had already heard what had happened. Sanders told them the story, leaving out Vince's initial carelessness. Vince later told T.J. the whole story, including his mistakes.

"I told you, Vince, you got to be careful! You can't make mistakes here. The price is too high. You're one of the lucky ones, you know. You get a second chance."

"Yeah, I know. It won't happen again, I can promise you that."

Later that night, at the EM Club, everyone was talking about the booby-trapped truck. They needed to hear over and over how Sanders handled it, and what made him suspicious. The story was told again and again, until, by the end of the night, not only was the truck booby-trapped, but they had fought a pitched battle with a squad of V.C. in the village. Vince and T.J. sat in a corner of the club, listening to the tale as it was retold by the others.

"Amazing how this is getting blown out of proportion," Vince said. "Does this always happen?"

"Yeah," T.J. replied, "all the time. Once, my squad was

out on patrol, and took a couple 'a sniper rounds. Nobody got hit, and we never even returned fire, but the next day the story had us in a company-sized action, fightin' NVA regulars. I don't know why it happens, it just does."

Vince said, "Makes me wonder how much of the stuff I heard back home was true."

Vince finished his beer, then walked back to his hootch. He saw Sanders reading on his bunk, and walked over.

"I want to thank you for what you did today. I guess you could say you saved my ass. I won't forget it, Sanders."

"Don't worry about it. Besides, you might be able to pay me back someday. We all got to rely on each other, you know. We're all we got. You remember that, Torelli, you remember how important your partner is to you, and you to him."

"I'm beginning to realize that, Sanders. I won't forget."

"Good. Now, we better get some sleep. We got a long day tomorrow."

"Goodnight, Sanders."

"'Nite, Newbie."

Later that night, Jackson approached Ski, and told him how Gilchrist had been acting while on the checkpoint, but Ski could do nothing about it. He had his orders from the LT, and they were clear. Everyone, unless physically unable, was assigned to street duty. No exceptions. Ski told Jackson he would try to give Gilchrist duties that kept him away from a lot of people, and out of the city, if he could, but that he couldn't promise anything. He told Jackson to watch Gilchrist closely, and report back to him each day.

"It's out of my hands, Jackson. We'll just have to deal with it."

"I don't like it, Ski. We're gonna regret this."

"I know, Jackson, I know. Let's just hope nothin' happens."

Vince had trouble falling asleep. The events of the day

kept replaying in his head, and he realized how lucky he was to have Sanders around to teach him how to survive. He had volunteered to go check out the truck, only because he wanted to show the others he would do his part and that he was not afraid. He was also intimidated by Sanders, and did not want to look bad in his eyes. He knew now how foolish his actions were, and swore to himself he would never do anything like that again. He was just beginning to realize that bad things could happen to him over here, and he shivered involuntarily at the thought. He could hardly believe that it had only been six months since he had received his draft notice. He remembered how difficult it had been for him and his family to say goodbye as he left for boot camp. All of them knew where he would end up.

It took him almost two hours to fall asleep.

December, 1966 1420 hrs.

Vince watched the familiar city pass by the window of the military bus as he and 57 other inductees were driven to the Oakland Airport to board a chartered airplane bound for the Sea-Tac, Washington, Airport. From Sea-Tac, they would be taken to Ft. Lewis, where they would be assigned to their respective basic training companies. All he had with him was the clothes he was wearing, and a small bag containing his razor, shaving creme, toothbrush and toothpaste, and a hair brush. After they arrived at Fort Lewis, they were formed into platoon sized groups. They then were marched to the replacement area, issued bedding, and assigned a barracks. A buck sergeant then came in and called roll again. Then, satisfied that all his charges were present, conducted a quick class on how to properly make up a military bunk. Having demonstrated the correct method, he then ordered the inductees to make their bunks. He strolled up and down the barracks, watching them with a critical eye. Every so often he would stop and berate one of the inductees over the allegedly "sloppy" bunk, pull the blankets and sheets off, and dump them in a heap on the floor, screaming at the unlucky person, "do you have shit for brains, boy? Didn't I just show you how to make up a proper bunk, maggot? Get your candy ass in gear, and do it right this time!" After 45 minutes of this, during which most everyone, including Vince, were the target of the Sergeants' wrath, the bunks finally met with approval. They were then told to form up outside in columns of four, and marched to the mess hall for dinner. The next morning, they met their drill sergeant, Master Sgt. Rodmore, were issued their clothing, more bedding, and gear, and taken to another barracks that would be their home for the next 10 weeks.

Two weeks later, Vince was made a squad leader, wearing a cloth armband with corporal stripes sewn on it, and one week after that, he was made the company Sergeant. He was given another cloth armband with buck sergeant stripes sewn on. He was one of the few in his company that had some college education, and his intelligence, common sense, and sense of humor, along with his personality, made him a natural selection for the position. In fact, it was his sense of humor that got him in trouble a couple of times. Though his stripes were never taken away, he was assigned KP duty for his little transgressions.

Once, while at chow in the mess hall, he was caught fooling around, laughing and talking while eating, which was absolutely forbidden in basic training. With over 500 soldiers to feed, time was of the essence, and each basic training recruit was to move through the line as quickly as possible, getting their food and eating without any delay, then bussing their trays and moving out to make room for the next soldier. Any time wasted during meals was frowned upon, and the offender would often be assigned

KP duty or extra physical training.

That day, Vince and a couple of his buddies were eating, and Vince was joking around, imitating one of the drill sergeants, making the others at his table laugh, which caught the eye of the mess sergeant. He saw that Vince was responsible, and decided to make an example of him. He walked up behind Vince, and announced to the mess hall, "Since Private Torelli has all this extra energy and time, he will be more than happy to demonstrate the proper way to eat in my mess hall. Isn't that right, Private?"

"Yes, Sergeant," Vince shouted in reply.

"Now, Private, first of all I want you to place your fork in the proper hand." Vince was left-handed, so transferred the fork to his right hand.

"Good. Now, place some food in your mouth, then put your fork down. Now chew your food thoroughly, swallow, and pick up your fork. Get some more food, place it in your mouth, put your fork down and chew."

Vince could hear the snickers of the other men in the mess hall, and could barely repress his own grin. The mess sergeant continued until Vince's plate was empty, then said, "Now, place your utensils in your tray, push your chair back, and stand up. Now, pick up your tray, and excuse yourself from the table." Vince dutifully did as he was told, picking up his tray as he stood up. He then leaned over, looking directly down at the table top and said, "Excuse me, table." Everyone in the mess hall watching this display immediately burst into peals of laughter, including Vince. The mess sergeant grabbed Vince by the collar, and hustled him into the kitchen.

"Sit here, and don't move, smart ass. I'll be back."

Vince had stopped laughing when he saw the Sergeant was serious, though he could still hear the other soldiers' laughter. For that little remark, he was on KP all the next day, starting at 0430 hrs. washing pots and pans, mopping floors, and peeling potatoes. His day ended at 1930 hrs.

After 9 1/2 weeks of basic training, they received their orders for AIT, Advanced Individual Training. Vince had applied for the MP school at Fort Gordon, Georgia, and was assigned there along with four others from his company. At the end of basic training, Vince and several others were promoted to Private First Class.

From the first day he arrived at Fort Gordon, his Company Sergeant kept telling them not to expect orders for anywhere but Vietnam, regardless of where they had applied to be assigned, preparing them for the worst.

Their training now consisted of a lot more classroom than basic training. They were schooled in such things as military traffic control, prisoner escorts, both peacetime and in war, counter-insurgency, military law, MP patrols and jurisdiction, report writing, and guard duty, along with the usual physical training, defensive tactics, arrest techniques, and weapons training, including the Colt .45 pistol, M-60 machine gun, M-79 grenade launcher, and M-14 rifle. After 10 weeks, they graduated as full-fledged MPs, having received their next duty station orders and a 14 day pass. Out of the 55 soldiers in his training company, 51 received orders for Vietnam.

24 June, 1967   1143 hrs.

Vince sat in the jeep, wishing for some shade. The temperature was approaching 100 degrees, and they were sitting on a checkpoint on Hwy 316 about 5 miles south of Long Binh. They had stopped several American military vehicles, checking cargo and I.D. of the drivers and passengers. They were checking to make sure that the drivers were properly licensed, and were going where they were supposed to be going, carrying what they were supposed to be carrying.

Sanders told Vince, "Some of the GI's are getting rich from dealing on the black market. They buy up cigarettes, hair spray, chewing gum, and candy at the PX, then resell it at a profit to the Vietnamese. It ain't easy to get large quantities of some stuff, like cigarettes or stereos, 'cause we're issued a ration card that limits how much we can buy. It's difficult, but not impossible. There are ways to get around it, and the black marketeers know how. Other stuff, such as food, medical supplies, even ammunition and weapons are stolen, then sold on the black market. It ain't unusual to find a jeep or quarter ton truck, and sometimes even a deuce and a half, on its way to Saigon loaded with stolen supplies. Sometimes the drivers are ARVN soldiers, but most of the time, they're Americans.

"Why do they do it, Sanders? They got to know that stuff goes to help the enemy. Is the money really that good?"

"They are very well paid in MPC, and the money can be sent home to their stateside accounts, just waitin' for their return. If they get caught, it means a court martial with a reduction in grade and pay, or maybe a stay in the Long Binh Jail, depending on the type of stuff they sold. They're willin' to chance it, though, 'cause of the large amounts of money they can make. The fact that most of the medical supplies, munitions, and weapons go directly to the VC or NVA does not seem to concern them. The promise of easy money is too great. The local VC command makes sure of that."

They had stopped about 20 vehicles, mostly American, since setting up the checkpoint at 0800 hrs. Only one had been found to have contraband. An airman from the Bien Hoa Airbase was found to be taking 5 cases of steaks to a contact in the Cholon District of Saigon. Sanders took him into custody for theft of government property, and they transported him to the Long Binh PMO for processing. A CID investigator was called, and once he was done questioning the airman, he would be released back to his company.

On this day, their ARVN counterpart, a Quan Canh named Nuyen, was less than enthusiastic about his duties. He mostly just sat in the jeep, dozing or visiting with the many vendors that set up their stalls along the highway. Once in a while, for appearances sake, he would wave over a Vietnamese military vehicle, briefly check the driver's and passenger's I.D., then wave them on.

"Is that all they do," Vince asked, "just sit around? He hasn't hardly stopped any vehicles."

"I know. Word has it that he is heavy into the black market himself, so he ain't gonna do nothing to stop it."

"Doesn't anybody know about him?"

"Yeah, it's no big secret. You gotta remember, we're "guests" here, and have no authority over the Viet Nationals. All we can do is report it, and hope for the best. What the Vietnamese choose to do about it is their business. I know that a lot of the high ranking ARVN officers are on the take, one way or the other, either black marketeering, drugs, or prostitution. Same with the local police and government officials."

"And nothing ever gets done about it."

"Nope, and probably never will, either. There's too much money involved."

They were interrupted by the arrival of another jeep, driven by Ski with the Lieutenant riding as passenger.

"Sanders," Ski called, "you guys are relieved from this post. Go back to the company and pick up a gun jeep, get some chow, then report to MACV headquarters. Pick up Williams on the way. You guys are on escort duty this afternoon. I'm assigning Baines' jeep to go with you. You'll be escorting a bus load of officers to Saigon. There's some kinda honcho meeting tomorrow morning. When you get there, turn the bus over to the 716th M.P.'s, then come back. Shouldn't take you more than a couple 'a hours. You get the rest 'a the day off after that."

"O.K., Sarge. Let's go, Torelli."

At a roadside cafe just off Hwy 316, in a small village the G.I.s call Gasoline Alley, three Vietnamese sat huddled over their coffee, whispering intently.

"My cousin said the bus would be leaving about 2 o'clock. That means it will arrive at the Newport Bridge around 2:30. You must be in place by 2:15, ready and waiting."

"Yes, Dai Uy, we will be ready."

"Fool, do not call me that. I am only a simple merchant to these people."

"Yes, Dai.. er, friend."

"That's better. Now are you sure you know the proper location?"

"Yes, the creek 300 meters before the bridge. We will be set up 30 meters off the road. Nguyen and Tung are the riflemen, Than and Song will man the machine gun, and I will have the B-40's."

"You must take out the MP jeeps first, then the bus will be unprotected. Use the first rocket on the lead jeep, while the machine gun fires on the second. If your first rocket is accurate, use the next ones on the bus. Nguyen and Tung will fire on anyone that makes it off the bus. Than should also use his machine gun on the bus once the rear jeep is disposed of. You must not spend more than a couple of minutes there, then take your weapons and disappear into the jungle. Hide your weapons, and return to your homes. Tell no one of this. We will hear if you do."

"Do not fear, friend, this is not our first assignment."

"It is the first from me. There must be no mistakes. My superiors have determined there will be several key American intelligence officers on the bus that must be eliminated. Do not fail us. The price for failure is too high, Liam."

Sanders kept their speed at a steady 35. He had told Vince and Williams to be especially alert. He knew there

45

were several good ambush sights along the highway, but doubted there would be any problems in broad daylight. He looked back to make sure the bus and other gun jeep were keeping up and were maintaining a proper interval. He looked at his watch, and saw it was 1423 hrs.

"We'll be at the bridge in about 7 or 8 minutes, Torelli. Keep your eyes open."

Two miles up the road, a poppa-san in a Lambretta chose that moment to try a u-turn in front of an ARVN deuce and a half filled with Vietnamese Rangers returning to their base outside Saigon. The resulting collision killed Poppa-san, and severely injured three passengers. The ARVN Rangers felt the impact and heard the collision, and believing they had been ambushed, immediately jumped from the truck, and deployed into defensive positions on each side of the road.

Liam heard the crash and the groaning of metal. He could see the collision and twisted metal that was the Lambretta, and saw the Rangers deploying from the truck toward him. He signaled the others to fall back with their weapons, and re-group. He joined them 200 meters back from their original position.

"What do we do now, Liam?" Than asked.

"We hide our weapons and go home."

"But you heard the Dai Uy. The bus will be here any minute, and we can't fail."

"Do you not see the Rangers? We can't get close enough to be effective, and there is not enough time to find a new location. We would not serve our cause by uselessly dying in a failed situation."

"But we have our instructions. We are not allowed to fail."

"I will take responsibility. After all, we did not fail. Circumstances merely interfered with us. I'm sure the Dai Uy will understand that. The decision is mine alone. Now go, there will be another time."

46

A couple of minutes later, the two gun jeeps and the bus came to a halt in the traffic jam caused by the accident a half-mile up the road. After a 45 minute wait, the Vietnamese Military and National Police opened one lane to traffic. Seven minutes later, Sanders' jeep started up the approach to the Newport Bridge.

Three days later, a patrol from the South Vietnamese Marine Battalion at Thu Duc found a body in the jungle east of their base camp. It appeared to be a peasant, his hands tied behind his back, shot once in the head. There was evidence of torture on the body. The South Vietnamese authorities were unable to identify the corpse, and it was buried along with hundreds of other unidentified bodies, in the Government cemetery outside Saigon.

While Sanders, Torelli, and Williams were arriving at MACV Headquarters, T.J. and Jackson were heading north on Hwy 1 to check out the report of a group of American soldiers that had gotten drunk at a roadside café, and started breaking up the place. The cafe was supposed to be off limits to American military personnel, as it was located in a known VC controlled area. It was about 15 miles north of Bien Hoa, and it took them about 20 minutes to get there.

As they pulled up, T.J. could see a small group of Vietnamese cleaning up broken chairs and tables. When the Vietnamese saw them, they came running over, all talking at once, gesturing to the cafe, quickly surrounding the jeep. Jackson stood on the driver's seat, telling them to be quiet, and asking if anyone spoke English. A young girl stepped up and said, "I do, MP." She appeared to be about 15 years old, though it was hard to tell her age. She was tall for a Vietnamese, and was slender, with long, straight black hair, large brown eyes, and a band of freckles on her cheeks, running across her nose. Her eyes were

47

rounder than normal for a full blood Vietnamese, and that, along with the freckles, suggested some French blood in her veins.

"Can you tell me what happened, Co?" Jackson asked.

"Three Soja come heah, drink beaucoup Ba Mui Ba, tell Poppa-san 'we want girl, you get.' Poppa-san, he say, 'no hab girl.' GI say, 'you no get girl, we be beaucoup angry, we maybe smash up you bar.' Poppa-san say, ' I no hab girl, you go Bien Hoa, get girl.' GI get beaucoup mad, throw bottles, smash chair, table. Poppa-san, he beaucoup scared, he run away until GI leave."

"Which way did they go?"

"They go that way," she answered pointing north. "They hab jeep."

"Do you know where they're from, or see their shoulder patches?"

"They hab horse standing on back legs."

"Sounds like either the 11th Armored Cav or the 1st Cavalry Division," T.J. said.

"Yeah, though from the direction they went, I'll bet they were with the 11th. They're stationed at Xuan Loc. It fits. These guys were probably on their way back from leave in Saigon."

"What do we do now, Jackson?" T.J. asked.

"We go after them. I guess it will take about 45 minutes or more to get there."

"We goin' alone?"

"Yeah. Don't think we'll need any help with this. I'll call the PMO, and let 'em know what's goin' on. As it is, we'll be spendin' the night there if we don't get this wrapped up quickly. I don't want to be travelin' this road at night. Let's get a description of the guys and get goin'."

An hour later, they were in the company commander's office of the 11th Armored Cav.

"So you think some of my boys smashed up that place, huh?"

"Yes, sir. We checked with Division, and they said your company had just come outta the bush a few days ago, and a bunch of your guys were granted passes to Saigon. The girl also described your unit patch pretty well, and they came in this direction."

"It's true some of my guys are on leave, but are you goin' to believe some lying little gook whore who's only working a scam to get money out of us?"

"Well, Sir, I do believe her. I saw the bar, and I don't think she's working a scam."

"Well, Corporal, I don't know of anyone who could have done it."

"Excuse me, Sir, I don't believe you."

The captain stood up quickly, sliding his chair back, leaning on his desk on both hands.

"Are you calling me a liar, son? 'Cause if you are, I'll have your ass. You'll be digging latrines the rest of your tour, as a private."

"Again, Sir, with all due respect, don't pull rank on me, and don't threaten me. It's been tried before, and didn't work then, either."

"Why, you wise ass little punk! You are gonna regret..."

"Excuse me, Sir," Jackson interrupted, "But if there is a problem, I would be happy to call my Provost Marshal at Long Binh, Colonel Robbins, and tell him how we are conducting a criminal investigation here, and that your cooperation has been less than helpful. You can explain your side to him, Sir, and lodge any complaint you want. May I use the phone, Sir?"

After a slight hesitation, the Captain said, "That won't be necessary, Corporal. I apologize for losing my temper, but I won't apologize for trying to protect my men. They've just come out of the bush after a particularly rough time, and are just blowing off some steam."

"I understand that, Sir. Now, can we take care of this?"

Forty minutes later, they were on their way back to the

49

cafe to give Poppa-san the equivalent of $75 in Piasters as payment for the damages. Jackson had identified the three Gis, and they admitted to causing the damages. He collected $30 from each, which was all they had. The other $15 was contributed by the Captain. Jackson called Ski to get his o.k., then thanked the Captain, and left for the cafe. Poppa-san was more than eager to accept the money to forget the whole matter. So ended another episode of military justice.

2245 hrs., 557th Company Area

The first mortar round landed inside the motor pool, destroying a small storage shed. 4 seconds later, the second round cratered the road adjacent to it. The next three rounds "walked" toward the EM Club, and the sixth round hit dead center on the club itself, ripping through the sheet metal roof, exploding over the bar. The explosion blew out the doors and windows, and the shrapnel shredded the tables and chairs, and shattered the glasses and bottles on the shelves behind the bar. The club caught fire from the blast.

SFC Weston, the club manager was in his office behind the kitchen, and when the first rounds exploded, he dove under his desk and was not injured in the explosion. He ran out the back door before the fire got out of control. Since the club closed at 10 p.m., it was deserted. By the time the fire company arrived, the building was fully engulfed. They could only keep the fire from spreading as the club burned to the ground.

Torelli, T.J., Sanders, and several others from the company walked over to the Club after the all clear sounded to see what had happened and watch the fire. Vince found a jagged piece of metal about the size of a silver dollar imbedded in the blown out door 40 meters from the Club. He pried it loose, and put it in his pocket. It was still warm to the touch. Later, back at the hootch, he showed it to Sanders and T.J. T.J. told him it was piece of shrapnel from the mortar shell that destroyed the Club.

Vince was unable to sleep that night. He was too keyed up over the shelling of the base and the destruction of the EM Club. The closeness of the mortar shells made his loneliness and despair all the worse. He wondered what he had gotten into, and what the future held for him. Would it always be like this? Would things get worse or better as time went by? Would he ever get used to it? The uncertainty of not knowing if he would survive the night, the next day, or the next month, made him uneasy. Vince did not fear death, because he believed death was final. What worried him more was that he could be maimed or crippled for life. He did not want to return to his family and fiancee in a wheelchair, or missing an arm or a leg. He didn't know if he could cope with that, and hoped he would never have to find out. He thought of these things as he lay in his bunk, and sleep did not come easy. Finally, he fell asleep, dozing fitfully until T.J. awakened him in the morning.

13 mortar rounds had fallen on Long Binh that night. There were no casualties in the attack, and the only damage was to the motor pool shed, the EM Club, and a latrine in the II Field Force area. Bien Hoa Airbase received 16 rounds, several of which landed in the helicopter park, destroying one Huey, and damaging two others. One Chinook had been slightly damaged by shrapnel. A security bunker near the flight line had suffered a direct hit, killing the two airbase Security Police inside.

Ton Son Nhut Airbase outside Saigon was also struck that night, not only with mortar fire, but 122 mm rockets, followed by sapper probes along the perimeter. Three Air Force Security Police were slightly injured in a brief fire-fight with the sappers along the northern perimeter in which two sappers were killed. 22 mortar rounds struck the airbase, setting off two secondary explosions in a fuel dump. Several buildings were damaged in the attack.

Other American installations at Cu Chi, Xuan Loc, Phuc Vinh and Lai Khe were struck with mortar fire and sapper probes that night.

Though damage was slight, with very few injuries, this seemed to the intelligence people to be a "test" of the defenses of the bases, and it appeared to them that something extraordinary was up.

29 June, 1967 0637 hrs. 557th MP Co. Area

"C'mon, T.J., we got buses to go get," Wild Bill said, as he loaded his gear in the gun jeep.

Jackson, T.J. and Wild Bill had been assigned to escort the buses from the airbase to the 90th Replacement Battalion, along with a second gun jeep manned by Booger Baines, Renfro, and Andy Anderson. There were several flights scheduled to arrive during the day, and because of the increased enemy activity in the area, it had been decided to escort two buses at a time with two gun jeeps, instead of three buses with two jeeps. That meant more trips, but better control and less of a target, should the VC decide to ambush them. They also had been told that an ARVN platoon would be patrolling the most likely ambush sites for added security.

"T.J., you'll be riding shotgun today. Wild Bill will be on the gun. Your job is to watch for any gooks that try to come up on motorcycles. They like to ride double and shoot up the jeep or bus as they pass. Wild Bill will be watching the buildings and fields and any likely ambush sites. I'll be driving, so if you see something, let me know right away."

"What if I see someone comin' up that doesn't look right?"

"You let me know, and keep your 16 locked and loaded and ready to go. 4 or 5 weeks ago, me, Gilchrist, and Sanders were on bus escort like this one night when the

52

Gooks opened up on us from the paddies near the 90th. Shot up one of the buses and one of our jeeps."

"Yeah," Wild Bill said, "that's when Jonesy and Baker got hit. In fact, I think you and Vince were their replacements."

"What happened to them?"

"The Gooks opened up with a couple'a AK's at the lead jeep and the first bus. Jonsey was drivin', and got hit in the knee. Baker was the gunner. He got grazed in the neck. Last I heard, he had healed up o.k. and was sent home. He only had about 4 weeks left, anyway. Jonesy's knee was smashed up pretty good. I'd be willing to bet he has problems with it for a long time to come."

"I think he'll be lucky to keep his leg," Jackson said. "I patched him up, and it was a real mess. He's lucky we were so close to the hospital. We were able to get him , Baker, and the new guy from the bus to a doctor right away. The new guy got gut shot. Man, what a way to start your tour, huh? I'll bet he wasn't in country more than two hours, and he ends up in the hospital, probably with a ticket home, too!"

"Were you guys able to return fire at all?" T.J. asked.

"Yeah," Wild Bill replied. "We could see where the ambush came from. Fired a bunch of M-60 at 'em, and Sanders put 3 or 4 grenades right on top of 'em. The ARVNs and 199th did a sweep of the area a half hour later, but didn't find anything, not even any blood trails. I think the Gooks di di mau'd as soon as they quit firin'."

"Seems like it's always that way. When I was with the 25th, there were lots of times we'd take some fire, and we'd fire back. Most of the time we weren't even sure where the fire came from. Didn't know if we hit anyone, though sometimes we'd find blood trails. We usually only saw the VC when we set up ambushes, or surprised them when we were on patrol."

"I know. We've had convoys hit along Hwy 316, and

Hwy 1, and we always fire back, but never see anyone. The grunts and ARVNs would always sweep the area without findin' nothin. Gets real frustratin'. I'd rather have a stand up fight than this hit and run shit. It's real hard on the nerves."

"Yeah, but I'll tell you one thing," T.J. said, smiling crookedly, "it's sure nice comin' back to the Post every night. I got real tired of sleeping out in the jungle for days."

Jackson agreed. "I do have to admit we got it pretty good. When I first got in country 5 months ago, I asked Ski if this was a safe area. Know what he told me? He said, 'There ain't no safe areas here, son, just some a whole lot shittier than others.' This is one of the less shitty areas, and I sure am glad I been stationed here. We still got to be real careful. I've seen too many of our guys get hurt."

"You guys ready?" Booger said, as he drove up. "First flight landed at 0630 hours, so let's get a move on."

About that time, Vince, Sanders, Parker, and Gilchrist were arriving at the 93rd Evac helipad. They had been assigned MedCap duty, escorting a doctor and two nurses to the orphanages in the area. Every week, a similar medical team made the trip to the orphanages by helicopter to provide free medical care to the children. The orphanages were run by the Catholic church, and were staffed by Vietnamese, French, and American nuns. The children living at the orphanages were not only orphaned by the war, but were the illegitimate half-caste children fathered by American and other allied soldiers. Most of the mothers were prostitutes who would leave their babies at the orphanages to be cared for.

The U.S. and South Vietnamese governments provided birth control devices to the soldiers and the prostitutes, but few took advantage of them. The government's purpose was to stop the spread of venereal diseases, and to slow the high pregnancy rate among the prostitutes, which resulted in thousands of unwanted babies.

The helicopter, a "slick" Huey marked prominently on both sides and the bottom by a large red cross on a white background, lifted off and headed in a north-easterly direction. The first orphanage was located in the countryside about half way between Bien Hoa and Phouc Vinh. From there, they would fly west to the second orphanage about 3 kilometers outside Lai Khe. The third orphanage was 1 kilometer outside the large base at Cu Chi, and the last was 5 kilometers west of Long Binh, completing the circle. The entire trip was expected to take 5 or 6 hours.

Each of the orphanages was located in areas referred to as "Indian country", as they were areas of high VC activity. As the Huey flew toward the first orphanage, Sanders told Vince that two of them would stay with the chopper pilot at the chopper, while the other two escorted the doctor and nurses to the orphanage.

"We ain't gonna sneak up on anyone in this chopper, and it's all Indian country out there, so you got to believe that Charlie is gonna know we're there."

"You think they'll cause us a problem?"

"Usually don't, but there have been times he has. This chopper ain't armed, and he's expectin' us, so we ain't a threat. They know why we're there, and probably will come to take a look at us, just to make sure we ain't pullin' a fast one."

"Anything in particular I should watch out for, since I'm probably going to be guarding the chopper?" Vince asked.

"Yeah, you are. I will tell you, though, you keep your eyes open and your head down. Stay under cover, and if you hear or see anything, don't get trigger-happy. They usually won't bother you, so don't give them a reason to. Don't forget, there'll be a lot more of them than us. You and Parker will stay with the pilot. I'm gonna take Gilchrist with me, seein's how he's been actin kinda squirrely lately."

"Good idea," Vince agreed.

Talking was difficult, as the doors to the chopper were open, and the wind, engine, and rotor noise made talking a chore. Vince leaned over and looked out the door. He could see the jungle passing some one thousand feet below them. The sun reflected off the hundreds of streams criss-crossing the countryside, and the jungle was like a brilliant green blanket, covering the land. Every so often, they passed over a peasant's garden, or a small rice paddy, or an opening in the jungle, sometimes natural, sometimes a bomb created clearing. The temperature was already over 90 degrees, with 100% humidity. The wind blowing in the open doors cooled the sweat on his face, but Vince knew that as soon as they landed, the heat would be stifling. This was the first time he had ever flown in a helicopter, and he did not like it much. Too noisy, too windy, and it just didn't seem possible they could be flying around in such a flimsy, awkward looking machine. He did not like flying on commercial jet liners, much less this. It was not something he wanted to do very often, and he was thankful the flight only took 20 minutes. He sat back and silently stared out the door, watching the jungle pass underneath them.

The two gun jeeps arrived at the terminal, parking near the buses. T.J. and Jackson waited in the jeep while Wild Bill went inside and contacted the bus drivers. This was the first time T.J. had been on the air base, having arrived in country at Ton Son Nhut in Saigon. He was surprised at its size, and at the constant activity going on. He could see F-4's taking off, heading out on combat missions, and all types of helicopters coming and going. There were troop transports, combat aircraft, and supply planes all arriving and leaving at a constant pace. He saw the bunkers at the gates, manned by the Security Police. An M-60 machine gun was mounted at the firing port, and each carried a .38 revolver as well as an M-16. They had passed two artillery emplacements as they drove to the terminal, and Jackson said the big guns were used as fire support for infantry operating in the surrounding countryside, and as harassment fire. They passed other bunkers, some empty, some manned, along the winding road through the base. T.J. thought the security was very good for an Air Force operation.

When the new arrivals were all on the buses, they started off, T.J.'s jeep in the lead. They drove out the gate and turned left, heading up Hwy 1 through Bien Hoa City, through Plantation, then turning right onto a secondary road heading toward Hwy 316. To their right was a large rice paddy. To the left was a smaller marsh. A creek wound its way out of the brush and across the marsh, passing under the road through a drainage pipe. It was from this area that the VC liked to ambush the buses, and this day there was a Cobra gun ship patrolling the area. Unknown to the MPs, an ARVN patrol had earlier made contact with a squad of VC moving through the area. After a brief firefight, the VC had broken contact and fled into the bush, with the ARVNs in close pursuit. The ARVN squad leader had called for assistance, and the gun ship had responded from Bien Hoa. T.J. knew they would have an uneventful escort with the Cobra in the area.

The MedCap chopper landed in a clearing about 150 meters from the orphanage. Vince, Parker, and the pilot, a 1st Lieutenant named Paciotti, stayed with the helicopter while Sanders and Gilchrist walked to the orphanage with the medical team. There were two foxholes about twenty meters apart on each side of the chopper that were used by previous MPs as cover. Vince and Parker went to one, the pilot to the other. After checking for booby traps, they jumped down inside, and tried to get as comfortable as they could. Not a breath of wind stirred the air, and the temperature had climbed to close to 100 degrees. Vince could see that the pilot had promptly laid down and gone to sleep. He was feeling the energy-draining effects of the heat, and sweat continually trickled into his eyes. His uniform was soon soaked, which added to his discomfort. Wearing his helmet and flak jacket did not help matters.

"Man, it's hot," Parker said, taking off his helmet and flak jacket. "I'm gonna take a little nap. You keep watch for a while."

"OK, but I'm going to wake you if anything happens."

"No problem. Oh yeah, when you hear Sanders coming, wake me up. He doesn't like us sleeping, and it'd be better for both of us if he didn't know it, OK?"

"Alright, but you better not snore."

Parker laughed, slid down in the hole, and using his flak jacket as a pillow, went to sleep.

Vince sat in the foxhole, scanning the edge of the jungle as the sweat ran down his forehead into his eyes. He listened to the various clicks, chirps, and whistles of the jungle insects, and after a little while, his eyelids began to droop and his head nod as he dozed off.

He had been dozing for a couple of minutes when he awoke with a start. He was instantly awake, though he could not figure out what had startled him. He looked over at the helicopter, at the sleeping pilot, then looked down the path Sanders had taken, but nothing seemed out of place. He shrugged, took his helmet off, and wiped the sweat out of his eyes. He stopped suddenly, realizing what wasn't right. The jungle was quiet. There were no sounds, no insects, no birds.

As he listened to the silence, he heard a slight sound. Clothing brushing against the jungle foliage, a shoulder rubbing against a tree trunk, or perhaps a rubber sandal slipping on the ground as its wearer stumbled. He slowly put his helmet back on and slid deeper into the hole, leaving only his eyes above the rim. He picked up his rifle, and clicked off the safety, scanning the jungle where the sound had come from. He listened carefully, but heard nothing. He saw no movement, only the shades of jungle green and shadowy grays. As he stared, the sweat again dripped into his eyes, causing him to blink and wipe them clear. When he looked back, it seemed something was different. Had the shadows changed, shifted maybe? There! Was that a face looking out at him? Was that a branch sticking out, or a rifle barrel? Vince shifted his gaze to one side, to use his peripheral vision, focusing on a point a few feet to the left. As he did, the "branch" slowly moved in an upward direction. He could see a face that gradually receded until it and the "branch" faded out of sight into the jungle. Vince continued listening and watching, but saw nothing else. The only sound he heard was the pounding of his own heart. He felt a lump of fear in his stomach, and his throat felt constricted and dry. After a minute, the natural sounds of the jungle returned, and Vince let out the breath he had been holding. He turned around and slid down, sitting on his heels. He took his helmet off and leaned back, resting his head against the side of the foxhole, taking several deep breaths.

"You OK, Vince?" Parker asked, as he sat up yawning.

"Yeah, I'm alright. Just a little hot."

"Take a rest, if you want. I'll watch for a while. How long has Sanders been gone?"

"About a half hour or so."

"They oughta be comin' back in a bit. Anything goin' on?"

"Nah. All quiet."

"Usually is. I hate these details. It's too goddamn hot, and boring as hell, unless you get to go into the orphanage."

"Yeah, real boring," Vince echoed to himself.

Thirty minutes later they were airborne again, heading

toward their next stop.

T.J. saw the Cobra suddenly bank and turn parallel to the road about 400 meters in. Suddenly, the minigun opened up, saturating the jungle with 7.62mm bullets. The gun fired so fast that T.J. saw an almost unbroken stream of red tracers arcing out of the helicopter. Once the Cobra finished its firing pass, T.J. could hear small arms and automatic weapons fire, punctuated every now and then by a grenade explosion.

"Looks like Charlie ran into a bit of trouble," he said.

"Sure does. Go get 'em, boys," Wild Bill yelled, as they drove past.

"There always seemed to be something going on in that area," Wild Bill said. "A few days ago, a patrol from the 199th Infantry sweeping the fields found a fresh arms cache in a patch of brush near the creek several hundred meters off the road. There was 122mm rockets, rocket propelled grenades, AK-47 assault rifles, grenades, mortar rounds, rice, medical supplies and all kind of shit. It was all collected and taken to the III Corps Compound in Bien Hoa. It was put on display, photographed by some reporter, then taken out to the range, and blown up."

"Will those the photographs be shown in the U.S.?" T.J. asked.

"Yeah. My folks said they're in the papers and some magazines as proof we're winnin' the war. Who knows, maybe we are winnin'."

The chopper gently set down on the helipad at the 93rd Evac. Sanders, Vince, and the others gathered their gear and weapons, and prepared to load them into their jeeps.

"You OK, Torelli?" Parker asked. "You've been awful quiet today, and you don't look so good."

"I'm alright. Just don't like flying in these choppers. Makes me queasy."

"You sure? We can stop at the dispensary on the way back, if you want."

"Thanks, man, but that's not necessary. Trust me, I'm fine."

"OK, if you say so. Let's load up and get outa here. I'm starvin'!"

Parker grabbed his gear and walked to the jeep while Vince collected his stuff from the chopper. Sanders took that opportunity to walk over and quietly say, "I heard Parker, and that's bullshit. We'll talk later. I think there's something you need to tell me."

Sanders then walked toward the jeeps, saying, "C'mon, you guys. Let's get goin'. I wanna be back in time for chow."

While Vince was stripping and cleaning his weapons, T.J. and the others drove into the company area. T.J. saw Vince at the cleaning tables, and came over.

"How'd it go, T.J.?" Vince asked.

"Real quiet today, Vince. We did see a Cobra working over Plantation today. Musta been somethin' goin' on in there. Made eight runs back and forth from the 90th. We did get to eat at the air base, though. Man, what great food. Those guys sure got it knocked. Everything was fresh, no powdered eggs or milk. Got army chow beat to hell! How'd your day go?"

Vince was done cleaning his weapons, put his .45 in his holster, then picked up his M-16 before heading to the arms room.

"Meet me in the mess hall when you're done. Gotta tell you what happened today."

"What's up?" T.J. asked.

"I'll tell you at chow. See you there."

Before T.J. could ask anything else, Vince walked off to the arms room.

40 minutes later, Vince and T.J. had their trays of food, and found a table away from the other guys. They sat down, and as they started to eat, Sanders walked over.

"You looked kinda far away out there today. I know that

61

look. You want to tell me about it?"

"Yeah. Have a seat." Vince took a deep breath and said, "You remember what you told me on the way to the first orphanage, about the VC knowing we were there, and if I saw or heard anything, not to do anything foolish?"

"Yeah, so?"

"Well, I saw 'em. At least I'm pretty sure I did. I think."

"What do you mean, 'I think'?" T.J. asked.

Vince told them what had happened, including the fact that Parker was sleeping when it happened. He knew he could never explain to Sanders satisfaction why he saw what he did and Parker was unaware of it, unless he told the truth.

"At the time, I was sure I saw him, but now I'm not so sure. The jungle was so thick, and it was so hot and all, and with all the shadows, I just don't know now."

"Trust your instincts, Vince," Sanders said. "If you believe, deep down inside, that you saw him, then believe it. I'm sure glad you didn't do nuthin' stupid. You don't know how many others there were around. Maybe he was just a single scout sent to check us out, but he may have been with a squad or platoon. You just never know. You do realize that they have those holes you guys were in ranged. You wouldn't have stood a chance. You made a wise decision, Vince. I guess there's hope for you, yet. You keep usin' your head like that, and you just might make it outta here in one piece. You guys wanna join me for a beer at the 615th club? I'm buyin'."

"Hell yes!" T.J. piped in. "Long as you're buyin, I'm drinkin'. How about it, Vince?"

"Sure, I could use a couple of cold ones about now."

"I said a beer, you two. You want more, you better bring some money. Let's go."

Later that night, Vince was watching a poker game in one of the hooches. Sanders, T.J., Renfro, a friend of

Renfro's from the 615th MPs, and a clerk from the 212th MP Sentry Dog Company were playing five card draw. The clerk, Norton, seemed to be in the middle of a lucky streak, winning about every third hand. He was a cautious better when one of the others was dealing, but bet more liberally when it was his turn to deal.

It was still very hot out, and most everyone was wearing only their fatigue pants or shorts and shower shoes, with no shirts, getting what little comfort they could from the heat. A large fan was at one end of the hootch, turned on high, and a radio was tuned to the Armed Forces Radio Network. An early Beatles song was playing softly in the background. There were numerous empty beer cans littering the area around the poker players. Vince watched a few hands when he suddenly realized Norton was cheating.

He saw Norton would start a running patter of small talk as he scooped up the discards from the previous hand to divert the others attention from what he was really doing, which was stacking the deck in his favor. He very deftly would separate three cards of the same value, and as he put the deck back together, would slip the cards in so they would be dealt to him. He was careful when shuffling not to mix them up with the rest of the deck, and never offered the deck for cutting. If someone said he wanted to cut the cards, he would merely put the two halves back the way they were without anyone being the wiser. After about an hour, he was two hundred dollars ahead. None of the others seemed to notice what was obvious to Vince. They merely complained about their losses and his run of luck.

When the players took a break to stretch and get another beer from the ever-present hootch refrigerator, Vince approached T.J. and Sanders.

"That Norton's cheating, guys. He's stacking the deck every time he deals."

"You sure, Vince?" T.J. asked. "I ain't been payin' too much attention, but he has been awful lucky."

"Yeah, I'm sure. I was able to call his hand the last four times he dealt. Doesn't it seem strange to you that he always seems to win with three of a kind, or a full house?"

"Now that you mention it, that's right! Sanders, we need to have a little talk with this guy."

"We ain't gonna do nuthin."

"What? This guy is cheatin' us blind!"

"I know he has. I been watchin' him, too. Don't you worry about it, T.J. Let's go back and finish the game. Not a word out of you, either, Vince. T.J., you got to act like nuthin's wrong, understand?"

"If you say so, man."

"Good. Let's get back to the game."

When the game resumed, Vince got another deck of cards, and stood where Norton couldn't see him. Each time Norton got the deck, and was ready to deal, Vince would hold up a card to indicate Norton's three of a kind. He was always right. Vince watched for another hour or so, and when he left, Norton was another $150 up. Vince went to his hootch and wrote some letters, then took a shower and went to bed, intending to read a book he bought at the PX. He was asleep within two minutes, the book having fallen to the floor.

Vince awoke to Ski shaking him. "Wake up, Torelli. Some people wanna talk to you."

"What's up, Ski? What time is it?"

"Oh dark thirty in the a.m. Get dressed, and meet me in my office in five minutes. I've got coffee there, if you want it."

Five minutes later, Vince was sitting in Ski's office, sipping from a steaming mug of coffee.

Ski was sitting at his desk, and two other chairs in his office were occupied by a couple of E-5's from the 615th MPs.

"What's this all about, Sarge?" Vince asked, yawning. The clock in Ski's office said it was 0430 in the morning.

"Seems a guy was found in a field a ways from here a couple of hours ago, beat up pretty bad. Turns out he's with the 212th MPs, a clerk or somethin'. These boys here tell me he was here last night playing poker. They talked to him, but he says he don't know who or how many jumped him. He says he wasn't robbed, and doesn't know why this happened. The sergeants here talked with the other poker players, and they say the game broke up about one a.m. They claim this guy was O.K. when he left. He had about $50 on him when he was found, and the other guys said he didn't lose much during the game, and didn't have a whole lot of money. Now, you answer these boys' questions, son. He's all yours, Sergeant. Keep it civil, understand?"

Vince told them he had watched the game for a couple of hours, then left about 2230 to write some letters and take a shower. He said the game was kind of dull, and he didn't recall anyone winning or losing much. They asked about the other players, and Vince told them who they were, knowing they already knew the answer, and had talked to them before him. Vince maintained his ignorance of the matter, and in a little while, they finished their questioning and left, admonishing Vince to contact them if he remembered anything else.

After they left, Vince asked Ski, "You got any idea what happened?" probing for information.

"No, Torelli, I don't. Can't understand why anyone would want to do that, unless they had some sorta grudge against that boy. He wasn't robbed, cause he had some money on him. No, son, I don't know. Only thing I do know is, you got to be real careful who you play poker with. Now, go get some chow. See you at guard mount."

As Vince started to leave, Ski said, "By the way, Sanders says you're about done with your training. He thinks a couple more days oughta do it. Startin' this morning,

65

you're driving. Sanders will ride shotgun, and tomorrow you guys go on nights for a while to complete your training."

At the mess hall Vince got his food and found T.J., Sanders and Renfro sitting together. He joined them, and as he sat down, Sanders asked, "How'd it go in Ski's office?"

"O.K., I guess," Vince replied. "Those two Sergeants didn't seem too interested in finding out what happened, though."

"I think they know." T.J. said, "That guy apparently has a bad rep when it comes to poker. They just don't know for sure who did it, and ain't tryin' too hard to find out."

"Well, they didn't get much from me. Ski managed to tell me most of what you guys said before they could ask me any questions, so it was easy for me to go along with your story."

Vince turned to Sanders, and asked, "think they'll be back?"

"Nah. Norton's not gonna tell 'em nothin', and without his statement, they're not gonna be interested. Besides, he wasn't hurt that bad, and he knows what would happen if he told. It's over, now. So, you guys ready to go to work? Vince, You're drivin' today, so when you're done with guard mount, you go get us a jeep. No gun jeep today, though. It's just you and me on town patrol."

2 July, 1967 1023 hrs.

Vince was driving south on Hwy 1 through Bien Hoa, heading toward the bridge over the Dong Nai River. Sanders wanted to show him the bunkers and security points on the riverbanks and bridge, and introduce him to some of the PBR guys that tied up near there. They might even get a ride on the PBR itself, if they were lucky. The flow of traffic was going about 20 miles per hour, and as they drove along, every so often Vince would see a woman or man sitting by the side of the road, holding their heads, some with blood running down their faces. There were several other people milling about, talking excitedly.

"Can you see what's going on, Sanders? Do those people need some help?"

"Keep drivin'. I know what's goin' on, and we're gonna take care of it."

"Where to?"

"Just keep goin'. Speed up a bit, and pull up alongside that motorcycle with the two guys on it."

Vince looked where Sanders was pointing, and saw two teenage boys riding a small Honda. The one on the back carried a four foot long bamboo pole in his right hand, and Vince now saw that the driver would suddenly swerve toward the shoulder of the road when passing a group of people, at which the rider would club one or two with the pole as they drove past, striking them in the back of the head. He did not seem to care who his victims were. Men, women or children, it was all the same to him. Each time he struck someone, causing them to cry out, and most to fall to the ground, both he and the driver would laugh uproariously. The pain they caused their unsuspecting victims did not seem to matter to them, as they continued to drive along, choosing their victims at random.

As Vince neared the motorcycle, Sanders took out his billy club, holding it in his right hand across his lap so it was mostly hidden. When they pulled abreast of the motorcycle, Sanders yelled, "Hey, cowboy!," and when the rider turned his head to look at him, Sanders whipped out the club and struck him on the left side of the head, causing a two inch gash, and knocking him off the cycle. As he hit the ground, he was immediately surrounded by an angry crowd, who began beating him with their fists and feet. The driver saw what had happened, and tried to accelerate away from the crazy MP's jeep, but before he could, Sanders struck him across the forehead with a backhanded blow. The force of the blow caused the driver to do a backward somersault off the motorcycle. He landed on the shoulder of the road in a sitting position, blood pouring down his face from the cut on his forehead. The motorcycle continued on for about 20 meters before it fell over.

"That oughta make them think twice before they try that again," Sanders said, as Vince continued driving, leaving the fate of the two to the angry crowd.

They drove all the way through Bien Hoa, and soon Vince could see a three-lane bridge arcing over a muddy, slow flowing river. It was about 100 meters wide, and as he parked the jeep off the roadway at the approach, he could see numerous clumps of brush and other debris floating slowly down the river. Vince heard several shots ring out, flinching involuntarily at the sound.

"Easy, Vince. Nothin' to worry about," Sanders said, smiling at him.

"What are those shots?"

"Just the ARVNs shootin' up the river. C'mon, lets walk up the bridge, and I'll show you."

They joined the steady stream of people walking over the bridge, passing a sandbagged bunker at the foot of the bridge. Vince saw 3 ARVN soldiers in the bunker, which had both an M-60 and .50 caliber machine gun inside. There were several other ARVNs sitting around outside the bunker, each armed with an M-16 or grenade launcher. There was an identical bunker on the opposite side of the road, and two more on the other side of the river.

They walked across the bridge amid the throngs of pedestrians, and approached another small sandbagged bunker midspan on the upstream side of the river. There was a single ARVN in it, watching the river flow past. Whenever a clump of vegetation or branches would get near the bridge, he would fire several shots into it.

"What the hell's that all about, Sanders?"

"The VC sometimes like to float bombs and booby traps down the river in those clumps, hoping it will damage the bridge or one of the PBRs. A few months ago, one hit one of the bridge supports, and exploded. It wasn't powerful enough to cause much damage, but it shut down the bridge for a day while the engineers checked it out. The gooks shoot at 'em when they're still far enough away not to do any damage if they do explode. See the flood lights? They use those at night for the same reason, 'cept at night, the VC will float down the river hidden in the brush, grab onto one of the supports, and plant a bomb, then float away before it goes off. Shootin' at the brush kinda discourages them from tryin' that. This bridge has been standin' for almost a year now without serious damage. Once in awhile there's an explosion, but it don't happen too often any more."

"Man, it's amazing what they will think of. You just can't take anything for granted here. You never know what's safe and what isn't."

They walked back to the jeep, with Sanders lecturing Vince on the way things were in Southeast Asia. He reminded him to be careful and suspicious of everything from the unusual to the ordinary, and everything in between. Over the last few days, Vince had heard this same lecture many different ways. As they walked up to the jeep, Sanders reminded him to check it out before getting in and starting it up. Vince slowly walked around the jeep, checking inside and out, looking for anything unusual or out of place. Seeing nothing, he got in to start it up. Just before hitting the ignition, he looked over at Sanders, and saw that he was standing a few feet away with his fingers in his ears and his eyes squeezed shut.

"Not funny, Sanders, not funny at all," Vince said, as he started the engine. Sanders chuckled and got in the jeep.

"Drive along the river. I'll show you a PBR base."

Vince drove back into the city, and followed route 314

69

along the river to Buu Long Village, where Sanders told him to turn onto a dirt road that paralleled the river. He passed a flat, hard packed dirt area that sloped gently down to the river. It was swarming with young boys, most 6 to 12 years old, and there were several jeeps and trucks of all sizes parked close to the river being washed by the boys. As they passed, several boys ran alongside their jeep, offering to "wash jeep cheap, MP." Sanders ignored them as Vince drove on.

"How much do they charge to wash a jeep?"

"Usually a hundred Piasters or so. You can usually bargain with them on the price."

"Hardly seems worth their while," Vince remarked.

"Oh, it's worth it to them. Sometimes they can wash 10 or 15 vehicles, on a good day, if they work hard and do a good job. The GIs will pay 'em, 'cause then they don't have to do it themselves when they get back to their company."

Vince drove along, passing several huts and shacks, and a small village, with patches of dense jungle in between long stretches of marshland. They passed a squad of ARVN infantry patrolling along the river, checking the village and the villagers. They saw no other vehicles.

After driving for 20 minutes, they rounded a curve and saw a small outpost a quarter mile up the road. He could see several small buildings, and two large power boats were tied up at the dock. The outpost extended from the bank of the river two hundred meters inland. The brush and trees had been cleared on three sides, and there were three barb wire perimeter fences spaced about 10 meters apart surrounding the base. The compound even had a helipad, with a Huey parked on it. As Vince drove up to the gate, one of the gate guards shouted, "Hey, Sanders, you big asshole. You still alive?"

"Yeah, Murph. I'm surprised some whore hasn't cut your throat by now."

"Guess I been lucky. You here on a friendly visit, or is this official hot-shit MP business?"

"Just a visit. Got a newbie here, and I wanna show him your toys."

Turning to Vince, Sanders said, "See this sorry excuse for a soldier, Vince? A couple of months ago, he tried to drink all the whiskey at the Cherry Bar. Got real wasted, and when he stepped outside to take a leak, got his ass jumped by a bunch of Cowboys. He'd laid a couple of 'em out, and was holdin' his own until one 'a them broke a board over his thick Irish skull. Knocked him cold. They was just goin' through his pockets when I drove up."

"That's right," Murph laughed. "Know what this guy did? Kicked the shit outa a couple of em', and kept another from knifin' me, which he was just gettin' ready to do. Then this asshole arrests me for bein' off limits! He was nice enough to take me to the doc's first. Got five stitches in my head, and spent the rest of the night in a cell at the PMO. Tell ya one thing, though, Sanders treated me OK through the whole thing, even though I don't think I was too nice to him." Turning to Sanders, he said, "Seriously, I owe ya a lot. All you gotta do is ask."

"OK, I'm askin'. Can you fire up one 'a them tubs, and take us for a little ride?"

"No sweat, GI. They just put one of 'em back together and gotta take her out on a test run. Be goin' in a few minutes, so you're welcome to come along. I'll get someone to cover for me here, and go with you."

"Thanks, Murph. Mind if we look around a bit while we wait?"

"Nah, go ahead. Come down to the dock when you hear 'em fire up the engines."

Vince drove into the camp and parked by one of the larger buildings. Above the door was a hand painted sign saying "Hollywood Pavilion", and they could hear music coming from inside. Vince got out of the jeep, and walked up to the front door, pulling it open.

"Hey, Sanders, can we get a beer in there?"

"I don't think you want to go in there, man."

"Why not?"

"Well, let's just say they wouldn't be too happy to see us walk in there, considering what they're smoking. It's so thick, you could get high just standing in the doorway."

Walking back to the jeep, he said, "Why do these guys do that, Sanders? Don't they realize how dangerous it is?"

"Yeah, they do. They just don't care. Who knows, maybe they've had enough of this place. It's just a way for them to escape for a while, Vince. Sometimes the things they have to do, the things they see, get to be too much and causes an overload. This is their way of copin'. Makes 'em forget for a while where they are. Course, others are just plain ol' dopers and don't care. Either way, it ain't none of our business. Let's go wait at the dock."

They grabbed their weapons and ammo, and walked down to the dock to watch the mechanics working on the boat's engines.

The boat was a Mark I V-hull power boat with an open sided canvas cover over the deck. It was piloted from the center, and sheets of half inch armor plating had been erected on the sides to protect the driver and crew. The boat was armed with two M-60 machine guns mounted amidships on each side, and each crew member carried the standard issue M-16 or M-79 grenade launcher. The crew normally numbered no less than five, but for this shakedown, they numbered four, plus Vince and Sanders.

Most of the time, the PBRs main mission was to provide security along the river through active patrols, and by checking the Vietnamese sampans for contraband or weapons, they hoped to deny the enemy the use of the river. At times, they served as transportation for SEAL teams being inserted deep into the enemy-controlled area north of the PBR base. They also served as rescue or pickup boats for infantry patrols that ran into trouble along the river, or those needing transportation out. They would retrieve bodies floating down the river, and sometimes provided active combat support for American or ARVN patrols operating in the area.

As Vince and Sanders watched, they saw Murph walk over to the boat and talk to the Lieutenant, pointing at them. The Lieutenant nodded his head, and Murph turned to them, grinning. He walked over and said, "Get your stuff and let's go. We'll be movin' out in a couple'a minutes."

As if on cue, they heard the powerful engine roar to life, then throttle down to a rumbling idle. They picked up their weapons and ammo, and boarded the boat.

As they got on board, the Lieutenant said, "You guys stay out of the way. You will ride there," he said, pointing to the aft deck. "I hope you know how to use those weapons. If anything happens, duck down behind the gunwales. You'll be alright."

The boat moved slowly away from the dock, and turned up stream. They drove along the winding river for a half mile before the pilot opened up the engines, causing the boat to leap forward.

They rode up river for more than a half hour, passing isolated huts and small villages along the banks. The people watched them carefully as they passed. Murph told them that most of the men were hard core VC, and that there was a major VC base camp a few miles inland. He told them that two months ago, they inserted a SEAL team a short distance from there. They dropped them off at 0200 hours, and returned for them at 2300 hours. He said they carried a large cloth bag when they returned, and when they dumped it on the deck he heard a moan from inside. He learned later that a high-ranking VC officer was inside. The SEAL team had infiltrated the base camp, drugged and kidnapped the officer, and gotten away without being detected. The team hid out during daylight hours a mile from the river, listening to the searching VC scour the countryside for their missing leader. Not knowing what had happened to him, they were not being very quiet, and were easy to avoid. When darkness fell, the team made its way to the river to await the boat's arrival.

"What happened to the VC officer?" Vince asked.

"Don't know. As soon as we got back to the base, the team loaded him into a chopper, and took off."

The boat suddenly slowed and headed out to the center of the river.

"What's goin' on, Murph?" Sanders said.

"Just up from here is a favorite ambush site for the VC. If they hear us comin', they'll start snipin' at us when we go around that bend up there. I think we'll probably turn around and head back now."

As if he had heard them, the pilot turned the boat around and headed back the way they came, the Lieutenant satisfied that the engine was performing normally. It took them 35 minutes to return to the base. They had been out for about an hour and a quarter.

Sanders and Torelli thanked the Lieutenant, then walked back to their jeep with Murph.

"Anytime you want to do this again, you let me know," Murph said. "I still owe you, Sanders, and I won't forget it."

As they drove away, Vince said, "That base doesn't seem very safe, Sanders. Aren't they afraid of being overrun?"

"It's more secure than it seems, Vince. All that cleared area outside the inner perimeter is heavily mined, plus there are pre-registered artillery fire zones all around it with the 8th Artillery in Bien Hoa, and assault choppers can be here in minutes, if needed. There's two platoons of grunts there, too. They'll be OK."

Later that day, they drove to the docks at Newport, and ate lunch at one of the small Vietnamese cafes nearby.

"Two months ago," Sanders began, "I was on convoy escort. We had run a bunch of trucks down here to pick up some munitions, and while they were being loaded, we walked over here for a beer. Baines, Frenchy, and I were sittin' at this same table. At that table next to us was a couple of GIs that worked the docks. One of them had a camera sittin' on the table, when all of a sudden this kid runs by, grabs the camera, and takes off. The GIs chased him, but lost him in the alleys. Man, was that GI pissed! A few days later, we were back here, sittin' at this same table. Over by that hootch with the white door was a group of teenagers hangin' around, includin' the one that stole the camera."

Sanders paused to take a long swallow from his beer. Vince lit a cigarette and signaled the barmaid to bring two more. He could see Sanders was bothered by this, and was having a difficult time telling the story.

"I looked over and saw the GI that lost the camera walking toward the kids. When he was within a few feet, he pulled a .38 from under his shirt, stuck it in the thief's face, and pulled the trigger. Just walked up and killed that kid! Then, cool as you please, he walks over to the river and throws the gun out as far as he can. He just sat on one of the pilings, waitin' for the MPs to come."

"Did anyone go get this guy?" Vince asked, "to make sure he didn't leave?"

"Yeah, a friend of his went over and sat with him until the MPs arrived."

"Didn't you do anything?"

"Nah. Besides, what could we do? It happened too fast for us to prevent, and once he shot him, he didn't try to get away. The kid was dead before he hit the ground. Anyway, we had a convoy to escort to Long Binh, and couldn't hang around."

"I wonder what happened to that GI?"

"Don't know," Sanders said, "But the MPs took him

away."

"Jesus, man, that's a tough thing to deal with."

"Yeah, it is, but you know, there's a lot of stuff that goes on here that ain't right. People get beat up, tortured, murdered, and nuthin' gets done about it. They get killed dealin' drugs or whores. GIs sellin' stuff on the black market, supply trucks hijacked or flat out stolen. Did you know there's millions of dollars worth of stuff stolen from us every year? Some goes to the black market, some makes its way to the VC and NVA."

"Don't we investigate those things? I know we got a CID unit here."

"Yeah, we do, but most of the time nobody will say what happened. Too many people, American and Vietnamese, are gettin' rich off it. The gooks ain't gonna say nuthin', and most of the GIs that could help us don't want to get involved. Everyone wants to make their time here as easy as possible, and the less involved they are, the better off they are. Put your time in as best you can, and get the hell out."

"Sometimes, I think I know how they feel," Torelli said, shaking his head. "I've only been here two weeks, and it's getting me down, too."

"Wait till you been here six months. It really gets bad. Enough, man. Let's get outa here."

They spent the rest of the day on town patrol in Bien Hoa. It was a relatively uneventful day, and Sanders had Vince drive to the air base, where they spent an hour and a half looking around and talking with the Air Force Security Police. They went to the EM club and had a couple of cold sodas, since it was over a hundred degrees out. While they were there, T.J. and Refro walked in.

"Hey, T.J., over here, " Vince called.

T.J. saw them and walked over, saying, "What's up, guys?"

"Nothing much. Been pretty quiet in town. We got to

ride on a PBR today. It was really great. Rode up the Dong Nai for an hour or so."

"Oh, man, are you ever lucky. How'd you get to do that?" Renfro asked.

"Seems Sanders knows a guy assigned to the boats. Helped him out a few months ago, so he let us ride along on a shakedown cruise."

"Man, I'd love to do that sometime," T.J. said. "I got dibs on the next ride, Sanders."

"OK, T.J., you're up next."

Vince and Sanders spent the next half hour in the air conditioned club, then left to return to Long Binh, to check in off duty. Since they were to start night patrol the following evening, they were off the next day. They planned to go with T.J. to the PX to stock up on some necessities, and Vince wanted to look through the PACEX mail order catalogs for a stereo system, and some china for his fiancee.

In an attempt to cut down on black marketeering, each soldier was issued a ration card when they arrived in country, limiting the amount of merchandise they could buy. Each card allowed the holder to buy four cartons of cigarettes a month, as American cigarettes were in high demand on the black market. They would bring a high price, and non-smokers would often buy their monthly ration, and resell it for a profit to others who would, in turn sell them for even more on the black market. Hair spray, bars of soap, candy, and gum were the other most popular items. Sometimes it was hard to find them at the PX, as they were bought up by the GI's, and sold in town.

Vince hoped there were still some bars of soap left, since he was almost out, and didn't like the thought of having to buy it in Bien Hoa on the black market.

Guess I'll find out tomorrow, he thought.

3 July, 1967   0817 hours

Vince, T.J., and Sanders had finished their breakfast a few minutes earlier, and were walking to the PX. They stopped at a barber shop behind their company area where Vince and T.J. got haircuts, GI style, then walked the half mile to the PX where they shopped around for a half hour, buying what they needed. From there, they walked across the base to MACV Headquarters. A friend of Sanders from the 194th MPs was on guard duty, and he took them to the lunch room where they bought ice cold Cokes and a couple of bags of chips.

Sanders led them up to the roof of the building, which was on top of a small rise. They could see almost all of the base from there, and some of the surrounding country-side. Two Cobra gun ships were visible a mile outside the perimeter, firing rockets into the brush.

They sat there for a hour and a half, talking, then headed back to the company for lunch. Vince thought he would take a nap that afternoon, since he would be up all night on duty, so after lunch, he went back to his hootch and wrote some letters, two of which were to his fiancee, one to his parents, one to his brother, and one to his best friend, Hank Perry, who was in basic training at Fort Lewis, Washington.

Hank had written to him two weeks ago, saying he had applied for MP school because Vince had made it sound like such good duty. He said he figured he would be getting orders to Vietnam eventually, and wanted to be doing something useful, rather than just beating the bush waiting for someone to shoot at him. Vince wrote that MP duty was better than being an infantry soldier, but it wasn't a walk in the park, either. When he was done, he turned his fan on high, stripped to his shorts, and lay down to sleep. He had asked Sanders to wake him at 4:30 so he would have time to shower and shave before evening guard mount.

Their hootch maid, Kim, was polishing boots, sitting in a corner of the hootch. She looked to be about 20 years old, but her true age was anyone's guess. Vince knew she had a couple of young children, and had heard her husband had been a captain with the ARVN Rangers. He had been killed six months earlier in an ambush near Phu My, so she had gotten a job as a hootch maid to support her family. She had borrowed a fan from one of the guys on day shift to keep cool in the stifling heat of the tin roofed hootch. She did not smile much, and wouldn't look any of the MPs in the eye. Vince would often take some extra fruit from the mess hall at breakfast or lunch, and give it to her for her children. That was the only time he would see her smile, a shy half-smile as she bowed and murmured "thank you".

T.J. came in a few minutes later, and found Vince sound asleep. Sanders was laying on his bunk with his radio playing softly, reading. There were eight others sleeping in the hootch who had worked the night shift. It was a quiet, restful time of the day, and T.J. found it easy to forget for a time where he was.

3 July, 1967   1817 hrs.

Guard mount was over, and they had been dismissed for duty. Vince and T.J. walked to the motor pool to check out their jeeps. This night, there were four two-man jeeps assigned to Bien Hoa patrol, three 3 man gun jeeps assigned as bus escorts, and three more 3 man gun jeeps on convoy escort duty. Several other MPs had been assigned to gate duty at the 90th Replacement, the combined police station, or CPP, in Bien Hoa, and the PMO in Di An. Vince had been assigned to town patrol with Sanders. The other three patrol jeeps were manned by T.J. and Jackson, Gilchrist and Parker, and Baines and Mason.

As Vince drove into Bien Hoa, Sanders told him that the

first thing they would do is meet with the Quan Canhs, the Vietnamese MPs, and the Cahn Sats, the Vietnamese National Police, and sweep the bars and whorehouses in the city. They would take care of any Americans, and the QCs and CSs would handle any Vietnamese soldiers, civilians, and prostitutes. Sanders told him they usually didn't arrest the American GIs if they were cooperative, and the only charge was being off-limits.

"As long as there's no other criminal activity going on, we'll just I.D. them for our report, then give them a lift back to their company area," he said.

The sweeps of the whorehouses were done by Sanders, Torelli, T.J., and Jackson, three QCs and two CSs. Entry into civilian houses was only supposed to be gained by the CSs, though in reality, neither American nor Vietnamese military personnel paid much attention to that requirement. Whenever a joint operation like this one was planned, the CSs were always notified and asked to take part, for appearances' sake only. Sanders didn't like working with the CSs, and these CSs were obviously reluctant to do more than get the MPs and QCs inside. It had been made very clear to them that entry would be made with or without their help, so they may as well assist. The team ended up taking eight GIs back to their companies, and arresting three others, two for drug possession and one for being AWOL.

They spent the next two and a half hours working with the Vietnamese police. It was apparent to Vince that someone had tipped off the whorehouses and bars that they were coming. After they were done, Sanders told Vince the local police probably were the ones, since they were being paid "protection" money by the pimps and bar owners to prevent any disruption of their business.

"This happens all the time," Sanders said. "The only way we ever arrest anyone is when we don't tell them our plans. If you ever get good info on the black market, AWOLS, drug dealin', or anything else, don't tell the gooks."

They planned to meet T.J. and Jackson at the mess hall for midnight chow after they were done, then make another sweep of the bars and whorehouses. Sanders liked to go to the air base around 3:30 a.m. for coffee and to talk with the Security Police, particularly the dog handlers. He told Vince there was a dog there that had two confirmed kills of sappers coming through the wire, and had a rank of Master Sergeant.

Sanders talked as they drove along, "Part of the security for the air base is the sentry dog patrols along the perimeter and other isolated areas inside the wire. The dogs can detect intruders far easier and a lot sooner than their human handlers. Remember three nights ago? One of the dogs found some unidentified people on the air base, two hundred meters inside the eastern perimeter wire, east of the flight line. Some other SPs responded and found seven sappers heading toward the aircraft parking area. They opened fire, killing three, wounding two, and forcing them to abandon their mission and withdraw northward. I heard three of the remaining four were killed by a machine gun bunker near the northern perimeter, and one wounded sapper was captured. There was no damage or American casualties. They did a sweep of the area at daybreak, and found several satchel charges and two B-40 rocket launchers with three rockets each hidden in a clump of brush."

"No shit! How do they get in?" Vince asked.

"The little buggers are real good at infiltration. The wire don't keep 'em out, it just slows 'em down a bit. You remember that, Vince. You ain't safe anywhere."

After transporting the prisoners to the PMO, it was past 10 pm. Vince and Sanders went back on patrol, planning to cruise through the city, make some walk-throughs of the bars, and check out the EM club at the III Corps Compound. There was a Filipino band playing there, and

Sanders had heard they were pretty good. They drove down Hwy 15 past Three Doors, and as they rounded a curve, Vince saw the road had been blocked by a pile of wood and brush. He slammed on the brakes, skidding to a stop 20 meters from the makeshift barricade.

"I would suggest you back up, quickly," Sanders said, grabbing his M-16.

Vince jammed the gear shift into reverse, and backed up 50 meters. They got out of the jeep, kneeling behind it, with their M-16s covering the barricade. After looking over the area for a minute, Sanders radioed for assistance. Within five minutes, T.J. and Jackson, and Baines and Mason arrived, setting up a hasty perimeter, using their jeeps as cover, also.

After surveying the scene, Jackson said, "Somebody's gotta go check this out. Any volunteers?"

"Cut the crap, Jackson. I'll go, and Vince is comin' with me."

"What?" Vince asked. "Does this mean I just volunteered?"

"You heard me. Get the rope outa our jeep. The rest of you guys keep us covered."

Sanders cautiously led Vince along the front of the buildings toward the barricade. When they were close enough, he shined his flashlight over it, looking for explosives or trip wires.

"You see anything, Vince?"

"No, Sanders. Looks clean to me."

"Give me your bayonet. I'm gonna try something."

Sanders tied his and Vince's bayonets to the rope in an "X" shape, making a crude grappling hook.

"Jackson, bring your jeep up here," he called.

Crawling to within a few feet of the barricade, he tossed the improvised hook over the top of the barricade, gently pulling it back, while hugging the ground. Vince saw the bayonets come over the top, and heard them clatter onto the pavement in front of the pile. Sanders raised his head and looked at Vince, smiling crookedly. Vince saw Sanders' face was bathed in sweat, and he felt his own heart pounding in his chest.

Sanders again tossed the bayonets over the top, and pulled back on the rope. This time they wedged in the branches, and he pulled steadily until he was sure they were securely caught. He crawled back to Jackson's jeep, and tied the rope to the bumper.

"Get outa here, Vince. When you're clear, Jackson is gonna back his jeep up real slow and pull that barricade apart."

"I am? When did I volunteer to do that?"

"Can it, Jackson. Do it slow and easy. Go ahead, Vince is clear."

Sanders ran back to the other jeeps, and took cover. Jackson had laid the windshield down, put on his helmet and flak jacket, and slid down in the seat as far as he could. He put the jeep in reverse, and started backing up. The rope tightened and began to pull the branches forward. After a few feet, they broke loose, and the barricade collapsed with a crash. Vince flinched, expecting an explosion, but when nothing happened for a minute or two, he and the others slowly and carefully came out from behind their cover and approached the pile.

"Don't bunch up, guys," Sanders said. "Baines, you and Mason help us clear the road. You other two keep us covered, and look sharp!"

After the roadway was cleared, the MPs did a walk through of the area to make sure no one was lurking around. After clearing the area for any enemy, they stood around for a few minutes, talking, then each got back into their jeeps and went back on patrol. Sanders reported what had happened to the PMO over the radio, then had Vince drive to the III Corps Compound. Though it was primarily an ARVN installation, there were numerous

83

American military advisors and officers assigned there, and the ARVN Command encouraged the MPs to come into the clubs as a calming presence so that their American counterparts would behave. Sanders checked off the air with the PMO, giving their location. He was one of the few MPs that routinely did. Most would not bother, though SOP and common sense said they should. Sanders planned to stay for 10 or 15 minutes, then head in for chow, where they were to meet T.J. and Jackson. They walked inside the club to the beat of the drums and electric guitars.

Jackson and T.J. were driving around the south side of the city, checking the bars for off-limits Americans. It was a slow night, and they found no one. They had just checked the Cherry Bar, and as they walked outside, T.J. could see a group of Vietnamese men squatting in a circle, smoking and talking. They were all armed with Korean War vintage M-1 carbines, and were dressed in levis and t-shirts.

"Those guys make me nervous, Jackson," T.J. said, watching them closely.

"Yeah, I know. Don't ever trust them, T.J. I'd be willing to bet most of 'em are VC or VC sympathizers, and the South Vietnamese Government arms 'em and puts 'em to work as Popular Force town guards. They're supposed to supplement the ARVNs by guarding the city at night, but I think a lot of times they're the ones causing the trouble."

"Renfro told me sometimes the MP units get sniped at during night patrol. Think these PF guys are the ones doin' it?"

"I'd be willing to bet on it. Just be careful around em'. You ready for chow? It's 2350, so we can head back to Long Binh. It'll take us 15 or 20 minutes to get there."

"Yeah. We're supposed to meet Sanders and Torelli, so we better get goin'."

As Vince drove through the city, he was surprised at how dark it was. The only light was from the jeep headlights and the stars. There was no moon tonight, street lights did not exist, and almost none of the buildings had electricity. He stopped the jeep alongside the road, and just sat there, looking up at the sky.

"What's up, Vince?" Sanders asked, starting to reach for his rifle.

"Nothing, Sanders. Just wanted to look at the stars for a minute."

"Remind you of anything?"

"Yeah, it does. There was a place my girl and I used to go at night. We would park at the San Leandro Marina, and walk along the shore. Sometimes we would just sit in the car, not saying anything, watching the stars. It seems like forever since I was with her."

"I know. It's tough, especially when you start thinking about your family and loved ones. Gets real lonely sometimes."

"Got anybody waiting for you, Sanders?"

"Nah. Just my Ma. Had a girlfriend, but she broke it off when I told her I volunteered for 'Nam."

"How come?"

"Said I was stupid, that I was gonna get myself killed. Said she didn't want to have to go to my funeral. Told me she wasn't that kind, she couldn't handle it. She walked out on me that night, left town. I ain't seen or heard from her since."

"Shit, Sanders. I'm sorry."

"It's OK, man. Guess she didn't love me like she said." Sanders paused, cleared his throat, and said, "How 'bout your girl? She stickin' by you?"

"We hope to get married when I get home. If I get home."

"Don't talk like that, Vince. You'll be goin' home before

you know it."

"I hope so, Sanders. I really hope so."

"You just listen to me, pay attention and learn what you need to survive. You be smart, and you'll be OK. You'll be gettin' on that plane back to the world before you know it."

"Can't come soon enough for me."

"I know what you mean. Time sure does drag on here, don't it?"

"Yeah. This has been the longest four weeks of my life. It's depressing to think I've got almost a year left to go."

"Don't you worry. It'll go fast enough."

"Yeah, I suppose so. Let's go, man, I'm getting hungry."

Vince started the jeep, and headed out of the city, turning toward Long Binh.

An hour and a half later, they were driving back to Bien Hoa. The rest of the night was quiet, though they could hear outgoing artillery fire from Long Binh and the air base every once in a while. They spent the rest of the night driving along the back roads and alleys of the city, as part of Vince's training and orientation. They saw no one, and the radio was quiet. Sanders showed him some of the back roads to Long Binh.

"You remember these roads, Vince. Could come a time when the VC cut the main roads, and this is the only way you will be able to get back to the base."

All the roads were dirt tracks barely wide enough for a jeep. Some wound through the jungle outside the city, while others took them through open fields and marshes.

At 0530, they drove to the POL point on Long Binh and refueled the jeep, then drove to the company area and unloaded their gear. Vince drove the jeep to the motor pool and turned it in, walked back to the company area and joined Sanders at the weapons cleaning table. He cleaned and oiled his M-16 and his .45, turned them into the arms room, then headed to the hootch. Vince changed into a pair of shorts, made from a cut down pair of fatigue pants, sandals he bought in town, and a clean t-shirt. He asked Sanders if he wanted to get some breakfast, but Sanders declined, saying he was going to get some sleep. Vince walked to the mess hall, got a tray of food, and joined T.J., Jackson, and Renfro at their table.

"Well, how'd you like your first night shift?" Renfro asked.

"Wasn't really what I expected. It was pretty boring, after the great roadblock incident," Vince replied. "You guys do anything interesting?"

"Nah," Jackson answered. "Spent most of the time driving around checking things out. Went to Di An and spent time at the PMO there. We heard Ton Son Nhut got hit last night. Took some rockets. Didn't hear if there was any damage or injuries. Sure glad there wasn't anything goin' on here."

"Is it always this quiet at night?" T.J. asked.

"Not always, though we get our share of boring nights. That's just fine with me. The quieter it is, the better I like it."

Renfro interrupted, "Anyone know what's on tap for tonight?"

"I saw the duty roster in Ski's office," Jackson said. "Me, T.J., and Gilchrist got bus escort duty along with you, Wild Bill, and Booger Baines. Torelli and Sanders are still on town patrol. Parker and Anderson, Gonzalez and Wilson, and Daniels and Felman are on town patrol with 'em. That's all I could see."

"How much longer you guys gonna be in training?" Renfro asked, as he stood up and picked up his tray and plates.

Torelli said Sanders told him it would only be another day or two. Both he and T.J. were anxious to complete their training and get out on their own.

"You want a beer before bed?" Jackson asked. "I've got

87

some cold ones in the hootch."

Torelli declined, saying, "I'm turning in. See you guys later."

Vince washed and brushed his teeth, then set his fan on medium. He asked Kim to turn it on high in two hours, giving her an orange he had taken from the mess hall, then went to bed. He was asleep in less than a minute.

23 July, 1967, 1935 hrs.

Vince was already yawning, and it was only an hour and a half into his shift. He'd been on nights for the last three weeks, and hadn't slept well that day. It had rained on and off last night and all day, with high winds. The monsoon season was in full swing in the III Corps area. It wasn't raining at the moment, though the sky was overcast and threatening.

Vince was assigned to a town patrol gun jeep with Sorenson and Jackson. As they drove through the city, Vince heard a frantic radio call for help from another MP patrol unit.

"Muddy Hinges, Muddy Hinges, this is Charlie 6 Bravo. We're receiving sniper fire. We're pinned down just south of Cambo Alley. We could really use some help." Shots and yelling could be heard in the background, and the transmission was suddenly cut off.

"Le't's go, Sorenson," Vince said, "We're only a few blocks away. Jackson, get on the gun."

Sorenson sped up, and when they were a couple of blocks away, turned off the headlights. When they were within one block, he slowed down, putting the jeep in neutral and turning off the engine. They heard a shot from what sounded like a large caliber rifle, then a burst of return fire from an M-16. The jeep coasted to a stop by the alley, and Vince and Sorenson got out and took cover inside. Jackson remained in the jeep, training the M-60 at the two story building down the block. Vince could see the Charlie 6 Bravo jeep about 100 feet away, with two MPs crouched down behind it. Three shots rang out from the second story window of a building across the street from them. One of the MPs returned fire with his M-16, firing a short burst.

"Jackson, you see where it's coming from?" Vince asked.

"No. I need to get across the street."

"OK. Unhook that gun, and get ready. I'll go across first, then cover you when you're ready."

"Alright. Give me about two minutes."

Vince stood up, peered cautiously around the corner, then ran across to the other side of the street when the sniper fired at the other two MPs. Just as he ducked behind the corner of a building, the sniper spotted him, and fired two hasty shots in his direction. One struck the building, and one ricocheted of the street 10 feet away.

"Goddamn," Vince said, as he leaned back against the wall. He looked over at Jackson, who was draping a belt of ammo over his shoulders. He picked up the gun, and signaled Vince he was ready. Vince moved away from the building, and brought up his M-16. He stepped out toward the street just enough to allow him to see the sniper's position, and began firing single shots at the second story window as fast as he could pull the trigger. Jackson ran across the road into the alley, sliding to a stop behind Torelli. Vince retreated back into the alley, and knelt down, sweating profusely.

"McLennan, you and Tashimoto get outa there when we start firing," he yelled at the trapped MPs behind the jeep.

"OK. We go when you fire," McLennan yelled back.

"Alright, Jackson. I'll stay high, you stay low. On my signal, start pouring some fire into that window. Ready? GO!"

Vince started firing at the window as Jackson opened up a second later, the heavier staccato of the machine gun drowning out the M-16. Chunks of plaster began flying off the building around the window from the 7.62 slugs, and what little glass remained disintegrated along with the wooden window frame. McLennan and Tashimoto ran to a small alley between two buildings behind and to their left, taking cover around the corner. Tashimoto immediately turned and fired a grenade at the building from his M-79 launcher. The grenade struck just to the right of the window, blowing an 18" hole in the wall. Jackson continued to spray the window area, the heavy slugs easily penetrating the 6 inches of stucco. Tashimoto fired another grenade through the window. It exploded inside the room, blowing out the side and back windows. A scream of pain came from the room, immediately followed by several shots fired at the jeep. Jackson fired again, raking the front of the building around the window.

Vince heard the rumble of a large engine, and saw a ARVN V-100 armored vehicle drive up and stop in front of the building. Its twin miniguns opened up, spraying the second story with a sustained, lethal fire, knocking more chunks of stucco from the building, blowing large holes in the front. Tashimoto fired a third grenade into the room, while the V-100 continued its fire. After 20 seconds, the firing stopped, and all was quiet. There was no return fire, and Vince watched the building, smoke and dust rising into the air from the destroyed second story. A squad of ARVN Quan Cahns moved up the street from cover a block away, and carefully entered the building. After a minute, the squad leader appeared at the second story window, and shouted down to the V-100 and soldiers in the street below. Vince and Jackson moved out into the street, meeting Sorenson in the middle of the street.

"Guess that's taken care of," Sorenson said with a grin.

"Yeah. I'd be surprised if they find anything left of that guy," Vince replied.

He inserted a fresh magazine into his rifle, then walked over to where the ARVN MPs had gathered after searching the building.

"Excuse me, Sergeant," Vince said to the ARVN squad leader. "Find anything up there?"

"Yes. We find much blood, parts of body, clothes. Two VC dead."

"They were VC? I thought they just might be disabled vets," Vince said.

"No, they VC for sure," he said, then turned and walked away.

"VC my ass," Vince said. "If they were VC, then I'm the Easter Bunny."

"Yeah," Sorenson agreed. "Let's go file our reports, then get some coffee at the airbase."

As they drove off, Vince looked back at the destroyed building. Two ARVN soldiers were carrying a plastic body bag out of the building, laying it on the street. The soldiers stood around talking and laughing, lighting up cigarettes, gesturing at the body and the building. Vince shook his head sadly as the jeep rounded a corner.

4 August, 1967 0210 hrs

Sanders flipped on the lights as he entered the hootch, yelling, "Allright you guys. Everybody up."

A chorus of groans rose from the 13 Mps that had been sleeping until Sanders came in. Shouts of "bullshit" and "get outta here" rang out.

"Knock it off!" Sanders bellowed, effectively silencing the complainers. "Be in the company area in five minutes. We got a sweep to do at Plantation."

Sanders stalked out, obviously in a foul mood.

"What time is it?" someone asked. Vince looked at his watch, and saw that it was just after two in the morning.

Geez, he thought, *I've only been asleep for two hours?*

He yawned and made his way to the latrine, where he quickly washed and brushed his teeth. A few minutes later he was standing in the company area while Ski addressed the formation.

"One of the buses from the airport was ambushed out by Plantation by an estimated squad size enemy force. The driver and two troops were killed, and four others were wounded. The First Cav had a patrol out north of Plantation, and is starting to sweep south toward the highway. They need us to provide a blocking force in case they end up pushing the VC in that direction. Sanders, pick a half a dozen men, and check out an M-60, a grenade launcher, and M-16's for you and the other two. Get some flares along with the HE for the blooper. There's a truck waiting at the motor pool that will take you out to your post."

"Yes, Sergeant. Torelli, Jackson, Satler, Sorenson, Michaels and Johnson, fall out. Vince, you and Sorenson are on the 60. Jackson, you got the bloop gun. Get your weapons and equipment, and meet at the truck in five minutes!"

Thirty minutes later, they were quietly sitting in the underbrush 50 meters off Highway 1, south of the big rubber tree plantation. Vince and Sorenson had set up the machine gun to cover the most likely path out of the trees that led parallel to the highway and headed in the general direction of Bien Hoa. Sanders felt the VC were locals, and would try to make it back to the city to disappear into its maze of alleys. Jackson and Satler were 20 meters to their left with the grenade launcher and their M-16's, while Sanders and the other two were set up on Torelli's left, spread out at 5 meter intervals. Other groups had set up further along the highway, anticipating that the VC would be coming their way. No one talked, no one moved, and all kept a sharp watch on the trees in front of them.

O545 hrs.

Sanders crawled over to Vince's location, and told him he had just heard from Ski over the radio. The 1st Cav had no luck and were heading back to their base, so Ski wanted them to sweep the tea plantation to where the rubber trees started, and, if they found nothing, they were to return to the highway and await pickup at 0730 hours. Sanders said they all would start from their present locations and move on line at 10 meter intervals.

0603 hrs.

The sky was lightening in the east as the line of MPs walked cautiously toward the rubber tree plantation 300 meters away. They were walking through waist high brush and grass, keeping themselves in line as they went. Vince could see Jackson on his left and Sorenson on his right, and could just make out Satlers' form 10 meters beyond Sorenson. Suddenly, there was a loud crack, and Sorenson let out a yell, disappearing from sight. Vince and the others immediately dropped onto their stomachs, scanning the area to their front for the enemy, but all remained quiet.

"Sanders," Vince called, "What's going on?"

"I don't know. Where's the others?"

"They all took cover. I heard Sorenson yell, then he disappeared. I haven't heard anything else since. I'm gonna crawl over there and see if I can find him."

"OK, but be careful. Watch out for booby traps."

Torelli left the machine gun with Sanders, drew his .45, and began to crawl toward where he had last seen Sorenson, slowly and carefully feeling for booby traps as he went. Every few feet he would stop and call out Sorenson's name softly, listening for a reply. Not getting a reply, he resumed crawling nearing where he thought Sorenson had disappeared. As he felt the ground in front of him, his hand suddenly reached empty air. Vince stopped and reached as far as he could in front of him, then as far to the right and left as he could without touching the ground. He was about to back off when he

93

heard a soft groan coming from below him. He carefully crawled forward, and looked into the hole in front of him. With the coming sunrise, he was able to see Sorenson about six feet down, lying, on some crates. "Sorenson" he called, "you alright?"

"Yeah, I think so. Knocked the wind outta me."

"Stay still and keep quiet. I'm gonna check around and get the others. We'll get you out of there as soon as we can."

Vince crawled slowly around the hole, checking for booby traps and anything unusual and, finding nothing, stood up in the brightening dawn and called to the others. Five minutes later they had pulled Sorenson from the hole, and found he was none the worse for the experience, except for some sore ribs.

Satler had jumped down in the hole, and was handing crates up to the others who were stacking them alongside the rim. Sanders had pried one open, and found it contained 25 chicom hand grenades. Other crates were found to contain brand new AK-47's, ammunition, RPGs, and mortar rounds. Ski had arrived with the LT, and supervised the recovery of the arms cache. He had them stacked alongside the road, and an hour later, a squad of ARVN soldiers arrived and loaded the crates on a waiting deuce and a half. Once the cache had been loaded, Torelli, Sanders, Satler, and the others boarded another truck, and were taken back to their company area, where they cleaned their weapons, then went back to bed.

Later that afternoon, a press conference was held at the III Corps Compound in Bien Hoa. The captured weapons and ammunition had been laid out on the ground for photographers, and a prepared statement was passed out, detailing the attack on the bus and the circumstances of the finding of the cache. The photos and article appeared in the Stars and Stripes two weeks later, and in the September issue of Life magazine.

7 September 1967, 1745 hrs.

Ski's going away party at the EM Club was in full swing. The beer had been flowing since three o'clock, and Ski was pleasantly drunk. He had hugged everyone there at least once, had made one drunken, tearful farewell speech, fallen down twice, and now was doing his own unique dance to a Four Tops song blasting from the juke box. A Filipino band was due to arrive at 1800 hrs, and Vince, T.J., Jackson and Hickock were herding drunken MPs off the stage, and trying to remove the tables, chairs, and multitude of beer cans from the performers' area. Hickock's job was to watch for empty beer cans thrown at them by the other party goers.

"Incoming!" Hickock yelled, ducking under a table as a barrage of beer cans flew at them out of the crowd. The cans rattled off the tables, with several finding their targets, bouncing off Vince and T.J.

Ski's replacement, SFC Milar, was sitting at a corner table near the stage, nursing a beer, watching the proceedings, a frown on his face. He had just arrived in country a few days earlier. He was last assigned to the MP school at Fort Gordon, Georgia, as the first Sergeant for a training company. It was apparent he did not approve of Ski's party and the MPs behavior. After finishing his beer, he got up and walked out, shaking his head.

Having managed to clear the stage, after several more barrages of beer cans, Vince and T.J appropriated the front center table. The band had set up and was testing their instruments. Vince was already slightly drunk, his vision a bit blurry and his head spinning. T.J. came over, carrying two more beers for each of them. Hickok and Renfro joined them just as the band started playing "Louie, Louie". The club erupted into cheers, and several MPs jumped to their feet and began dancing wildly. As the singer walked onto the stage into the spotlight, the cheers changed into hoots and whistles. She was young and pretty, dressed in a tight white sweater, black mini skirt, and white go-go boots. When she started swaying with the beat, and audible groan filled the room. Vince sat there, his mouth hanging open, holding an unlit cigarette, staring up at her.

"Damn, T.J., she's gorgeous."

"That she is, Vince. Don't see much like that over here."

"She can sing, too. Ain't that a surprise!"

The singer was doing a passable job on the song, and driving the MPs in the club wild. Several more had started dancing, and the beer was flowing freely. By the time she was on her fifth song, Vince had drunk two more beers, and had a splitting headache. One of the MPs staggered up to the stage and began trying to climb up onto it. Having consumed the better part of two six packs, he was experiencing some trouble getting both legs up at the same time. He would get one foot on the stage, then try to lift the other before the rest of him, which would promptly cause him to fall flat on his back. He would lie on the floor for a few seconds, blinking his eyes, then struggle to his feet and try again, with the same results. After the fifth time, two of his friends came over and helped him up, handed him another beer, and led him back to his table.

Vince drank another beer, and when he looked at the stage, there were two singers.

"T.J., when did that other girl get here?" he mumbled.

"What other girl?"

"The other singer, stupid."

T.J. smiled, shook his head and said, "Time to go, Vince." He stood up and took Vince's arm. "There is no other singer, pal."

"What are you talking about T.J.? Yes there is, I can see her."

"O.K., Vince. C'mon, I can see it's time to get you to bed," T.J. said, as he pulled Vince to his feet.

"I don't wanna go," Vince slurred, weaving as he stood by the table.

"You sure, Vince? You got duty tomorrow, and guard mount comes awful early."

"Oh, shit. Do I have to, T.J.?"

"Yes, you do. Now be a good little soldier, and come with me."

T.J. helped Vince up, and pointed him toward the door. As they passed Ski's table, Ski looked up at them and said something unintelligible. He stood up and threw his arms around Vince, bursting into tears. He mumbled something else, gave Vince a big wet kiss on the cheek. He then threw his arms around T.J., hugged him, and fell back into his chair reaching for his beer.

T.J. guided Vince to his hootch, and dumped him on his bunk fully clothed. Vince was snoring softly almost before he hit the blankets. By the time the party ended two hours later, Ski had passed out on the floor. Renfro and Hickok carried him to his hootch and put him to bed, an empty beer bottle clenched in his hand.

9 September, 1967 0600 hrs.

This was SFC Milars' first guard mount as the company's new First Sergeant. He had everyone standing at parade rest while he addressed the group. As he made each point, he checked it off on a clipboard he carried.

"This company has been run too loose for too long. From now on, it will be run by the book. There is only one right way to do our job, and that's according to regulations. So, no more pissing out the doors of your hootch. Use the latrines. If you want to go to the movies, meet in the company area 15 minutes before show time, and we will march over as a unit. You will no longer park your jeeps in the company area when you come in for chow. They will be parked at the motor pool, and you will walk to the mess hall. Whenever you leave the company area, you will be in proper, full uniform, including soft caps. All cut-off utility trousers are to be disposed of. They are unauthorized, and it is against army regs to alter the prescribed uniform in any way. Food is not to be removed from the mess hall, and no food is allowed in the hooches. Soft drinks are OK, but no alcoholic beverages. Music will be kept low so it does not disturb others around you. There will be no loud, boisterous behavior in the company area. Proper rules of etiquette will be followed at all times."

"Is this guy for real, Vince?" T.J. whispered out of the corner of his mouth.

"I sure hope not, T.J. Man, is he in for trouble! The guys aren't gonna take this too kindly!"

"THERE WILL BE NO TALKING DURING GUARD MOUNT!!" Milar yelled, looking directly at Vince. "You will remain at parade rest until ordered otherwise during inspection. Weapons, ammunition, and uniforms will be in order before dismissal. Company; ATTENSHUN."

The company snapped to attention, and at the command "Present HARMS" drew their .45s, locked the slide back, and held them at a 45 degree upward angle 3 inches from their chest. SFC Milar made his way through the ranks, followed by Jackson, who had been promoted to Buck Sergeant three weeks earlier. Milar carefully inspected each uniform for proper creases, buttoned pockets, rolled sleeves, and bloused trousers above their polished jungle boots. When he found an infraction, he would note it on his clipboard. Every so often, he would inspect an M-16 or M-60, or ammo belt. Any weapons that didn't pass his scrutiny had to be cleaned and re-inspected before that MP went on duty.

After guard mount, SFC Milar returned to his office to transcribe the notes he had made into a report to the Lieutenant. He also made notations in the files of the MPs he found lacking. He had sent for the company artist, and when he knocked and walked in, SFC Milar stopped writing, placed his pen on the desk, and handed him a sheet of instructions written in his bold style. "This needs to be completed before 1800 hours," he said. "The materials have been stacked behind the arms room. Dismissed, Corporal."

SFC Milar picked up his pen and began writing again, as if the Corporal wasn't there. The Corporal stood in front of the desk, reading the instructions, then turned and walked out, shaking his head in disgust. SFC Milar did not see him leave.

Vince and Wild Bill had been assigned to gate duty at the 90th replacement for the first half of their shift. Their post was a round bunker big enough for 3 people to occupy comfortably. The walls were concrete, five feet high and 18" thick. Sand bags had been stacked in front and around the sides as extra protection, and a double layer was on top of the wall to the front. An M-60 was mounted inside, pointing toward the fields across the road, and a field phone had been hung inside to provide communications with the PMO at Long Binh. Railroad tracks ran alongside the entrance road past the bunker, in a 20' deep gully. This was well protected with wire, mines, and powerful floodlights at night to prevent infiltration by the VC. At night, the MPs would tie a mongrel dog, appropriately named "Charlie", to the wire above the tracks. If there was anyone or anything moving down there, Charlie would start barking. He was the guard posts' very effective early warning system.

The area in front of the guard post, across Hwy 1, was all a free fire zone. Anyone moving out there after curfew was fair game. The perimeter wire was thick, and interspersed with lots of trip flares and mines.

The MPs job was to carefully check all vehicles entering

and leaving the post. Travel papers and individual orders were carefully read to make sure those coming into or leaving the base had the authority to do so. If there was any doubt, a quick phone call was made to check them out.

Vince took his duties seriously, always checking the GIs' paperwork carefully. There was a steady stream of traffic in and out until about 1000 hours, when the number of vehicles slacked off. It had begun to rain, lightly at first, then heavily, and Vince and Wild Bill huddled in the bunker, trying to stay dry. The tin roof helped keep some of the rain out, but the strong winds blew it in through the open sides between the roof and the walls. They had not brought their ponchos with them when they left the company after guard mount.

"So what do you think of Sgt. Milar, Vince?" Wild Bill asked, wiping the rain off his face.

"He's the exact opposite of Ski, that's for sure. Too much by the book for my liking."

"Yeah, me too. A total Lifer. I don't think the guys are gonna be too happy with him."

"I think you're right, Wild Bill. After that speech this morning, I can hardly wait to see what else he's got in store for us."

At noon their relief arrived, and they headed back to the company area for lunch. After lunch, they spent the rest of their shift on town patrol. The rain had ended, and the sun had broken through the clouds, drying the streets. It was a slow day, with not much happening. They handled one accident in which a corporal from the 1st Cav driving to Di An rear-ended an empty Lambretta. Vince wrote up the report, had the Corporal give the Lambretta driver $10 in military payment script to appease him, since there was hardly any damage to either vehicle, and sent them on their way. The rest of the day was spent patrolling the city and along the river.

At the end of their day, Vince drove into the company

area to drop off Wild Bill and their equipment before turning the jeep in. The first thing he saw was a freshly painted sign on a stand in the middle of the gravel lot. It was made from wood, and painted OD green with white lettering that said "No parking in Company Area." There were four similar signs at various locations, declaring "Clean Your Weapons", "Quiet at All Times", another "No Parking", and one that announced "No Running in the Company Area."

"I don't fucking believe it!" Vince muttered.

"You better believe it, pal," T.J. said, as he walked up to the jeep. "Wait until you see the other ones all over the area. You're really gonna be pissed! Meet me at the hootch after you're done."

Vince dropped off the jeep, cleaned his weapons and turned them in, then walked back to his hootch. He dropped his gear at his bunk, and he and T.J. walked through the company looking at all the signs. There was another "Quiet" sign at the entrance to each of the hooches, several "Use the Latrine" signs, and a "Do Not Remove Food" sign at each entrance to the mess hall.

"This can't be happening, T.J. Does he think this is a basic training camp? A lot of these guys have been through some rough times, and aren't about to put up with this crap."

"I know, Vince. It ain't right, but he must have the Lieutenant's blessing. So we better get used to it. Milar is the boss now. You ready to eat?"

"Yeah. Wonder what signs are posted at the mess hall."

"Whatever they are, they won't make the food taste any better."

Vince chuckled softly. "Got that right. Let's go."

Vince listened to the grumbling of the other MPs during dinner and afterwards at the rebuilt EM Club. When asked his opinion, all he would say is he didn't like it but it did no good to just complain.

"What do you mean?" one of the others asked.

"Just what I said. It does no good if we just complain."

"What have you got in mind, Vince?" T.J. asked.

"Nothing. Just seems to me that complaining never solved anything, and action speaks louder than words, right? Anyway, who's buying the next round?"

He went to bed a couple of hours later, as he had MedCap duty the next day with T.J. and a newly arrived MP named Flannery.

The next morning Vince walked to guard mount, and placed his gear on the ground. Several of the MPs were huddled together, talking quietly, chuckling now and then. His curiosity aroused, he walked over to the group, and asked, "What's going on, guys?"

Wild Bill grinned at him, and pointed to the top of the water tower a short distance away. The tower was a 5,000 gallon wooden tank on a 50 foot high platform, and contained the potable water for the company. Arranged neatly around the walkway on the top edge of the tower were all the signs SFC Milar had placed throughout the company area the day before.

Vince laughed and said, "I don't think Milar's going to be too pleased about this."

"Guess we'll find out," Booger Baines smirked, under his breath. "Here he comes now."

SFC Milar stormed up to the hastily formed guard mount and yelled, "ATTEN-SHUN." When they were all standing rigidly in place, he began walking down the line of men, looking each in the face as he passed.

"I want to know who is responsible for this, and I want to know NOW! Somebody will pay for this act of insubordination. This is inexcusable, and I want the guilty party to step forward!"

All the MPs remained at attention. SFC Milar waited a long 30 seconds, and when no one moved, said, "Alright. If that's the way you want it. Whoever you are, you better pray I don't find you out. Hickok, front and center!"

Hickok moved up and stood at attention in front of Milar.

"PFC Hickok reporting as ordered, Sergeant," he shouted in his best basic training impersonation. Behind him, he could hear the snickers and chuckles from the other MPs, trying hard to maintain their composure. Vince managed, through great effort, to keep his face expressionless.

"Get my signs down, Private, now!"

"Right away, Sergeant," he replied, then ran to the tower and began climbing the ladder attached to the side. He stopped halfway up, waved at the group, grinned, then continued climbing. When he got to the top, he climbed onto the walkway, but "accidentally" stumbled into the row of signs, knocking three off the rim. They smashed to pieces when they hit the ground.

"Sorry, Sergeant," he yelled, "Lost my balance. I'll get the rest down."

He then backed up two steps, bumping into two more, causing them to follow the other three to the ground.

"Oops, sorry. Won't happen again, Sarge."

By now, the rest of the guard mount had given up trying to stifle their laughter. Milar turned to them, his face red and twitching, and yelled "GUARD MOUNT! YOU ARE AT ATTENTION!"

Hickok had gathered up the remaining signs, and was trying to climb down the ladder, cradling all 9 signs in his arms. About a third of the way down, his foot slipped off a rung, seemingly by accident, causing him to drop the signs so he could grab onto the ladder to keep from falling. The wood signs tumbled to the ground in a heap, pieces flying in all directions like wood shrapnel when they hit.

"Whoa, Sarge! That was close! I almost fell," he said, as he climbed the rest of the way down.

"Hickok, in my office. NOW. Guard mount,

DISMISSED."

Milar turned and rapidly walked to his office, following Wild Bill inside. The MPs could hear him shouting, but could not make out what he was saying.

Vince and T.J. walked to the motor pool, the new guy, Flannery, following behind.

"I hope Milar isn't too hard on Hickok," T.J. said, chuckling.

"Going to get a major ass-chewing, but that's probably all. What else can he do to him? C'mon, Flannery, we got work to do."

"Any ideas as to who put the signs up there?" Flannery asked.

"I think it was a cooperative effort," T.J. replied, grinning, "don't know for sure, though. My guess is no one will ever find out. And don't go around asking too many questions, OK?"

"Sure, T.J., I understand."

Two days later, the signs were back. Sgt. Milar had the company artist work 12 hours repainting the new signs the carpenter had made. He personally placed the signs through out the company area.

At 0410 hrs. a loud "whoosh" and flash of light illuminated the area outside Sgt. Milar's hootch, waking him instantly. At first, he thought a mortar shell had landed close by, but when he cautiously looked out the door, he saw what had happened.

Thirty feet from his front door was a large bonfire blazing 50 feet into the air, fueled by several gallons of gasoline. Milar could see all the signs that had been repainted and repaired burning fiercely. Someone had gathered up all the signs, stacked them in front of Milar's hootch, doused them with gasoline, and set them on fire. Before anything could be done, the signs were totally destroyed.

Of course, there was hell to pay. Milar called a formation an hour later. As he made his way through the ranks, he sniffed each MP to see if he could smell gas on them, and yelled at the whole group, threatening them with article 15's or worse if any were caught doing anything wrong from then on. Each MP knew he would have to be on his best behavior until this episode blew over. There were no more signs posted in the company area.

September 12, 1967,   0710 hrs.

"Man, Vince, Milar has been a real asshole lately," T.J. said, as he forked some powdered eggs into his mouth. "He never really got over the sign bonfire."

"Yeah. I wonder who could have done that?" Vince asked, looking pointedly at T.J. over the rim of his coffee cup.

"Beats me," T.J. said, not looking at him, concentrating on his plate. "You should see what he's been doing."

"What's he been up to?"

"He keeps making 'surprise' inspections at all hours of the night, barging into the hooches, waking everyone up, searching their gear."

"Yeah, I know. I've been there a couple of times myself."

"Well, now whenever he hears a radio or tape recorder on, he comes stormin' in yellin' 'Turn down that narcotic music'. We all just laugh at him, and that really pisses him off. In retaliation, he makes us meet in the company area if we want to see the movie, and march over in cadence, as if we're still in basic trainin'. Get this, Vince. Every time he sees anyone with one of those Vicks inhalers, he grabs it from them, and tears it apart, lookin' for drugs."

"What's his problem? Does he think everyone with one of those things is a drug addict?"

"I guess so. Yesterday, I went to the PX, and bought about 25 of 'em. I'm gonna give 'em out to everyone for tomorrow night's guard mount. We're all gonna take 'em out at once and see what happens. Want one?"

"Why not. This oughta be good!"

T.J. lowered his voice so only Vince could hear him. "I got a case of smoke grenades, too."

"How'd you do that?" Vince asked, grinning, wondering what T.J. had in mind.

"You remember yesterday when they pulled the clerk, Givens, outta the office, and put him on the road? Well, the guy ain't been on patrol since he got here, and don't know how to handle his weapons very well. After shift, we were standing in line at the clearing barrel. He was behind me, and after I cleared my .45, he asks me how to clear his. I told him to eject the round in the chamber, point it at the barrel, and pull the trigger. I said not to worry if it fires, just keep pulling the trigger until it stops. Dumb shit just walked up to the barrel, jacks a round out, then starts firing the rest of the rounds off. Everyone hits the ground, the arms room sergeant comes runnin' out and around the side to see whats goin' on, and starts yellin' at him."

Vince started laughing, saying, "You're kidding! He really did that?"

"Yep. And he wasn't foolin' around. He really thought that was the right way to clear it! Anyway, I saw the arms room door open, ain't nobody around, so I just walks in and grabs the first case I see. Turns out, it's all smoke grenades. I stashed 'em on top of the ammo bunker."

"What are you planning to do with them?" Vince asked, looking around the mess hall.

"Not quite sure, yet. That's what I wanted to talk to you about."

He leaned closer and lowered his voice even more. They talked quietly for the next several minutes, laughing softly once in awhile, then agreed to meet outside Milar's office later that night.

13 September, 1967   0435 hrs.

Vince finished tying the smoke grenade to one of the struts just outside the screen covering the side of Milar's office. He straightened the pin holding the firing handle in place, and tied the string to it, passing the other end through the screen into the office. T.J. took the end and stretched it across the office, tying it to the entrance doorknob. He then left through the back door, relocking it as he left. The clerk on duty in the outer office did not hear them, as he was happily sleeping, his head on the desk.

SFC Milar arrived at the office at 0545, and stopped in the clerks' office to pour himself a cup of coffee from the pot next to his office door. He walked to the clerks' desk and removed the dispatches and reports from the previous day, scanning the top sheet as he walked to his office, turned the knob, and pulled the door open. The string tightened, pulling the pin from the grenade. The firing handle popped off, igniting the fuse, and three seconds later, the grenade went off with a loud "pop", spewing smoke throughout the office.

Milar had taken three steps into the office when the sound of the grenade igniting caused him to look up, just as a cloud of purple smoke billowed over him. Coughing, he stumbled backwards, dropping the papers and his coffee cup. He bumped into the clerk, who had run into the office to see what had happened, knocking them both to the floor. Coughing and choking, they crawled out of Milar's office, through the clerks' office and out into the open. They got to their feet, and staggered into the company area, wiping the tears from their eyes and trying to get their breath back, to the accompaniment of the laughter of the 15 MPs preparing for the morning guard mount. Purple smoke poured out the doors and sides of the offices.

"THIS IS NOT FUNNY!" Milar bellowed. "STOP THAT LAUGHING RIGHT NOW!"

The sight of Milar, the clerk, and the office only made the MPs laugh harder, having been joined by several others from the mess hall who had heard the shouting.

"C'mon, Vince, let's get outa here," T.J. said, looking guiltily around.

"Not yet, T.J. No one knows it was us, but it may cause some suspicion if we suddenly disappear."

"Yeah, guess you're right." T.J. looked at the smoke-filled office, and laughed softly.

"This was a good one, Vince."

"We are the best, T.J., aren't we?"

"Yeah, and we ain't done yet. We're gonna have to cool it for a bit, though. He's gonna be on the warpath, and we're all gonna pay for this."

Several MPs were walking off, headed back to the mess hall or to their hooches, so they quietly left with them, walking casually away.

Three and a half hours later, the cleanup crew selected by Milar finished with his office. A second crew, sent to relieve them and to clean the clerks' office, arrived and began moving stuff outside from the office. Everything had to be taken outside and aired out to rid it of the smoke smell. The walls, floor, and ceiling had to be washed down, not only to remove the smell, but the purple tinge that covered them. The MPs on the cleanup details were those unwise or unlucky enough to have remained too long in the company area that morning. Milar immediately suspected them of being involved in the prank, and figured he could extract a small revenge by making them clean up the mess. The MPs didn't mind too much, because it was such a great joke they felt it was worth it.

At guard mount that evening, Milar was still in a foul mood. Every little thing he could find wrong resulted in that person being on report. He ripped off buttons that he found unfastened, dinged others over the cleanliness of their weapons, and put others on report because they hadn't, in his opinion, shaved close enough. By the end of guard mount, he had filled two pages on his clipboard.

"Guard mount, DISMISSED!" he shouted.

As the formation broke up, all the MPs pulled out the inhalers T.J. had given them earlier, took the caps off, put them to their noses, and began to noisily sniff the contents. Milar watched them, turned beet red and, with his face twitching, turned without a word and walked away. Once he entered the office, the MPs burst into laughter, the sound following Milar as he made his way to his desk.

23 September, 1967   2020 hrs.

Milar made his way to the shower, wearing his robe, carrying his towel and soap. He preferred showering at night, as there usually was no one else in the shower. He knew he didn't fit in with this company, and had no desire to try. He did not make friends easily, and felt his authority would be undermined if he became too familiar with the men under his command. He stepped into the shower room, and saw it was empty. He put his robe and towel on a bench by the door, and turned on the shower. He was happy to find there was hot water tonight. More often than not, cold showers were the order of the day, as the heating unit was constantly breaking down. He stood under the spray, letting the water run over him, luxuriating in the soothing warmth, oblivious to his surroundings.

The shower door slowly opened a few inches, and a hand tossed a canister into Milar's shower. The canister burst, and yellow smoke began to fill the room. Milar opened his eyes at the "pop" of the smoke grenade igniting, and as the acrid smoke enveloped him, groaned "not again", beginning to cough. He moved toward the door, feeling for his robe and towel as he went, but they had been taken from the bench after the canister was thrown in. He stumbled outside, rubbing his eyes. Several flashbulbs went off as he staggered naked away from the shower room. Before he could clear his vision, whoever had taken the pictures had disappeared. Milar found his robe on the ground outside the shower, picked it up, and walked back to his hootch without putting it on. Taped to the door was a crudely lettered note that said "There's lots more where that came from. You will never know when or where the next one will come."

One week later, his transfer request to the 29th General Support Group was approved. He wasted no time packing, and was gone that same day. No one was there to see him off, and no one but the Lieutenant bothered to say goodbye.

By then, U.S. combat deaths in Vietnam had almost doubled from the year before, sparking protests all over the United States. Students and non-students regularly demonstrated at the University of California, Berkeley, often resulting in rioting and acts of civil disobedience. Local Police and California Highway Patrol officers did their best to maintain order and disperse the demonstrators, arresting scores of protestors and using dogs, tear gas, and riot squads. Other protests at the University of San Francisco, though smaller, were just as boisterous, and in the nation's Capital, thousands of protesters gathered on a regular basis, and on Oct. 21, over 50,000 people demonstrated in Washington D.C. against the war.

During this same time, Operation Shenandoah II was underway in Binh Duong Province northwest of Saigon. Almost 1,000 VC and NVA were killed by the 1st Infantry Division. Operation Swift involving the 1st Marine Division in Quang Nam and Quang Tin Provinces, I Corps, accounted for over 500 enemy dead in just eleven days, and Operation Kingfisher near the DMZ involving the 3rd Marine Division, killed over 1100 NVA. American casualties were listed as "light" by MACV.

Thanksgiving Day 1967

Dinner was set for 1600 hours. Vince and T.J. were lucky enough to be off, and walked over to the mess hall a few minutes early. Vince wasn't feeling very good, as he had just finished reading letters from his mother and fiancée, and was feeling homesick. Though they kept their letters full of happy news, that only made him more homesick. He was feeling sorry for himself, hating being where he was, and wishing he could go home. He picked up his tray and moved down the line. The servers plopped mashed potatoes, creamed corn, turkey slices, cranberry sauce, and stuffing on his tray, not caring that it all ended up in a pile. The last server ladled gravy over the whole pile, covering everything.

"Why don't you just put all this in a blender, turn it on, and I'll drink it?" Vince said, disgustedly, stopping in front of the mess sergeant at the end of the line.

"Move on, MP. Be happy you got that."

"I can't tell you how happy I am, Sarge. I'll be sure to mark this day as one my favorites," he said, walking to his table.

As he sat down, T.J. looked up and said, "Seven months, Vince, then back to the world. We're gettin' short, man."

"Yeah, we are. God, it seems like I been here for years."

"You? I been here six months longer than you, ya know."

"Yeah, but that's your own damn fault. You could have left here after the second time you got wounded, but you decided to stay. You're crazy. If it was me, I'd have been outta here on the next plane."

"I couldn't leave, Vince. Who was gonna look out for you, bein' such a dumb-ass newbie and all. Why, you just mighta got in trouble without me here to protect ya. Besides, it knocked time off my enlistment when I extended. I get an early out."

111

"Yeah, right."

"Well, whatever works. Besides, the scars give me character."

"I can do without the 'character'. And I'm much prettier than you, anyway. I don't need the help."

"Well, like I said before, whatever works."

"Seriously, T.J., what're you going to do when you get out?"

"Don't really know, Vince. Haven't given it much thought. I do know I ain't gonna settle in Riggins. Maybe I'll go down to Boise. I kinda like the army, though. Even thought of stayin' in, makin' it a career."

"See, you are nuts. I can't wait till my time is up. I've had enough of soldiering to last me a lifetime."

"I don't know, Vince. It don't seem so bad an idea. After this is over, we ain't gonna get involved in another war for awhile. Could be a nice, quiet life. Steady pay, three meals a day, always got a roof over my head. It ain't so bad. Wanna re-up with me?"

"Nah, I don't think so. I'm going back to my family, my fiancee. Sanders is going to be a cop. Maybe I'll do the same."

"Now who's nuts? I wouldn't be a cop for all the money in the world."

"Beats army life. Got a letter from my dad yesterday. He says San Francisco PD is hiring, looking for veterans. I guess that will mean me, soon enough. Me and Sanders, two old vets turned cop. Kinda has a poetic ring to it."

"What have you got left when you get outa here, Vince? Six months?"

"Yeah. I'm trying to get a duty station near home. I hear the army will usually let you spend your last few months close to home, so I hope I get Oakland Army Base or the Presidio in San Francisco. I could live at home until I get out, then maybe join a police department somewhere. I'd like to stay in the Bay Area if I could."

"I'd like to be an officer. Maybe I'll apply for OCS."

"You WHAT?" Vince cried, shocked at this statement from his friend. "All I've heard from you for the last five months is how shitty army life is, and now you're talking about becoming a lifer, and an OFFICER at that! Man, if that doesn't take the cake!"

"Who knows, Vince. I may end up a General some day. Wouldn't that be a bit of news."

"Heaven help us and the U.S. Army."

Vince lit a cigarette, then said, "You ever get homesick, T.J.?"

"Yeah, sometimes. I miss my family and friends, though there were few enough of them in Riggins. Place ain't that big."

"I miss my family, too. Sometimes it aches so bad I can hardly stand it. I start to hate this place all over again, and I can't stop thinking of home, my mom and dad. I wonder what my brother's up to. My fiancée writes me all the time, but it doesn't help. It's just not the same, and reading her letters only makes me miss her more. Rotation can't come soon enough to suit me."

"Me, neither. My luck is gonna run out if I'm not careful. I think I've pushed it to the limit. Can't wait to get outa here. Between you and me, I think extending my tour was a mistake." He sighed, smiled at Vince, and said, "How about a beer? I'm buyin'."

"Sounds good. Let's get out of here."

23 December, 1968   1834 hrs.

The entire company was standing in formation in the company area, listening to the LT giving out the next two days' duty schedule.

"The enemy has declared a Christmas cease fire through New Years day."

A series of hoots and jeers greeted this announcement, causing the LT to smile and hold up his hand.

"Quiet down, now. I know, I know, we've heard it before. How many of you were here for the Tet cease fire last year?"

T.J. raised his hand, along with several others. Looking around, the LT said, "Guess you guys oughta know better than any of us how good their word is. I know this is a tough time to be here, and it's even tougher having to work, but I'm posting the duty schedule in the clerks' office. Check it out. We aren't lettin' down our guard again, so we will remain at full compliment over the holidays. No one gets the day off unless it's your regular day, so don't ask. Sorry, guys. O.K., let's hit it. Dis-missed!"

The LT turned on his heels, and headed back to the office. The MPs walked away in groups, grumbling among themselves. Vince, T.J., and Sorenson headed for the EM Club for a beer, with several others. All three had the next two nights off, but were scheduled to start day shift on Christmas day.

T.J. bought three beers at the bar, and carried them over to their table. He sat down and passed one to Vince and Sorenson.

"I'm sure glad we're gonna be on days," he said. "Looks like we got bus escort for the next few days. I'd just as soon stay on that. It's easy duty, safe, too."

The sound of breaking glass caught their attention, and looking toward the bar, they saw one of the Vietnamese barmaids picking herself up off the floor. She started picking up the shards of broken glass from the drink glasses she had dropped when she had fallen, placing them on her tray. They could see she was crying. Three GIs Vince didn't recognize were standing at the bar, laughing. The tallest of them, the apparent leader of the group, turned to the barmaid, and said, "Next time, watch where the fuck you're going, you clumsy, goddamn gook," loud enough for them to hear. He turned back to the bar, said something to the other two, causing them to burst out

114

laughing again.

Vince got up and walked over to the barmaid. Kneeling on the floor, he started helping her clean up the glass. "It's all right, Thuy, we'll take care of it."

"Oh, Torelli, I so sorry. Thuy not clumsy. I not fall. That GI, he put foot out, he make me fall, then laugh at Thuy. Why he do that? Why he want hurt Thuy?"

"Are you OK? Did you get hurt when you fell?"

"No. Thuy all right. I very sorry," she said, starting to cry again.

"It's OK, Thuy, it's OK," Vince said, putting his arm around her shoulders, and pulling her to him. She sobbed softly, her face pressed to his shoulder.

"Well, now, ain't that touchin'," the tall GI said, watching them.

Vince looked up at him, and seeing the smirk on his lips, stood up and slapped him across the face, hard. Startled, the PFC clenched his fists and took a step toward him. T.J. and the others got up and moved to a position behind Vince as the PFC came at him. Vince grabbed him by the throat, squeezing hard enough to cut off his air.

"Back off, asshole," he said, pushing him back.

Gasping for air, the PFC rubbed his throat. Looking first at his friends, then at Torelli and the others, he gasped, "This ain't done with. I'll be waitin' outside when the club closes. Just you and me, punk. C'mon, guys, lets get outa here." He turned away and walked out, followed by the other two GIs. Vince and the others walked back to their table and sat down.

"That went well," T.J. said, grinning. "You know that guy'll be waitin' for you when we leave."

"Yeah, I know. Maybe he'll cool off a bit before then."

"What happened over there?" Sorenson asked.

Turning to him, Vince growled, "He's a punk. He trips Thuy, then laughs and makes fun of her when she falls. You saw her crying, didn't you?"

115

"Yeah. It ain't right."

"I know. It pissed me off."

T.J. stood up and said, "I'll be back, gotta take a leak," and walked out the door.

Sorenson went to the bar and got three beers, then returned to the table. They listened to the Filipino band play for a while until T.J. returned. The band was doing a decent job on one of the more recent rock tunes from the States, but seemed to play more songs from a few years earlier, in particular, the early Beatles and Stones stuff.

When the club closed two hours later, they walked out the side door and headed toward their hootch. As they rounded the corner and started walking between the rows of hooches, four soldiers stepped out from between the buildings on their left, and four more from the buildings on their right, blocking their way. The tall GI from the bar stepped forward toward Vince.

"I told you I'd be waiting for you. Time for some payback."

"You need all that help, or is it going to be just you and me?"

"It's gonna be whatever I want it to be." Turning to the others he said, "Let's get done with it, guys."

As the soldier stepped toward him, Vince moved into him, throwing a punch that connected with the GI's nose, breaking it. The GI staggered back, clutching his nose with both hands, as the blood began flowing through his fingers. Vince followed, punching him twice in the stomach, knocking the wind from him. He fell to his knees, gasping for air, blood dripping from his ruined nose. The other GIs, taken by surprise, started forward, anger etched on their faces. Before they could get to Vince, T.J. stepped in front of them. As he did, he reached under his shirt, and pulled out a .45 auto pistol. Jacking a round in the chamber, he pointed it at the first GI's forehead. They stopped suddenly, their eyes opening wide as they saw the gun.

"I think it's time we put an end to this."

"T.J.!" Vince said. "What are you doing?"

"Don't worry about it, Vince."

Turning to the GIs he said, "You guys wanna push it, or do you think it's time to end it?"

The group backed up a few steps. One of them held his hands up, palms toward T.J., and said, "Whoa, Cowboy. No need for that. We don't even like him very much ourselves. I think me and the rest of the boys will be leaving now, OK?"

"I think that's a good idea. I also think you better take your friend there, and forget all about this. I don't want to see you guys around here again, or at the club understand? You've worn out your welcome."

"Yeah, yeah, we get the picture. C'mon, guys, let's get outa here."

Two of the GIs walked over and helped their friend to his feet, supporting him as they walked off. T.J. kept them covered until they rounded the corner, then carefully lowered the hammer of the pistol, and tucked it back in his waistband, pulling his shirt over it.

"Where'd you get that, T.J.?" Vince asked, grinning.

"From a friend of mine in my old unit. I've had it for a few months. Knew it would come in handy some day."

"It sure did. Thanks, T.J. I thought we were in for a bad time there for a while. I tried to take the big guy out first. Figured the others might not be so anxious to fight with him out of the picture. I need a beer. Anyone else want one? I got some in the cooler in the hootch."

"Yeah, I'll have one," Sorenson said, walking toward the hootch. "I sure didn't feel like getting my ass kicked tonight. I haven't ever been in a fight, you know. I was the one everyone picked on in school."

Vince and T.J. looked at each other, then burst into laughter.

117

"Don't worry, man," Vince said, throwing his arm over Sorenson's shoulder, and chuckling, "it's over. We won't have any more problems with them, thanks to T.J. Let's get back to the hootch."

They walked off toward their hootch, talking quietly, as the company area settled in for the night. They had a couple of beers and played cards for another hour, then Sorenson and T.J. turned in. Vince stayed up for another 45 minutes, writing letters, before going to bed.

The next morning, Christmas Eve, Vince slept in, getting up at 0800 hours. He was too late for breakfast at the mess hall, but went to the back door and got some fruit from the mess sergeant. He planned to get a haircut and do some shopping at the PX. His fiancee had decided what china pattern she wanted, and he wanted to order it from the Pacex catalog at the PX, and have it sent directly to her. He found T.J. in the day room, and they set off, walking across the Post toward the PX.

As they crossed an open field, they saw an old pappa-san leading a water buffalo pulling a cart. The cart was loaded with halves of 55 gallon drums, and pappa-san was leading the buffalo toward a pit dug in the middle of the field. Since there was no such thing as a sewage treatment plant, or even any sewers, the army hired local Vietnamese to collect the half drums placed under the toilet seats in the latrines, and cart them to a pit where they emptied them, then poured diesel fuel on the waste, and set it on fire.

"There goes the honey wagon, Vince," T.J. said, as they watched the old pappa-san make his way to the burn pit.

"God, T.J., can you imagine doing that for a living? You could tell your grandkids, "Yep, I was a shit burner durin' the war"."

"Let's get outa here before he lights it, Vince. Ain't nuthin' worse than the smell of burnin' shit."

They walked a little faster, leaving the field just as pappa-san finished dragging the barrels off the cart and dumping their contents in the pit. He poured five gallons of diesel fuel over the mess, and set it on fire. Heavy, black smoke began rising into the sky as it burned. Once the fire was burning good, pappa-san loaded the empty barrels back on the cart, and set off to take them back to the latrine he got them from, then moved on to the next latrine to empty their barrels in the pit. He did this three times a week, for which he was paid $20 a month.

Vince spent an hour at the PX ordering the china, paying for it, and arranging to have it delivered to his fiancee. They bought some other things, had some lunch at the PX snack bar, then walked to the base theater to see the movie. "Hush Hush Sweet Charlotte" with Betty Davis was playing, and even though Vince had seen it twice already, they went inside, where they could get out of the heat for a couple of hours. There was a show scheduled at the EM Club later that night that they wanted to go to. The band was an American rock band sponsored by the USO, and was supposed to be pretty good. They mostly wanted to go in the hopes that there would be American female singers or dancers with them. It had been a long time since they had seen a round eye woman.

Vince fell asleep during the last half of the movie. Afterwards, they walked back to the company area, arriving just in time for mail call. Vince received three letters, two from his fiancee and one from his mother. Placing the other letters in his pocket so he could read them later in private, he walked over to the weapons cleaning area and sat on the bench. Opening the letter from his mother, he began to read.

PART II
TET

24 January, 1968

Fifteen miles northwest of Long Binh, a Long Range Reconnaissance Patrol, or LRRP Team, on a training exercise spotted two platoons of VC heading south through the jungle. They remained hidden while the VC passed, as they were greatly outnumbered, and had instructions to avoid contact if at all possible. They noted the VC appeared well fed and rested, and were carrying much more equipment than usual. 81mm mortars, 122mm rockets, RPG's, and crates of ammunition were distributed among the VC soldiers. The LRRP team took note of the weaponry and size of the enemy force, and after they had passed, faded back into the jungle to continue their exercise.

Two days later, they returned to their base camp at Lai Khe, and reported the sighting to their CO at the de-briefing. The CO turned in his handwritten report to his clerk the next day for typing. The clerk did not get it typed until late that afternoon, and since he was late in meeting his buddies at the EM Club, he put it in his out basket to send to Division HQ the next day. The next morning, the report missed the morning courier, so it was not picked up for delivery until that afternoon. It was not delivered until the following morning. The Major who received all such reports was in a staff meeting until after lunch, and was unable to read it until that afternoon. After reading the report, he felt it was important enough to forward to headquarters. He called his assistant, and told him to put the report with several other unusual contact reports, and get them on the chopper to MACV Headquarters at Long Binh. At Long Binh, the reports became part of the mass of paperwork awaiting attention, and it was another day before the report was read. The intelligence officer thought it important enough to forward to Saigon, and on the afternoon of Jan. 29th he put it in the courier bag for delivery. The report would not be delivered until Jan. 30.

The VC spotted by the LRRP team were mostly combat-hardened veterans of the 273rd VC Regiment known as the Loc Ninh Regiment. On that day, they were moving weapons and supplies to a secret base 5 kilometers southwest of Bien Hoa. Capt. Thuong kept the two platoons on the march 16 hours a day, delivering the weapons, ammo, and medical supplies his company would need to accomplish their mission the following week. He hoped to have all his supplies and men in place with a few days to spare, to allow the men to rest, train, and prepare their weapons. He also needed time to brief his platoon leaders on their individual missions. A model of the Bien Hoa Air Base had been prepared for his use, with bunkers, ammo and fuel dumps, buildings, and aircraft storage areas marked. His mission was to attack the air base by overrunning the perimeter defenses, then make his way to the aircraft storage area to destroy as many planes and helicopters as possible along with any fuel or ammo dumps he came across. His would be one of several companies attacking the air base. The objective was to create as much destruction and confusion as possible, and to prevent any American air support or response.

Communications centers were priority targets, and the sapper teams assigned to destroy them were prepared to sacrifice everything to accomplish their mission. A secondary goal was to prevent or delay any response to the attacks from the base at Di An, a few miles from the air base, or from Long Binh. Other units from the regiment were to attack the Ton Son Nhut air base, and selected targets in Saigon. They, too, were transporting last minute supplies and weapons to their assigned assembly points in preparation for the planned offensive. By January 28, all the units were in place, resting and waiting the last couple of days until the signal to attack came.

30 January, 1968 1745 hours

Vince and T.J. finished dressing, and collected their gear for guard mount. They walked to the company area and stacked their gear in the formation area, then went to the arms room to check out their weapons. They got their M-16s, .45s, and ammo. T.J. checked out a grenade launcher, 8 HE grenades and 4 parachute flares. They went to the cleaning table, and wiped each weapon down with an oily rag. They checked each weapon's action several times, making sure it worked properly, then checked each magazine, making sure they were fully and properly loaded, and that each would feed the rounds properly if needed. Each MP went through this pre-duty check, being careful to do a thorough job.

Vince carefully placed his ammo on his flak jacket, making sure it did not fall on the ground. He put on his helmet liner, and made sure his web belt and MP arm band were straight. When all was ready, he walked over to a group of MPs talking with Sanders.

"So there's supposed to be this Tet cease-fire goin' on," Sanders was saying, "but the gooks have never honored it before. Somehow, I don't think this year will be any different."

"I've heard of it before, but exactly what is Tet, Sanders?" Vince asked.

"It's the Vietnamese lunar new year. Supposed to be their biggest holiday. The North always calls for this cease-fire for the holidays, then uses the time to resupply, rest, and infiltrate. Last year, they took advantage of the time to move supplies down the Ho Chi Minh trail. Gave us hell for quite a while after that. I expect this year will be the same. We're gonna be in for a rough time before much longer, so you guys gotta be extra careful off Post." Looking over his shoulder, he said, "Here comes the LT. Fall in, guys."

2015 hours

Vince was riding shotgun tonight. It gave him the opportunity to really look around. He found that the city looked different at night, without all the people and noise. He and Sanders had decided Vince would ride the first half of the night, taking over the driving after midnight chow. They were enroute to the Cherry Bar to assist Daniels and Felman on a disturbance call. They had hit off on a bar check about five minutes earlier, and a couple of minutes later Felman came back on the radio, out of breath, asking for another two units, saying they had a half dozen drunk GIs detained, and were having some trouble controlling them. Sanders heard the call, and started heading that way, knowing he would be sent anyway. Parker and Anderson were also en route to help, but were a few miles farther away.

Sanders pulled up in front of the bar, and parked next to Daniels' jeep. He and Vince got out and walked to the front door. Just as Sanders pulled it open, a body came flying out, landing on the ground, unconscious. Sanders rolled him over and saw he was a PFC, his shoulder patch indicating he was with the 199th Infantry Brigade.

"Vince, cuff him to the jeep, then come inside," Sanders said, as he walked into the bar, pulling his billy club from its holder.

Vince could hear yelling coming out the open door, both in English and Vietnamese. He quickly dragged the PFC to Daniels' jeep, and cuffed one hand to the steering wheel. Pulling his own club, he rushed inside the room. Vince saw several things at once as he entered the room. Felman had two GIs leaning against the back wall in the search position, covering them with his .45. Daniels was sitting at the bar with a bloody towel pressed to his mouth, and two other soldiers were handcuffed together, lying face down on the floor at his feet. Sanders was standing facing a buck sergeant, who had a .38 revolver pointed at him. Sanders had his .45 out, pointing it at the Sergeant's head.

"Need some help, Sanders?" Vince asked, moving slowly to one side.

"Well, Sgt. Phillips here doesn't believe it's in his best interest to come with us, Vince. I'm tryin' to convince him, but he's full of firewater, and I do believe that's cloudin' his judgment."

Vince had by now drawn his own .45, holding it down alongside his leg.

"I'm gonna try once more to convince him," Sanders continued, "that he's got about 30 seconds to drop that weapon, or I'm gonna blow his fucking head off. Ever see what a .45 at close range can do to a person's head, Vince? Makes a real mess. Good thing the Sergeant here's got his dog tags, cause that's the only way he'll be identified. You got your .45 out, Vince?" Sanders asked, never taking his eyes off the Sergeant.

"Yeah, Sanders."

"Good. You take careful aim at the Sergeant, and if he shoots me, I want you to blow his head off. It's real important he realizes that his only option to come out alive is to drop that gun, and give up peaceably. You do understand that, don't you, Sergeant? Well, don't you?"

Vince could see the fear on the Sergeant's face. His eyes darted all around the room, as if he was looking for some unexpected help to materialize out of a dark corner. He was sweating profusely, and the gun shook badly in his hand.

"LOOK AT ME!" Sanders shouted, causing the Sergeant to flinch and snap his eyes back to Sanders' face.

"Do you believe I will shoot you?" Sanders asked, in a

quieter, almost conversational tone.

The Sergeant nodded slowly, once, his eyes never leaving Sanders' face.

"Good. Now you might be thinkin' you can pull your trigger first. Maybe so, but my friend over there will shoot you anyway. It don't matter if you give up after, he's gonna kill you. So you see, Sergeant, you drop that gun, and we all walk outa here alive. You don't, and for sure you'll be goin' home in a body bag. Now, I'm gonna count to three, and if that gun don't hit the floor, I'm gonna shoot you. One..."

The Sergeant swallowed heavily, his eyes darting from Sanders to Vince, and back.

"Two..."

His hand began to shake even more, and the sweat was running off him in rivulets.

"Thr..."

"OK, OK, I'm dropping it. Don't shoot," the Sergeant said, dropping the gun like it was on fire.

Sanders slowly lowered his .45, and placed it in his holster. The Sergeant sat down in a chair, hanging his head, breathing heavily. Sanders walked over to him, pulling his cuffs out. As Sanders handcuffed him, the Sergeant raised his head and said, "I'm gonna barf", and promptly threw up all over his own boots.

It was close to 2330 when they got everyone booked at the PMO and finished their reports. Daniels had gone to the aid station to have a couple of stitches put in his split lip, while Sanders and Torelli sat in the PMO drinking coffee, completing their paperwork.

"Would you have killed him, Sanders?" Vince asked, gathering up his reports.

"In a heartbeat, Vince. Tell you what, if I thought he was gonna shoot me, I would have done it a lot sooner. I ain't gonna let no drunken asshole grunt kill me. But I could see in his eyes he didn't want to pull the trigger, so I gave

125

him an opportunity to drop it. Now, let me ask you somethin'. If he'd 'a shot me, would you have shot him?"

"I've done a lot of thinking about that the last couple of hours. You know what? I would have dropped him where he stood. It kind of bothered me, 'cause I've never felt like that before. He made me afraid, Sanders, and for that I hated him. I thought for sure he was going to shoot you, and that really pissed me off. If he had shot you, I think I would have killed him whether he dropped the gun or not."

"I'm glad to hear you say that, Vince. I would 'a done the same thing for you. Some people would say that's wrong, that it's nothing more than murder. They would be right, but that's just the way it is over here. People do things they would never do back in the States. There's a different set 'a rules in a war. I'm not sayin' it's right, and I ain't sayin' you should do anythin' you know is wrong. What I am sayin' is, you got to watch out for yourself and your partner. When we are out here, we're all we got. It's just you and me against all the bad guys, American as well as Vietnamese, that don't like us and want to do us harm. Don't expect anyone to help you if you need it except your partner. That way, you won't ever be disappointed."

"Yeah, I know that. It's just hard for me to deal with those feelings. I don't like it very much."

"Me neither, partner, but after awhile, it'll stop botherin' you so much. There's stuff I done over here I ain't proud of, but I know it had to be done. I got over it, Vince, so will you. We made it through this one OK. There's gonna be more times like this, and we'll get through those, too."

"You know, I believe you're right, Sanders. I do believe you're right. I'm gettin' hungry. You ready for chow?"

"Yeah, partner, let's go eat."

2041 hrs.

T.J. drove to the air base, and stopped by the Security

Police bunker inside the main gate to talk to the SPs. They didn't have to be at the air terminal for their next escort for another 15 minutes. Renfro's jeep was already there, having come through the gate a few minutes earlier.

"Hey, MP, how many more trips you got tonight?" an SP named Mortenson asked. He had been on duty the last couple of nights, and had gotten to know T.J. well enough for them to want to shoot the bull every now and then.

"Don't know, Sy. We'll be in and out the rest of the night. Made four trips already, and it ain't even 11 yet. Anything goin' on?"

"Nah, been real quiet. The CO has ordered some extra bodies on the line for the next few nights, though. We've been getting probed along the perimeter most every night lately, and the CO is gettin' kinda nervous." Mortenson lowered his voice, then continued. "He's had us lay more mines and flares, claymores and stuff like that. He's increased the dog patrols, too."

"Sounds like you guys are expectn' some trouble."

"The CO must be. He's the one that ordered all this stuff. Guess he's gettin' tired of losin' aircraft to the sappers."

T.J. looked toward the runway more than a mile away, then looked at his watch.

"Listen, Sy, we gotta get goin'. Here comes our plane. We'll be back around 2:30 or so, after we dump these buses and get somethin' to eat. Will you still be here?"

"Yeah, I get off at 3. If you can, meet me here, and we'll go get some GOOD coffee, not that army kerosene."

"OK, if I can I'll be here. I don't think there's any more escorts scheduled until 0500 or so. See ya later."

31 January, 1968   0208 hours
"Anything seem strange to you, Vince?" Sanders asked, as they drove slowly through town.

"Seems awfully quiet. Where's all the PFs?"

"That's what I'm wonderin'. We should be seein' them at their usual places. I ain't seen anyone for the last hour."

"You're right. Wonder where they could be? Maybe we ought to look around a bit, huh?"

"Let's go back to Cambo Alley. There should be three or four hangin' out there."

Sanders turned the jeep around and headed back the way they had come. As he neared Cambo Alley a couple of minutes later, he cut the engine and turned off the lights.

"I got a bad feelin' about this, Vince. In all my time here, I never remember there not bein' some PFs around. Make sure you're ready for anything, and watch yourself."

Sanders coasted to a stop a few buildings away from the mouth of the alley. He and Torelli quickly dismounted the jeep and crouched down along each side, their M-16's locked and loaded, the selectors set on full auto. Sanders signaled Vince to cover him, then ran in a crouch to the entrance of the alley, flattening himself against the building next to it. After waiting 30seconds, he waved Vince over. Vince duplicated Sanders movements, crouching down when he came up next to him.

"What now, Sanders?" Vince whispered, just loud enough for Sanders to hear.

"We gotta check it out, so on my three count, we go around the corner. I'll go high to the other side of the alley, you stay low on this side. If nuthin' happens right away, we'll use our flashlights to look around. If somethin' does happen, we get the hell outa here quick as we can, and hoof it back to the jeep for cover," Sanders whispered back, leaning over with his mouth close to Vince's ear.

"You ready?"

Vince swallowed hard and nodded twice. His heart felt like it was trying to pound a hole in his chest, and he felt a lump in the pit of his stomach.

"One."

Vince rose to a stooped position, tensing his muscles for

the dash into the alley.

"Two."

He hit the charging lever of his rifle with the heel of his hand, making sure the first round was fully seated in the chamber.

"Three."

Vince took the three steps necessary and turned the corner, hugging the near wall. He crouched down, sweeping the alley with the barrel of his rifle. Sanders was about four feet further down, hugging the far wall. Vince waited quietly, staring into the inky darkness of the alley. The silence was complete. He could hear nothing moving.

"Got your light, Vince?" Sanders asked, quietly. "Let's take a look around."

Sanders and Torelli snapped on their flashlights, and slowly played them around the alley.

Vince could see it was empty except for the usual trash. Several rats ran squealing from their lights toward the darkness further down the alley.

"There's no one in there," Sanders said, walking away from the wall, and heading down the alley.

"Sanders! Wait!" Vince called, as he walked down the alley. "How can you be so sure?"

Sanders turned to examine one of the walls, and said, "Those rats wouldn't have been around if anyone was in here. C'mere, take a look at this."

Vince stood up and walked to where Sanders was crouched down, examining a darker area on the ground. He shined his light on it, and saw it was a pool of blood. It was still fresh, though the edges had started to coagulate.

"What's that from?"

"Don't know for sure, but whatever it came from ain't here no more. I'd like to think it came from some animal, a rat or a cat, but it looks like there's too much for that. Might be the PFs got after each other, and one ended up cut, but we'll never know for sure. Let's get outa here."

129

When they got back to the jeep, Sanders told Vince he was going to drive through the downtown area to look for other PFs, then stop at the CPP to report what they found.

"When we're done with that, you can drive over to the air base so we can get some coffee."

31 January, 1968   0252 hours

The SPs had passed T.J.s' jeep through the main gate, and he parked next to the bunker to wait for Mortenson to get off duty. He expected Sanders and Torelli to show up any time now, and figured they all could go for coffee together. A couple of minutes later, Vince drove in, saw T.J.s' jeep parked by the bunker, and pulled up next to him.

"How's it goin', Vince?" T.J. asked, as he pulled up.

"OK, T.J.," he answered. "You copy the call at the Cherry Bar?"

"Yeah. Got a little hairy in there, did it?"

"You ain't kiddin'. I thought Sanders was going to blow that Sergeant's head off! Man, I'm sure glad it turned out all right. This has been a really strange night! Must be something in the air, 'cause we've been real uneasy all night."

"Yeah, I know what you mean. You guys seen any PFs around town? The ones usually hanging out around plantation and the north side of town haven't been there all night."

"Same with us. No PFs downtown, either."

Sanders broke in, saying, "We checked Cambo Alley, but didn't find anyone. Did find some blood, though we don't know where it came from. I don't like this at all."

"Sanders has got me all nervous, now," Vince said, grinning at T.J.

"That's good, Vince," T.J. replied. "It'll keep you awake tonight."

"Hey, guys," Mortenson called from the bunker. "One

of our dog handlers is reporting unidentified personnel inside the east perimeter not too far from here. Wanna go check it out with us?"

"Sure," T.J. said. "We'll go with ya. How 'bout you and Sanders, Vince? Wanna go along?"

Sanders declined the offer. "We'll meet you at the mess hall in a bit. There's somethin' else I wanna do first."

"OK. See ya in a little while."

The SP jeep drove off, followed by T.J.s' jeep, heading toward the reported contact area.

"Let's drive over to the flight line, Vince. I wanna see if a friend of mine is working tonight."

Vince started the jeep, and drove off into the air base along the main road.

Rockets began falling all along the flight line, ammo dump, fuel dumps, and aircraft park areas. A direct hit on a jet fuel storage tank caused a tremendous, fiery explosion. Two cargo planes were destroyed and several others damaged in the initial attack. More than 30 122mm rockets struck the air base in the first few minutes, followed by almost a dozen 82mm mortar rounds.

T.J. was following the SP jeep, approaching the reported contact point when the first rockets struck the air base. The explosions were deafening, and the SP jeep veered away from the perimeter, and sped up, heading for a bunker a couple hundred meters away. T.J. followed as Mortenson's jeep screeched to a stop by the bunker, and they ran inside. T.J. slammed on his brakes, sliding to a halt next to Mortenson's jeep. He, Gilchrist, and Jackson jumped out, grabbed their weapons, and followed them inside. There were two other SPs on duty there already, so their group, plus Mortenson and his partner brought the total occupants to seven.

Vince was driving north near the east end of the flight line when the rocket attack began. The concussion of the first two rockets, landing 100 meters away, caused him to jerk the steering wheel away from the explosions, probably saving both their lives. The third rocket exploded close enough to lift the jeep onto its left wheels, almost causing it to overturn, and throwing Vince out of the driver's seat. He hit the ground on his left shoulder, hip, and knee, shredding his uniform, and scraping away large patches of skin where he hit the pavement. He bounced twice and rolled off the road into a shallow ditch. His ears were ringing so loudly he could not hear the other explosions, and his shoulder and knee burned fiercely, bleeding freely where the skin had been abraded.

He lay on his back for a minute, dazed, trying to gather his wits. He rolled over and tried to stand up, making it to his hands and knees before the dizziness and nausea overcame him, and he fell onto his uninjured side. He lay there another half minute until the feelings passed, then gingerly felt his knee and shoulder. His hand came away wet with blood, but he was reasonably sure nothing had been broken, and he could feel no unusual bumps or protrusions. He slowly flexed his knee, and though it hurt, it seemed to work OK. He worked his shoulder with the same results. Though the pain was bad, everything seemed to function normally, and he again got to his hands and knees, then slowly stood up. Another wave of nausea and dizziness rolled over him, but quickly faded this time, and he was able to stand upright, though he swayed side to side.

As he looked around, he could see several fires burning around the air base, and figures running in the distance. He saw the jeep 50 feet away, near a small shed. He could see there was no one in it, and wondered where Sanders was. He began to slowly limp to the jeep, dreading what he might find when he got there. When he got close enough, he could see his M-16 was still in the back. He grabbed it and a bandolier of ammo as he walked past and turned toward the shed. He could see a darker shadow against the wall and stopped, bringing up the M-16.

"Sanders, that you?"

The figure waved at him, and Vince limped over, lowering the rifle. He saw that it was Sanders, sitting on the ground, leaning against the shed. He was holding his right side, and Vince could see his shirt and hand were wet. There were several other small bloody spots on his right leg, arm and shoulder. Vince carefully sat down next to him, leaning back, resting against the shed.

"You all right, Sanders?"

"I think so. Took some shrapnel in the side, though I don't think it's too bad."

It sounded like Sanders was talking from a long distance away, and Vince had to lean toward him to hear over the ringing in his ears.

"Messed up my shoulder and leg a bit," he said. "Nothing's broken, though. Can't hardly hear, and I've got one hell of a headache. You got your weapons with you?"

"Yeah, but only one magazine for my '16. Couldn't find the bandoliers. Must've been tossed out when you were."

"I found one in the jeep. You feel like looking for help?"

"In a minute. I gotta rest a bit first."

Neither could hear the rattle of small arms fire from other areas of the air base.

T.J. and the others waited a minute or so after the last explosion before emerging from the bunker. They could see fires burning in the distance, in the area of the aircraft park and flight line.

"Man, that was one bitch of an attack!" Mortenson exclaimed. "I never seen nothin' like it the whole time I been here."

"What now, Sy?" T.J. asked.

"Guess we better check out that infiltration report. Don't seem so unlikely now, does it?"

Sy and his partner had climbed into their jeep, and started the engine when the first bullets struck. Sy was hit in the upper arm, his partner struck in the side, shoulder, and neck, and one of the SPs from the bunker was hit in the hand. Gilchrist had his ribcage furrowed by a bullet, and the M-79 was knocked out of TJ's hands by an AK round.

Sy rolled out of the jeep onto the ground, and quickly crawled the few feet behind the bunker where the others had taken cover. His partner remained seated in the jeep, his body jerking to the impact of other bullets. He slowly fell out of the jeep and lay motionless, a pool of blood quickly spreading on the ground.

"I think Snyder's dead, T.J., and I've been hit. I'm bleedin'."

"Take it easy, Sy. I'll fix you up," T.J. said, pulling a field dressing from his first aid pouch.

Bullets continued to whip through the air above their heads, thunking against the two jeeps. One of the SPs had started to return fire from the bunker with the M-60, shooting toward a field between them and the east perimeter. T.J. recognized the heavier thump of the machine gun, interspersed with the rattle of an M-16. He quickly tied off the dressing on Mortenson's arm. The wound bled freely, but was through and through, the bullet missing the bone. Jackson was laying behind a wheel of the jeep, firing his rifle at figures running through the field. T.J. could see the muzzle flashes of the VC rifles as they ran diagonally in front of him. There was another burst of fire from the M-60, and several of the figures fell like rag dolls.

T.J. reached into the jeep, and grabbed Mortenson's and Snyder's M-16s. He handed one to Sy, saying, "They're gonna be comin' after us, Sy. We gotta stop 'em."

Sy nodded slowly, taking the rifle. He rolled over to the front wheel of the jeep, and began a controlled fire at the running figures.

T.J. reached back into the jeep, and felt around until he

134

found the extra magazines. He grabbed several, tossing a couple to Mortenson, and placing the rest in the thigh pockets of his fatigues. When he looked out over the field, he saw a group of four VC break away from the main force and charge the bunker, firing their weapons. He fired a magazine on full auto, knocking three down. One continued the charge, apparently unscathed, pulling a satchel charge from a pouch he was wearing. He got to within 10 meters of the bunker when a burst from the M-60 on T.J.s' jeep almost cut him in half. T.J. slammed home another magazine, then looked up and saw Gilchrist standing in the back of the jeep, firing the machine gun, screaming at the top of his lungs.

Gilchrist was suddenly knocked from the jeep as if a giant fist had punched him in the chest. He landed flat on his back on the ground behind the jeep, but immediately jumped to his feet, climbed back up on the jeep, and resumed firing. T.J. could see a dark stain spreading down the back of his uniform. Several more VC were cut down by Gilchrist before he was again knocked out of the jeep. This time, he had difficulty getting to his feet, and he staggered as he walked. As he tried to climb back into the jeep, he collapsed in a heap. Jackson crawled over to him, grabbed a handful of his collar, and dragged him behind the bunker, where he was out of danger for the moment.

T.J., Mortenson and the bunker M-60 provided cover fire, and T.J. saw more figures fall. They were having a devastating effect with their combined fire. T.J. could see over a dozen bodies laying in the field by the dim light of the parachute flares that had been dropped over the air base. He heard Mortenson yelling at the others, directing their fire at the attacking figures. Suddenly, the enemy fire slacked off as the VC melted into the ground.

"Hold your fire, guys," T.J. shouted. "Stay alert, something's up."

T.J. used this time to crawl to the jeep and grab the

bandolier of grenades out of the back. He looked for the grenade launcher, and saw it on the ground a few feet from Jackson.

"Jackson, toss me the '79."

Jackson flipped it to him, and he broke open the breech. Though the stock was splintered, the firing mechanism seemed to be OK. He loaded a parachute flare, and fired it into the air over the field. As it burst and slowly floated down, he saw crawling figures coming toward them. He quickly loaded a grenade, and fired, immediately loading and firing another. Both exploded among the figures, causing a group of ten to jump to their feet and run toward them, firing their rifles.

Bullets struck all around T.J., clanking against the jeep. Mortenson and Jackson were firing steadily, and the M-60 in the bunker opened up again. Several more VC fell dead or wounded from this withering fire, and after a few more steps, the charge broke. The remaining VC retreated back into the field, and the fire from the enemy stopped.

Silence lay over that corner of the war.

31 January, 1968 0308 hours

"You ready, Sanders?" Vince asked, flexing his knee several times to keep it from stiffening up.

"Yeah, guess now's as good a time as any."

Vince started to get up when Sanders suddenly grabbed his arm and yanked him back down.

"Wha-?" Vince started to say as Sanders clamped a hand over his mouth, smothering the words. He pointed toward the road north of them, and Vince saw a group of six soldiers moving cautiously down the road toward their jeep. He nodded, and Sanders removed his hand from Vince's mouth, placing his finger to his lips.

They were sitting against the shadowed side of the shed, and the figures walked toward them without seeing them. When they got closer, Vince could see by their size and weapons that they were VC. As they approached, two broke off and came toward the jeep, which was between them and the VC, about 10 feet away. The other four moved to the side of the road and crouched down, speaking softly among themselves.

Sanders pointed at Vince, then at the two approaching VC. He pointed at himself, then at the four crouched across the road 25 feet away. He slowly brought his M-16 up, and Vince did the same. Vince carefully set his selector switch to "auto" and tensed his muscles, gathering his feet beneath him, ignoring the pain in his knee and shoulder.

When the VC were 15 feet away, he jumped to his feet, swinging his rifle around, and fired a full magazine. He saw their bodies jerking as if in slow motion as the bullets struck. One dropped his rifle as he grabbed his stomach, half turning and falling heavily to the ground. The second flung his hands up as the .223 bullets stitched him from his left hip to his right shoulder, knocking him to the ground.

As Vince jumped to his feet, Sanders opened up on the group crouched across the road. They were close together, and his burst dropped two immediately, while the other two tried to stand and bring their weapons to bear on their unseen enemy. Another stumbled, wounded, as Sanders adjusted his fire. The last simply blew up, Sanders' bullets having detonated some explosive charge he was carrying. The blast pushed Sanders into the side of the shed and killed the other wounded VC. Sanders got to his feet, pulling his .45 and told Vince, "Check those two, I'll check these."

Vince pulled his .45, and cautiously walked around the jeep. The first VC was obviously dead, his eyes wide open in shock, staring into nothingness, a look of surprise on his face. The second was lying on his side, a large pool of blood spreading from under his body through fingers clutched against his stomach as if he was trying to prevent it from escaping. Vince nudged him onto his back with his boot, covering him with his 45. There was no movement, and no pulse when Vince pressed his fingers to the VC's neck.

Vince was suddenly overcome by a wave of nausea, and had to sit down, taking several deep breaths. Sanders walked over and sat down next to him. He could see the look on Vince's face, and the greenish pallor to his skin.

"They're all dead," he said. Looking down, he said, "You did good, Vince. Came through when you had to, man. You did what you had to do, 'cause if you didn't, it would be them standin' over our bodies right now. Let's get outa here. You gotta shake it off, Vince, and stay alert, there's bound to be more of them around."

T.J. remained crouched behind the jeep and the bunker with the others. There were flares all along the perimeter now, back lighting the field in front of them. They could hear other fire fights around the air base, and now and then an explosion would erupt. There were fires burning in the distance, and they could see tiny vehicles driving back and forth hurriedly, silhouetted by the fires.

"Sy, you OK?" T.J. asked.

"Yeah. How're you guys doin'?"

"I'm all right. Jackson, you hit?"

"Nah, not a scratch. Gilchrist is in bad shape, though. We gotta get him to a medic soon, T.J."

"I know, but I don't think our friends out there are gonna let us just walk away from here."

"Someone's gotta get him outa here. Either one of the jeeps still workin'?"

Mortenson said, "I think our SP jeep is. Looks OK. Took some bullet hits, but the tires are alright, and nuthin's leakin' outa the engine compartment. One of my guys took a bullet in the hand. Lost two fingers, so he ain't gonna be much help. I got him patched up for now, but he should see the doc before much longer, too. Maybe he can take Gilchrist, and go for help in the jeep."

138

"Good idea." T.J. turned to the wounded SP and said, "You up to it, man?"

"Yeah, I'll take him. You wanna go too, Sy? Get that arm looked at?"

"Nah, I'm OK. Think I'll stick around here for awhile."

"OK" T.J. said. "Jackson, help me get Gilly into the jeep."

Jackson crawled to where Gilchrist was lying, and carefully dragged him to the jeep. Gilchrist moaned softly when they lifted him into the passenger seat. The front of his uniform was soaked with blood. Jackson tied him to the seat with a couple of field dressings to make sure he wouldn't fall out along the way.

"Ready, T.J.?" Jackson whispered as he finished tying off the dressings.

"OK," T.J. said. He turned to the wounded SP, and said, "Head directly to the main hangar area. It's well lit, and there's bound to be lots of friendlies there. Keep the bunker between you and the field as long as you can, and drive like hell. Stay away from rovin' groups along the way, 'cause you don't know if they're ours or theirs. Tell someone where we are, and what's goin' on. We'll stay here as long as we can, but we're gonna need some help soon. After the jeep leaves, those guys out there are gonna come after us with everything they got. I think we better move while their attention is on the jeep."

T.J. turned to Mortenson. "Sy, go in the bunker, and tell Ramirez what we're gonna do. Have him bring the M-60 and all his ammo with him. Is there any place around here that can give us some cover?"

"There's a cement culvert about 50 meters behind us. That oughta work."

"It's gonna have to. OK. Sy, you and Ramirez go first and get set up. Jackson and I will cover you, then fall back to your position while you cover us. We'll give you three minutes, then we're comin'. Don't fire unless it's absolutely necessary. I want 'em to think we're still here. Take my '16 and the '79. I'm gonna get the other '60 off my jeep."

T.J. carefully and slowly crawled to his jeep, and got to his knees, keeping the jeep between him and the hidden VC. He reached in the jeep and took the ammo can with the M-60 ammo out, placing it on the ground. He took the ammo belt out and draped it around his neck, then reached up and unlatched the gun from the mount. All his movements were done with the utmost care, slowly and quietly. He lifted it to the ground, then, laying on his belly, cradled it in his arms and crawled the few feet to the bunker. He set the M-60 up in the space between the jeep and the bunker, and loaded a belt of ammo.

"I'll fire a short burst to cover the noise of the engine starting up. You drive like hell, man. Be careful, and don't let us down."

"I won't," the SP replied. "Ready."

"OK. Sy, you and Ramirez start movin'."

Turning to the SP in the jeep, he said, "Go!" and fired a burst into the field where the VC lay hidden. At the same time, the SP started the jeep and sped off and Sy and Ramirez started crawling toward the culvert.

As the jeep drove away, several VC rose up and began firing at it. A burst from T.J.'s M-60 dropped two of them, while Jackson brought another down with a short burst from his M-16. The others melted back down into the field, and the firing stopped. The only sound T.J. could hear was the receding engine noise from the jeep.

"They made it, T.J., they made it!" Jackson exclaimed.

"Yeah, Jackson. I hope to God they get some help. We're in deep shit here. Grab your gear. Let's get outa here."

Every so often, a VC would pop up and fire a burst toward the jeep or bunker. T.J. could hear the bullets whipping overhead and thunking against the jeep. He cradled the M-60 and began crawling after Jackson, toward the culvert.

Vince nudged Sanders with his elbow, and pointed toward the fires. He could see a large group of men moving cautiously toward the hangar area some distance away.

"I don't think they're our troops, Sanders."

"I'd bet you're right, man. We better get going before we get cut off."

"We taking the jeep?"

"Can't. Tires got blown out by that rocket. We gonna be hoofin' it now."

"Where to?"

"Well, I figure the hangar area is probably our best bet. We better go around, cause I don't like the looks of those guys between us where we wanna go. How much ammo we got?"

"I got a bandolier with five magazines for the 16's. That plus our .45's is it."

"It'll have to do. From now on, we fire controlled bursts only, 3 to5 round bursts, like they taught us. Follow me."

Sanders cautiously peered around the shed, then walked along a course at right angles to the hangars some 700 meters to their right. Vince followed a few feet behind. They walked for a hundred meters before Sanders stopped and knelt down. Vince knelt next to him, but did not say anything. Sanders took several deep breaths, his head hanging down. He raised his head, and appeared to be listening carefully, looking around the field they were walking through. The grass and weeds were about 18" high, and every 30 or 40 meters there was a clump of bushes.

"Gotta rest, Vince. It's hard to breathe, and I'm bleedin' again." He pulled his hand away from his side, and Vince could see it was wet with blood.

"Let's get to those bushes, Sanders. I'll fix you up, but I

don't like being out in the open like this," Vince whispered, his mouth close to Sanders' ear.

They limped to the bushes, and crawled in a few feet until they were hidden from anyone passing by in the field or on the road. As Sanders sat down, Vince pulled a field dressing from his web belt, and knelt down next to him. He pulled up Sanders' shirt, and looked at the wound. He saw a 3/4" laceration, and probed around it gently with his fingers. Sanders groaned softly when Vince pressed on his ribs. Vince began bandaging the wound, wrapping the dressing around his body, pulling it tight.

"Hold your hand on the dressing. Press hard. That should stop the bleeding. I think you might have a broken rib, so I'm going to tie this tight. Why didn't you tell me you were hit so hard?"

"Didn't want to slow us down. We're in deep shit here, Vince."

"Yeah, I know," he replied, as he tied off the dressing, causing Sanders to groan again.

"Sorry, man, but I gotta do this."

"Yeah, it's OK. Actually, it feels better now. It's a little easier to breathe."

Vince checked several other small wounds in Sanders' side and arm, and saw that they were no longer bleeding, and didn't seem to be serious. As Sanders pulled his shirt down, he looked at Vince's shoulder.

"Your turn, Vince. Take your shirt off, and let me check your shoulder."

Vince gingerly took off his shirt. Sanders saw a large abrasion three inches long where the skin had been scraped off almost down to the muscle. The wound was still bleeding slightly, and clear fluid oozed from the raw flesh. Sanders applied a dressing from his own pouch.

"How's the knee?"

"Hurts, but I can handle it. Wish I had some water, though."

"Me too. Let's get goin'. The sooner we get there, the better off we'll be."

Vince stood up and stretched his muscles, trying to loosen up the stiffness that was setting in. He hurt all over, and his shoulder and knee burned fiercely. The bandage was already wet with blood and fluids. The ringing in his ears had faded, and he could hear better, but his head still ached badly.

Sanders crawled past Vince and out into the open, stood up and started to walk toward the well lit hangars a half mile away. There were several helicopters flying over the base, some firing at targets on the ground. As he turned to call to Vince, who had just emerged from the bushes behind him, a figure rose up from the grass, and began raising his rifle.

"Sanders! Look out!" Vince yelled, bringing his own rifle up.

The VC hesitated at Vince's shout, shifting his attention and his rifle toward him. Vince pulled the trigger a second before the VC. His first round struck between the VC's feet. The next broke his shin, and as he started to fall, the third and fourth struck him in the stomach and chest. The last round in the magazine blew out the VC's throat, blood spraying from the gaping wound. The VC fired three rounds, mostly by reflex, as he fell dead. One struck Vince in the left leg, passing through the muscle, knocking him to the ground.

At Torelli's shouted warning, Sanders had dropped to the ground, rolled over, and sat up, bringing his rifle up. As Vince fell, two more VC stood up less than 15 feet away. Sanders fired two quick bursts, knocking both of them down.

"Vince, you OK?" Sanders asked, looking over the field for more enemies.

"I'm hit, Sanders. My leg."

"Can you get back in the brush?"

143

"Yeah, I think so."

"Go, then, I'll cover you."

Vince painfully crawled the few feet back into the brush. He pulled out his last dressing, and pressed it against his leg. He heard someone coming, and pulled his .45.

"Easy, Vince. It's me," Sanders said as he crawled in the bushes. "We gotta get outa here. There's bound to be more of 'em out there, and they're gonna come looking for their friends. I don't wanna be here when they find 'em.

"Let me get this bandage on, Sanders. It's gonna be hard to walk."

"I'll help you, but we gotta get goin', now! It won't take 'em long to figure out what happened and where we are."

Sanders thought for a minute, then said, "Stay here, I'll be right back."

As he crawled away, Vince grabbed a fresh magazine and loaded it into his rifle. He crawled to the edge of the brush, almost blacking out from the effort and the shock. When his head cleared, he could see Sanders crawling among the dead VC, stopping at each for a few seconds. He crawled back, carrying an AK 47, several magazines of ammo, and two grenades he had taken off one of the bodies. Vince thought he saw grass moving out in the field, as if from crawling bodies, 30 meters away.

"Let's go, Sanders. There's more of them coming."

"You able to walk?"

"Don't worry about it. The bleeding's stopped, and nothing's broken. I'll walk."

"Alright. We crawl out the back side of this brush, and head directly toward the hangars. We got a lot of open ground to cover, so let's be quick as we can, and stay alert!"

They crawled through the brush, and cautiously peered out. They saw figures in the distance, probably Americans from the way they were running around, silhouetted against the lights and fires. The field in between seemed empty. Sanders slung the AK over his shoulder, pulled his

.45, and helped Vince to his feet. He put his arm around his waist, supporting his weight, and said, "Here we go, man, ready or not." They stepped from the brush into the open.

31 January, 1968   0337 hours

Mortenson passed around a canteen he had grabbed from the bunker before pulling back. It had been quiet the last couple of minutes, and T.J. and Jackson had made it safely to the culvert. T.J. set up the M-60 to cover the right flank. The other SP, Ramirez, had set up his M-60 to cover the left flank, with interlocking fields of fire to the front. Jackson and Mortenson set up between the two machine guns, Jackson taking the M-79.

"How many grenades you got, Jackson?" T.J. asked.

"One flare, two H.E.'s."

"OK. I got about a hundred rounds for the '60. How about that other gun, Ramirez?"

"About the same, man."

Mortenson said, "I've got three magazines for my '16."

"I've got four," Jackson said.

"Alright. We need to conserve our ammo, so don't fire unless it's necessary. Our M-60's can handle anything, for now."

Suddenly, rifle fire erupted from the field, striking the bunker and the jeep. A B-40 whooshed toward the bunker, exploding above the gun port, blowing sand and bits of sandbag into the air. A second rocket followed, this time entering the gun port, exploding inside.

"Looks like they think we're still there," Sy commented.

"Yeah. Hold your fire, guys. They're probably gonna go check it out. Wait for my signal, then hit 'em hard!" T.J. said. He could hear someone shouting in Vietnamese, and the rifle fire gradually slackened off.

About two dozen figures rose from the field and charged the bunker, firing as they ran. The VC ran up to within 10 meters of the bunker, then took cover in the grass. Two kept running up to it, lobbing grenades through the gun ports, then taking cover. The resulting explosions caused the bunker roof to collapse. The VC leapt to their feet and rushed the destroyed bunker, swarming over it, looking for bodies. Unable to find any, they began milling about while their leaders talked among themselves.

"NOW!" yelled T.J., opening up with the M-60. Immediately, Ramirez began firing the other machine gun, and Jackson fired a grenade. The grenade struck a VC in the chest, blowing him to pieces, killing two others close by, and wounding a couple more. Several VC had fallen to the fire from the M-60's before they reacted, taking cover behind the destroyed bunker and the jeep. Sy was firing single shots, and had knocked down two more before they made it to cover.

More than half the group had fallen, casualties of the withering fire from T.J.'s small group. The rest began returning fire, aiming at their muzzle flashes. At first, the bullets were high, passing a couple of feet over their heads, but soon began to strike the ground in front of the culvert, and ricochet off the concrete lip. Jackson loaded his last grenade, and fired at the pocket of VC, then grabbed his M-16. The grenade exploded on the disabled jeep, setting it on fire, followed by screams and shouts. The fire from the VC intensified, and four black clad figures ran to the right, trying to reach a small rise from which they could shoot directly into the culvert. T.J. saw them, and got to his knees, picking up the M-60. He began firing the machine gun at the running figures. Two were knocked down with his first burst, while a third staggered, fell to one knee, then got up and walked a few steps back toward his comrades before collapsing. The fourth turned and ran away from T.J.'s position. T.J. fired another short burst, and saw the VC knocked flat on his face. Bullets were whizzing all around him, and as T.J. ducked down into the culvert, two struck the M-60, knocking it from his hands. One ricocheted into his left wrist, nicking the bones, and exiting halfway up his forearm.

"Ah, shit," T.J. exclaimed, grabbing his wrist.

The machine gun was ruined, the two bullets having destroyed the breech. He could see several figures running toward him, some falling to the fire of the others. He drew his .45, and fired three times at the closest VC. He saw him spin and fall. As he turned to fire at another VC 10 feet to his right, a grenade landed on the ground in front of him.

"Grenade!" he yelled, throwing himself down as it exploded.

As Sanders and Torelli stepped from the brush, two Huey gunships passed low overhead, heading toward the east perimeter. They quickly walked another 75 meters, stopping to rest in a ditch alongside a road. They sat silently, resting for a few minutes. Sanders did not see anyone pursuing them, and felt they had, for now, eluded the enemy. He could hear firefights in the distance, and saw a stream of red tracers arcing down from an unseen helicopter a half mile from them.

"I never thought it would be like this, Sanders," Vince whispered, the exhaustion overwhelming him.

Sanders lay back against the side of the ditch, grunting softly, clutching his injured side. "What did you think it would be like?" he asked.

"I don't know. I thought I'd be doing police stuff. You know, like enforcing the law, arresting people, that kinda stuff."

"Guess it's turned out a bit different than you expected, huh? That's the problem with our training. We learn the law, how to enforce it, but we don't get proper combat training. They never prepare you for what it's really like. I learned the hard way, three weeks after arriving in the

147

country, same as you. We're lucky more of us don't get killed."

"I'm scared, Sanders."

"So am I, Vince. You'd be crazy not to be."

"That's not what I mean. It's a different kind of scared. Yeah, I'm afraid of dying, but I can handle that. What really scares me is I'm getting real good at this war stuff. I know I'm good at it, and it doesn't bother me, what I've done tonight. It's not that I like it, 'cause I know I did what had to be done. It's just that I feel like I should regret taking those lives, or feel bad or something, but I don't. I feel like I've been waiting for this all my life, that it's my destiny to be here. It's like I'm finally where I should be, doing what I'm supposed to be doing."

"You got any other family in the military?" Sanders asked, leaning back against the ditch, his eyes closed.

"Nah. I only got one brother, and he's partially deaf, but my dad was a Marine during World War II. Fought on Guadalcanal, Ie Shima, Saipan, and Okinawa. My Grandfather fought with the 82nd Division at Meuse-Argonne in France. His father was killed in the Spanish American War. I think we had family fighting in the Civil War, too.

"Sounds like you've got some warrior blood in you, Vince. Glad you're on my side."

"You know, I never imagined myself being in a war, but ever since I was a kid, I knew deep down inside I would be here someday. It seems like I've been preparing for this all my life."

"Wait, Vince! Listen. I hear a truck comin'," Sanders said, turning to look up the road.

Vince looked and saw a vehicle slowly approaching them, still a hundred meters away.

"Gotta be one 'a ours," Sanders said. "Wait till they get closer, then we'll go up to the road. Do it slow, and hold your weapon over your head. They might be a little trigger happy, and won't know who we are. Let's sit here, outa sight, nice and quiet for a bit."

They slid down into the ditch to wait. Vince watched the approaching truck, and saw it was a three quarter ton loaded with SPs, with a machine gun mounted in the back. There were six or seven in the back, and at least the driver in the cab. As he watched, he caught some movement from the corner of his eye. He looked to his right, and saw several shadowy figures moving through the field toward the road about 40 meters away. He reached over and tugged on Sanders' sleeve, pointing to the figures. They both watched as the VC approached to within 20 meters of the road, then melted down out of sight into the grass.

"VC?" Vince whispered.

"Count on it. Looks like they're settin' up to ambush that truck."

"We gotta do something, Sanders. We can't let this happen."

"Yeah, I know. Got anything in mind?"

"You still got those grenades?"

"Yeah."

"O.K. We move along this ditch closer to the gooks. On my signal, you throw the grenades. That ought to shake them up and warn the truck at the same time."

"Sounds o.k. to me. Let's do it!"

They crawled along the ditch as quickly and quietly as they could toward the VC. Vince looked back and saw the truck was only 50 meters behind them. Sanders suddenly stopped and peered over the top of the ditch. He signaled Vince to get ready, and took out the two grenades. Vince checked his M-16 as Sanders rose to his knees and threw the two grenades, then dropped back down into the ditch. The two grenades exploded within seconds of each other, followed by screams of agony and shouts in Vietnamese. Vince rose up, his rifle at his shoulder, and as the VC rose

149

from their ambush, he began firing short bursts. Each time he fired, a VC fell. Vince was aware of the heavier thump of Sanders' AK, and the chatter of the M-60 on the truck as the SP's joined the fight, firing at the now exposed enemy. The VC attempted to return fire, but in less than a minute, all had been killed or wounded.

The truck had stopped, and the SPs had taken cover on the opposite side of the road, except for the machine gunner. When the firing stopped, and all was silent for another 30 seconds, Sanders shouted "You guys in the truck. We're two MP's from the 557th. We're comin' out. Hold your fire."

"Keep your hands in sight, and move slowly. Come up on the road," the SP at the M-60 yelled back.

"You got it. We're comin' out," Sanders replied, standing up, holding the AK in his left hand, arms extended above his head. He walked up the embankment onto the road as Vince rose up.

Just as Vince started to climb out of the ditch, a burst of rifle fire came from the field behind him. He turned and saw a VC on his knees, holding an AK to his side with his right arm. His left arm was hanging uselessly at his side, the sleeve soaked in blood. He got off one more shot before Vince could bring his rifle to bear and shoot him, taking off the top of his head, knocking him on to his back.

Sanders was about halfway across the road when the first bullet hit, entering his lower right back just above the kidney, exiting his chest just below the nipple. The second bullet hit high on his right back, breaking his collar bone, and exiting the top of his shoulder. As he fell, he heard someone scream a long drawn out "noooooooo," and heard an M-16 fire. As he hit the ground, darkness overtook him, and he heard no more.

150

31 January 1968   0343 hours

The grenade exploded just as T.J. dove for the ground, killing the charging VC. The explosion was deafening, and the blast knocked T.J. against the back of the culvert. A piece of shrapnel sliced his cheek open from below his left eye to his ear. Another chunk hit him in the shoulder, lodging against the bone, and several smaller pieces peppered his face and head, causing superficial wounds. He rolled on his back, still clutching his .45, and tried to blink away the pain and shock. As he lay on his back, he saw a figure looming over him, raising a rifle. He brought up the .45, and fired one shot, just as several other shots rang out. The figure fell on top of him, and as consciousness faded, he heard voices talking, but was unable to understand what they were saying.

Jackson ducked as T.J. yelled, the explosion and shrapnel passing over him as he hugged the ground. He saw a VC run up to the culvert and raise his rifle. Jackson shot him twice, watched him fall into the ditch, then turned his attention back to the field. There were another two dozen VC advancing toward them, though still 75 meters away.

"Sy, you OK?" Jackson asked, in a stage whisper.

"So far, Jackson. Where's T.J.?"

"Don't know. He was over by you last I saw him."

"How's your ammo?"

"I'm low. Only one magazine left for the '16. Our 60's out, too. We still got our .38s."

"I'm low, too. T.J.'s 60 is smashed. We're in deep shit if they decide to rush us again."

"You see those guys comin'?" Sy asked, pointing toward the advancing VC.

"Yeah. They gotta know we're here. I think they're bein' careful 'cause they don't know how many of us there are, or how well armed. Hopefully they'll stay back. Can we get outa here?"

"Nowhere to go, Jackson. This culvert is only about a

hundred meters long, then it's open fields from there."

"That ain't good, Sy. Look, there's only three of us left. T.J.'s missing. Anybody that wants to go, better go now. I'll cover for you."

"What're you talking about?" Sy asked. "If we try to leave, we're dead, and so are you. We wouldn't get 10 meters. We're stayin'."

"You're dead if you stay, Sy."

"Yeah, I know that, too. We've been through a lot, tonight, Jackson. We ain't about to leave you out here by yourself."

"That's right, Jackson," Ramirez echoed.

"Thanks, guys. Better get ready, they're getting closer."

The approaching VC began to fire sporadically. It was obvious they didn't know their exact location, as they were sweeping the culvert with searching fire. Jackson, Sy, and Ramirez held their fire until the VC were within 30 meters, then opened up. Jackson began firing single shots, picking his targets. He could hear Sy's M-16 firing, and the louder pops of a .38 pistol. As soon as they started firing, the VC charged, firing at their muzzle flashes. They ducked down as bullets impacted all around them, ricocheting off the back of the concrete culvert.

Jackson loaded his last magazine, and prepared to rise up and fire off the last of his ammo. The VC were no more than 20 meters away when four 2.75 in. rockets fired by a Huey gunship blasted a gaping hole in the line of running men. Nine died instantly, and several others were cut down by the Huey's door gunners. The second salvo of rockets exploded further down the line, killing several more of the VC. The few survivors broke to the left, and ran toward the only cover close by, a large clump of bushes some 50 meters away. They never made it. They were shot down to a man before covering half the distance.

As the smoke and dust cleared, Jackson raised his head

and looked out over the battlefield. He slowly rose to his feet, and waved at the Huey, which was now hovering 50 feet off the ground. The pilot gave him a thumbs up, then signaled him to wait where he was. Apparently, help was on the way. Jackson lifted his rifle in the air, pointed at it, and shook his head "no". The pilot brought the chopper down to 30 feet, and the door gunner tossed a sack out, then waved at him. The Huey lifted up and flew off to toward the east.

Jackson walked over and picked up the sack, and found it was a canvas bag with eight full magazines for their M-16s, a first aid kit, and two full canteens of water. Jackson took the bag back to the culvert, distributed the ammo, then wearily sat down, lighting his first cigarette since the attack on the air base began. He inhaled deeply while opening a canteen to slake his raging thirst.

Vince ran to Sanders, laying face down in the road. He knelt by the big man, and gently rolled him over, cradling his head on his arm. Sanders looked up at him, grinned weakly and said, "The little bastard got me good, Vince."

"You're going to be alright, Sanders. Hang on, buddy, you'll be OK," the tears welling up in his eyes, spilling down his cheeks. "Stay with me, man, stay with me!" he said.

Turning to the SPs, he yelled, "Help me, please!"

Several jumped up and ran to him. Others formed a rough skirmish line, and moved into the field, checking the bodies and making sure there were no more hiding nearby. A single shot would ring out now and then.

Vince and the SPs lifted Sanders up, carried him to the truck, and gently laid him in the back. One of the SPs took off his flak jacket, folded it in half, and placed it under Sanders head. Vince climbed into the truck and sat down next to Sanders, wincing in pain. Sanders reached over and took Vince's hand, squeezing weakly. Vince saw he had his eyes closed, and was breathing shallowly.

"Open your eyes!" Vince yelled at him. "Do you hear me, Sanders? Open your eyes!"

Sanders eyelids fluttered, then opened. He looked wildly about, then fixed on Vince's face above him.

"Good. Stay awake, Sanders, we're going to get you to a hospital, but you got to help us. You're going to be OK, my friend."

The soldiers returned to the truck, having found only dead VC in the field. The driver turned the truck around and headed toward the main base.

Sy stood up and walked over to where the dead VC lay in the ditch.

"Hey, Jackson, give me a hand here. Looks like there's someone under this gook!"

Jackson and Mortenson lifted the dead VC, and rolled his body into the field.

"It's T.J.!" Jackson exclaimed. "T.J., you o.k.?"

T.J.'s face was covered with blood, and his uniform was drenched with both his and the VC's blood. His eyes were closed. Jackson could see the gaping wound on his face, and told Sy, "Get me a field dressing, quick!"

Jackson bandaged T.J.'s face, propping him up against the side of the culvert, then bandaged his arm, improvising a sling to keep it still. T.J. had regained consciousness, leaning weakly against the culvert.

"How you feelin', T.J.?" he asked, as he tied off the sling.

"Not so good, Jackson. My face is killin' me." T.J.'s words were muffled and slightly slurred.

"We'll be gettin' outta here soon, man. People know we're here."

Jackson told T.J. about the last attack and their rescue by the chopper.

"Way I figure it, that SP musta made it back with Gilchrist, and told someone about us. I hope they're sendin' a truck to pick us up."

154

"How's Sy and Ramirez?" T.J. mumbled.

"A little banged up, but still alive."

"The VC?"

"All gone, for now. Don't see any, and no shootin' since the chopper left.'

"Think they're gone?"

"Don't know, but I sure hope so. I'm dead tired, and I've had a bellyful of this shit."

"Get me my '16, Jackson."

"Sure, T.J."

Jackson picked up T.J.'s rifle, loaded it with a fresh magazine, laid it across his lap, and said, "Hope you don't need this anymore, man."

At the University of California, Berkeley, several thousand protesters clashed with riot police, decrying the immorality of the war. Carrying signs, North Vietnamese flags, and drawings of dead Vietnamese children, they marched through the clouds of tear gas toward lines of club wielding police blocking their path. Several protesters who tried to force their way past the line were clubbed back. 34 others were arrested during the day on riot charges, assault on a police officer, failure to disperse, and various other charges. 16 protesters and 7 police officers were injured.

31 January, 1968 0425 hrs.

The truck carrying Torelli and Sanders drove up to a hanger being used as a makeshift aid station. Two orderlies ran out and lifted Sanders off the truck, placed him on a stretcher, then picked it up and hurried inside. Vince tried to follow them inside, but an airman grabbed his arm and said, "You can't go with them, soldier. Come with me, you need some attention yourself."

He led Vince inside and off to the left, telling him to sit on the floor, and someone would be right with him. A minute or two later, a corpsman came over and started checking on Vince's wounds. He cleaned his leg and bandaged the bullet wound, then tried to check his knee. His uniform was stuck to the abrasions by dried blood, and the corpsman had to soak it with water, then cut off the pant leg. He washed the large, deep scrape as best he could, and covered it with a sterile dressing slightly dampened with water. He did the same to Vince's shoulder, and once he was done, gave him a penicillin shot. He left for a couple of minutes, then returned carrying a clean uniform.

"Here, put this on. When you're done, go over there, and find a bunk. Wait there for a doctor to see you."

The corpsman hurried off to another soldier being helped in by two airmen. Vince put the clean uniform on, taking a long time, as he was beginning to stiffen up from his wounds. By the time he was done, he was hardly able to walk. His calf and knee were so sore and stiff that they were barely able to support his weight. The forced inactivity while his wounds were being treated had allowed the exhaustion to catch up with him, and his injured knee had swollen to twice its size, and felt like a wooden leg when he tried to walk. The bullet wound to his calf burned, and the muscle ached terribly. He could only limp a few steps at a time before having to stop and rest. Still carrying his rifle, he slowly and painfully made his way around the room among the wounded, every so often calling out Sanders' name, hoping for a reply. He searched the entire room without finding him, and in desperation, grabbed a passing corpsman.

"Where are the more seriously wounded being treated?" he asked him, holding tightly to his arm.

"The next hanger, but you can't go in there."

"A buddy of mine was shot up pretty bad. I need to check on him."

"Sorry, soldier, but unless you need immediate medical

help, you are confined to this room."

Vince sneered, "Yeah, right," and started to limp away toward the door.

"Hold it, soldier," the corpsman said, grabbing the back of Vince's shirt, "You ain't goin' nowhere!"

Vince spun around, bringing up his rifle, jamming the barrel under the corpsman's chin, forcing his head back.

"You gonna stop me?" he growled.

"OK, man, OK," the corpsman said, releasing Vince's shirt, "take it easy. Go on if you want."

Vince pulled the rifle away, and slowly limped out the door.

T.J. lay back against the side of the culvert, listening to a distant firefight. Jackson and Sy kept watch, while he and Ramirez rested. The side of his face was numb, and his arm and shoulder ached. He was terribly thirsty, and drank almost a whole canteen of water. There was no more movement from the field.

The fight was now being waged just south of the flight line by an aircraft de-arming pad. T.J. knew his injuries weren't life threatening, but he did not know the extent of his face wound. His cheek felt like it was burning, and he could not move his wrist or his shoulder without white-hot bolts of pain shooting through them. He kept his rifle with him, ready to fire if need be.

Mortenson stood up, looking over the now dark and quiet battlefield. "I gotta go get Snyder," he said. "Can't just leave him out there."

"I'll go with you, Sy," Jackson said, placing his hand on Sy's shoulder. "We'll bring him back, o.k.?"

"Thanks, man." He turned to T.J., and asked, "Will you be OK here for a bit, T.J.?"

"Yeah, but be careful. Don't be gone long."

"Watch for us, Ramirez. I don't wanna get shot comin' back, you thinkin' we're VC!"

157

"Don't worry. We'll spot ya. Go ahead."

Jackson moved out slowly across the body-strewn field toward the ruined bunker. Mortenson followed a few feet to his left, stopping often to check bodies along the way. As they made their way to the bunker, they faded into the smoke and darkness until they were only shadows, briefly glimpsed as they moved from body to body, looking for Snyder's corpse.

T.J. watched them until they disappeared. He heard a shot ring out, followed immediately by two more from the area of the bunker, then silence reigned once more. A few minutes later, he and Ramirez saw shadows approaching.

"Jackson, Sy, that you?" Ramirez called out.

"Yeah, take it easy, we're comin' in."

They walked up to the culvert carrying Snyder's body. They gently laid him on the ground, covering him with a poncho they had taken from the bunker.

"I heard a couple a' shots over there," T.J. said. "What happened?"

"One of the VC by the bunker was still alive. Went for his rifle when we walked up. Sy shot him."

"Hey listen!" Ramirez interrupted. "You hear a truck?"

They listened carefully, and could distinctly hear a truck approaching. They looked toward the sound as it got louder, and saw a deuce and a half driving up to the destroyed bunker. The truck came to a stop and several people jumped down and started searching the area, looking through the bunker and the ruined jeep.

"Hey, guys!" Jackson yelled, "Over here, we're over here!" He stood up and waved his arms over his head.

"Stay there soldier, we'll come to you. Stay where we can see you," came a shouted reply.

Mortenson and Ramirez both stood up with Jackson as the soldiers cautiously approached, rifles at the ready.

When the approaching group could clearly see that they were Americans, a 2nd Lieutenant walked up, saying, "We werc told you were out here. You're sure a sorry lookin' group!"

A buck sergeant came up and said, "There's dead gooks all over the place." Turning to Jackson, he said, "You guys do all this?"

Jackson replied quietly, "We had a little help near the end from a gunship. Man, are we glad to see you!"

"Well, you guys sure did a number on ol' Charlie. C'mon, let's get you outta here," the Lieutenant said.

He had the Sergeant pick six men to remain there to count and search the VC bodies while they took T.J. and the others to the aid station, telling them he would return in a half hour to pick them up. Three minutes later, they were headed toward the main base and medical aid.

31, January, 1968 0428 hrs.

Vince limped into the adjacent hanger. Inside, three dozen cots were lined up. Most were occupied by wounded soldiers, both American and Vietnamese. Over half the wounded had IV bottles dripping lifesaving fluids into their damaged bodies. Most were conscious, some semi-conscious, moaning softly, and others lay so still Vince couldn't tell if they were dead or alive.

He painfully made his way from cot to cot, searching for Sanders. He would peer intently at each soldier until he was sure it was not him. His leg wound had started to bleed again, soaking through the bandage into his pant leg. He left a trail of bright red drops as he walked. It took Vince more than ten minutes to check all the cots. Sanders was not there. Vince began to panic, looking wildly around. Spotting a doctor nearby, he limped over to him as he was checking a soldier's pulse. The doctor, an Army Captain, looked up as Vince approached, and said, "Can I help you?"

"Yes, sir, I hope so. I'm looking for a friend of mine. A big, black MP? Got two bullets in the back. Would've been brought in a half hour or so ago. You seen him?"

"No, soldier, but I just got here a little while ago myself." He peered closely at Vince, noticing the paleness of his features.

"You o.k.? You don't look too well."

Spotting the blood soaking his pant leg, he guided Vince to an empty cot, helping him to sit down.

"Let me take a look at that leg." He said, starting to pull up Vince's pant leg.

"Can't, Sir, I haven't got the time. I got to find him."

"You haven't got much choice right now!" he said, cutting off the blood-soaked bandage.

"Look, there's a temporary morgue set up in that room," he said, pointing to the opposite side of the hanger as he re-bandaged Vince's leg. "Have you checked there yet?"

"He's not there, Doc. He can't be."

"Well, son, maybe you should make sure. Want me to help you?"

"No, thanks. I'd rather do it myself."

"I understand. For what it's worth, I hope he's not in there."

"Me, too," Vince replied, forcing back the tears that threatened to spill down his cheeks.

The doctor finished re-bandaging Vince's calf.

"That should heal nicely. You're gonna be mighty sore tomorrow, though. I've wrapped it pretty tight to help stop the bleeding. You should have someone check the bandage in an hour or so."

"Thanks, Doc, "Vince said, slowly standing up.

"Good luck, son," the doctor said, moving off toward a wounded soldier being carried into the hangar on a litter.

Vince turned away and slowly limped across the hanger. He stopped to rest at the doorway, leaning against the jamb, closing his eyes. Strangely, the pain in his leg and knee were fading as he walked more, loosening the damaged muscles. He was able to walk better, though still with a pronounced limp, but without having to stop every dozen steps or so to rest.

"You can't be in there, man, you just can't be," he mumbled to himself, the tears welling up in his eyes again.

He took several deep breaths, stood up, and walked into the room. There were seven body bags laid out in a row. He walked up to the first, knelt down on his good knee and grabbed the zipper. Summoning up all his resolve, he pulled the zipper down. As the heavy bag opened, he saw a shock of straight black hair, a brown forehead, and the two almond-shaped eyes of an ARVN soldier. He breathed a sigh of relief, and zipped up the bag. Moving to the next bag, he again knelt down, took a deep breath, and pulled the zipper down. This time, a blood-spattered tangle of blond hair appeared. Vince closed the bag, then moved on to the next in line. After checking six of the bags, he sat on the floor next to the last one, grabbed the zipper, and closed his eyes. He pulled the zipper down, held his breath, then opened his eyes.

T.J. lay on the operating table in the aid station while a doctor sutured the wound on his face. It took 27 stitches to close the cut.

"Well, my friend, this scar is gonna give you character," the doctor said.

"Gimme a break, here, Doc. This gonna mess up my good looks?" he asked, groggily.

"Nah. It'll make you mysterious. Could even be a topic of conversation to break the ice with the ladies. That shoulder is gonna give you more trouble, though. I'm gonna immobilize it, and ship you over to the 93rd Evac. I'll let them take care of it."

He finished suturing T.J.'s face, and applied a fresh dressing. The small shrapnel wounds in his arm had been cleaned and bandaged. The bullet wound to his wrist had also been cleaned and sutured, and his arm had been taped

161

to his midsection, effectively immobilizing it until it could be properly x-rayed and treated. The doctor gave him a pain killer shot, and had two orderlies carry his stretcher into the next hangar to await a Medevac chopper. An IV was hanging from a stand next to his cot, the tube snaking down, ending taped to the inside of his right arm, where the fluids dripped slowly into his vein. As he lay there, a figure suddenly loomed over him.

"Hey, T.J. How ya doin'?" Jackson asked.

"Jackson. I ache all over, man. Feel like I been run over by a V-100. How are you doin'?"

"O.K. Some scrapes and bruises, nuthin' serious. I was just over checkin' on Sy. He got a bullet through the arm, but it ain't bad. He'll be o.k."

"What about Gilchrist? You find out anything about him?"

It was getting difficult for T.J. to talk. The swelling to his face and the pain-killing drugs made it sound more like "Yoo hind out anyding abou' 'im?"

"Yeah, he's alive, T.J. The crazy bastard's alive! Been sent to the 93rd. He's in real bad shape, but I talked to the doc who first treated him, and he said he's got a chance to survive, though it's a slight chance. Said he was lucky to get to a doctor so quick. A few more minutes, and he would've died out there."

"Glad to hear it. I gotta rest now, Jackson. I'm so tired," T.J. mumbled, his eyes closing as he dropped off to sleep.

"You rest now, T.J. You've done enough for one night, my friend, so you just sleep. Everything's alright now."

Jackson knew T.J. couldn't hear him, but he kept on talking, anyway. He reached out and took T.J.'s hand, and started to tell him of his family's farm in Iowa.

Vince opened his eyes and looked down. He saw the body was an ARVN missing the top half of his head. He squeezed his eyes shut as he mumbled a quick thanks to

God, pressing his palms to his eyes as the relief washed over him. After a minute, he painfully got to his feet and limped out of the morgue back into the aid station.

"You find your friend, son?"

Vince looked up and saw the doctor he had been talking to earlier.

"No, Captain, no luck."

"I'd look at it as good news, soldier. You better sit down and rest. You look like you're going to pass out."

He took Vince by the arm, and led him to a cot, gently sitting him down.

"Tell you what, I've got some free time, so I'll ask around. What did you say his name is?"

"Sanders. Big, black MP from the 557th. We came in together about an hour ago."

"Alright. You stay here. I'll check it out, see what I can find out, and get back to you."

He checked Vince's bandages and, satisfied all was in order, walked off.

Vince sat on the cot, listening to the moans of the wounded and the murmured conversations between the lesser wounded. He turned to an airman lying on the next cot, his legs in casts, and asked, "I don't suppose you got a cigarette?"

The airman pulled a pack of Marlboros from his shirt pocket with a book of matches and tossed them to Vince. "Help yerself," he said.

"Thanks, partner," Vince replied, as he lit a cigarette, inhaling deeply. He placed the pack and matches on the cot next to the airman, who had laid down and appeared to be asleep. Vince, too, laid back on his cot, easing his battered and aching body down. He listened to the medevac helicopters arriving and leaving, as the more serious wounded were transferred to the 93rd Evac for more extensive treatment of their injuries. An orderly came by once and gave him some water, briefly checked his

163

bandages, then moved on to the next cot. Ten minutes later, the doctor came back.

"Well, I found the other doctor who was here before I got in. He said he treated a black MP corporal for two bullet wounds, and medevac'd him out right away. He'd been hit pretty hard, and the doctor said he didn't know if he'd survive the flight, but if he did get to the 93rd, he might make it. Listen, son, I wouldn't get your hopes up too high. From what I've heard, he was in real bad shape."

"Thanks, doc. What's the best way for me to get over there?" Vince asked, sitting up, gingerly.

"Only safe way is by helicopter, and the only ones going out of here are the medevacs. It's too dangerous to go by road. There's reports of heavy fighting in the city, and, besides, there are very few vehicles leaving the airbase. There's fighting all over the base. Seems the VC have penetrated the perimeter in force, and are attacking all over."

"Can you get me on a medevac?"

"Sorry, not just yet. I've got several more seriously wounded that need to go. Maybe in a few hours, but not until then" he said, as he stood up. "You just take it easy. You've done enough for one night. Good luck, son," he said, as he turned and started to walk away.

"Hey, doc," Vince called after him, "thanks."

The doctor looked over his shoulder, grinned, and gave Vince the thumbs up, then walked away.

Vince carefully got to his feet, gradually stretching and loosening his muscles. He walked in slow circles until the stiffness lessened. His shoulder and knee ached, but the painkiller shot blocked most of it. His calf hurt terribly when he walked, which made him take small, stiff legged steps.

"God, I feel like hammered shit," he said to himself. He walked outside just as a medevac chopper landed. Stretchers bearing the more seriously wounded were quickly loaded, and the chopper lifted off.

Vince finished his cigarette, field stripping it and placing the butt in his pocket out of habit. He stood in the warm night air, listening to the war. He could see fires burning along the perimeter, and sporadic gunfire erupted every so often, punctuated by an explosion now and then. Vince could hear firefights in the distance, coming from Bien Hoa City. Huey gunships passed overhead constantly, heading into battle. Another medevac landed, and three stretchers were loaded. One of the orderlies shouted at the pilot, "There's one more comin'. The doc's still workin' on him. Should be ready in a few minutes."

The pilot nodded, then unstrapped himself and got out of the chopper, leaving the engine running.

"Got a cigarette?" Vince asked, limping over to him.

"Sure, here ya go," he said, handing him one. "Name's Jeff."

"I'm Vince. You going to the 93rd?"

"Yeah, my sixth trip tonight."

"What's it like in the city?" Vince asked, drawing on his cigarette.

"All hell broke loose. From what I can see, the VC are attacking all over the place. Bien Hoa, Long Binh, Tan Son Nhut, Di An, anywhere there's a base. I've made two trips from Di An, and three from here. Hey, you o.k.? You look like you've had a tough time tonight."

"If you could call being blown out of a jeep and getting shot a tough time, I guess so. I'll be alright. Listen, I need to get to the 93rd to find my partner. He got all shot up earlier, and last I heard, he was in bad shape and had been taken there. Any chance I could get a lift?"

"Yeah, no sweat. Besides, you look like you should be goin' there yourself. Hold on a minute."

The pilot walked to the chopper, climbed in for a minute, then came out carrying two cold beers. He tossed one to Vince, popped his open, and took a long drink.

165

"What happened to you?" he asked, wiping his mouth with the back of his hand.

Vince opened his beer, took a mouthful, swished it around, then swallowed.

"Man, that tastes good!"

Vince talked for he next five minutes, telling him everything from the time he and Sanders drove onto the airbase.

"So, you see, I owe him my life. He kinda made it his job to teach me. Without him, I wouldn't have survived this long, and I've been in country a seven months now. I feel like it's my turn to take care of him. There's no one else he can rely on. Besides, he's my partner."

"Look, I'll get you there. I lost my co-pilot three months ago while on a combat medevac 15 miles west of here trying to evac a squad of ARVN Rangers from an ambush, so I know what you are going through."

"Sorry to hear that, Jeff. I really appreciate this. I owe you, and I won't forget."

"Don't worry about it. You got any ammo for that rifle? You might need it. The gooks don't care if we're a medevac or not. They're all over the city, and have been shootin' at me all night. If you want, you can count the bullet holes in my chopper."

"No, thanks. Might change my mind about flying with you. I've only got this one magazine. Let me hunt some more up before we go."

"There's a canvas bag behind my seat. Get a couple of magazines out of it. I like to have some extra with me, just in case. Grab us two more beers while you're at it."

Vince made his way to the Huey, and painfully climbed in. He took three magazines from the bag, and put them in the large pockets of his fatigue shirt. He grabbed two more beers from the small cooler, carefully made his way among the stretchers, and climbed down. The pilot had moved toward the door of the hangar, and was leaning against the wall next to the door.

Vince limped toward him, and called out "Hey, Jeff." The pilot turned toward him, and Vince tossed him one of the beers.

At that moment, the helicopter behind him exploded in flames, sending debris in all directions. The concussion knocked Vince down, his beer flying from his hand. He landed on his stomach, tearing the bandage from his knee, and starting it bleeding again. His rifle was torn from his hand, and skidded ten feet away. Vince saw the pilot lying at the base of the hangar wall, bleeding from the head, apparently unconscious. Several corpsmen and SPs began rushing out of the hangar to see what had happened. Vince heard small arms fire begin, the bullets impacting the hangar around the doorway. One SP grabbed his leg, and fell. A corpsman clutched his stomach, and as he toppled forward, Vince saw the top of his head disintegrate.

He lay flat on his stomach, and crawled to his rifle. He pulled the M-16 to him, thumbed off the safety, and slowly turned around. He could see muzzle flashes coming from a group of small storage sheds just off the tarmac 40 meters away.

As the enemy fire intensified, five figures broke cover and ran diagonally toward a fuel storage tank to Vince's right. He fired from a prone position, squeezing and releasing the trigger, firing short bursts. Two of the running figures stumbled and fell with his first three bursts. Another staggered, recovered, and kept running, disappearing with the other two behind the storage tank. Vince fired one more burst, for good measure, the bullets clanking off the tank. Several SPs had exited the hangar by now, taking cover and returning fire.

Vince crawled to the pilot, who showed signs of returning consciousness. His eyes fluttered open. Vince could see a two inch curved gash in his forehead, bleeding

167

freely. As he regained full consciousness, he started to sit up. Vince pushed him back down, saying, "Stay down, Jeff. We've got trouble."

"What happened?" Jeff asked, bringing his hand to his forehead. Bullets struck the building above them, and the rattle of rifle fire increased.

"We're under attack. Here, take this," he said, handing Jeff his .45 with a spare magazine.

"Can you move? We got to get to better cover."

"Yeah. Head hurts like hell, though," Jeff said, wiping the blood out of his eyes.

"OK. Follow me, and stay low."

Vince started crawling to the hangar door, followed by Jeff. As they crawled, bullets began to strike the wall above them, causing them to stop and hug the ground. He could see a VC shooting toward him, and fired a burst from his rifle, causing the VC to take cover behind the shed. The VC popped out and fired a short burst, then ducked back out of sight several times. Each time, Vince would try to return fire without success.

Bullets continued to strike all around him, and he knew it was just a matter of time before his luck ran out. He turned to tell Jeff to crawl to the hangar door while he covered him, and saw he had crawled half the distance toward their tormentor, angling to one side. He was now laying prone, both hands extended in front of him, carefully aiming the .45 pistol Vince had given him.

Suddenly, the VC popped out from behind the building firing a short burst toward Vince. Jeff fired three quick shots from the pistol. The VC hunched over from the impact of the heavy slugs, staggered back two steps, and fell on his seat, a look of shock on his face.

The pilot fired two more shots, knocking the VC flat on his back. Jeff rolled on his side and looked at Vince, raising his fist in a victory salute. Vince grinned, raising his own fist in reply.

168

He caught a movement out of the corner of his eye, and quickly swung around, bringing his rifle to bear on a figure running from shed to shed toward Jeff, who had started crawling back toward Vince, unaware of the danger. Vince took careful aim at the 15 foot gap between the shed the VC had run to and the next one closer to Jeff, sighting down the barrel. As soon as he saw the VC start his dash across the open space, he pulled the trigger, firing on full auto. The VC took two steps and fell forward, landing on his hands and one knee. He looked toward Vince, screamed in Vietnamese, and started to raise his rifle. Vince fired another burst, and saw the VC jerk as the .223 rounds struck, the impact knocking him over. He was dead before he hit the ground.

Vince waited until Jeff got back, covering his movements. Fire from the enemy had almost ceased, and Vince saw no more movement from the sheds. The destroyed chopper burned fiercely, lighting the surrounding area.

"That wasn't too bright, Jeff!" Vince scolded, as Jeff crawled up to him.

"Had to do something. That little bastard had us pinned down. He'd 'a got us both before much longer. Besides, they blew up my chopper, and that really pissed me off!"

"Still wasn't too bright, but I thank you, anyway. Let's get out of here."

Vince pressed the magazine release on his M-16, the empty magazine falling to the ground. He put a fresh one in, pulled back on the charging lever, then released it, chambering a round. He thumbed the safety on.

"Let's go!" he said, getting to his feet, running as best he could toward the other American position, followed closely by Jeff.

Their sudden movement drew fire from the area of the sheds. Several SP's returned fire, peppering the small buildings. One SP threw a grenade that exploded between two of the sheds, and two VC broke cover, charging toward them. They were immediately cut down by the SP's. Three more attempted to flee, but took no more than five steps before falling dead. There was no more movement, and no more fire from the sheds.

"Cease fire, cease fire!" one of the SPs yelled. He turned to Vince and said, "You guys ok?"

"Yeah," Vince replied. "What happened to the chopper?"

"I think the VC hit it with a RPG. Anyone on board?"

"Three wounded ARVNs. I had just gotten out of it before the explosion. Those wounded didn't have a chance."

"Yeah, tough luck, huh?"

Looking over at the sheds, he said, "We gotta go check out those buildings. Better make sure none of 'em are still around. I've got three SPs with me, and I could use your help."

"Alright, how you want to do this?"

"We move out in a skirmish line to the sheds, and take cover. Two of us will check for survivors, while the rest cover us. Since I'm the only NCO, I'll be in charge. By the way, who are you?" he asked.

"PFC Vincent Torelli, 557th MP Co., Long Binh."

"OK, PFC Torelli, you, me and Sanchez will provide cover. Johansen and Nevin are the search team. Let's go, and be careful!"

Vince turned to the pilot, and said, "Head inside, Jeff, and get a doctor to look at your forehead."

They moved in a line three meters apart toward the sheds. They cautiously crossed the open area, drawing no fire, taking cover alongside the sheds. They could see about a dozen bodies around and behind the sheds, none moving. The two SPs, Johansen and Nevin moved from body to body, carefully checking for signs of life.

After checking all the bodies, they returned to where the others were. Vince could hear rifle fire from other areas of the airbase. He crawled to the Sgt., and asked, "Anybody besides me see a couple of VC run to that storage tank over there?" pointing to where he last saw the VC. "I got a couple of them, but some made it behind the tank."

"How many did you see?" the Sgt. asked.

"Five or six. There's got to be three or four still there, unless they di di mau'd without us knowing it."

"We better go check it out, just to make sure. We can't have them out there runnin' around. Same as before, guys," he said over his shoulder. "Let's go."

They moved out toward the storage tanks cautiously, moving slowly into the area between the sheds and the tanks. After they had crossed halfway to the tanks, rifle fire erupted, causing them to dive to the ground. Vince was on the far right of the line, and saw a VC step from behind the tank and throw a grenade. He yelled a warning, and pressed his face to the dirt. The grenade exploded a few seconds later, followed by screams of pain. Dirt rained down around him as he lifted his head.

He brought his rifle up, and fired toward the muzzle flashes coming from the storage tanks. The other SPs also began to return fire. Vince rolled over several times to his right, and began crawling toward the tanks. All the enemy fire was being directed toward the SPs, and Vince knew the VC did not know he was there. He crawled as fast as he could until he was next to the tank opposite from the VC. He got to his feet, checked his M-16, and prepared to move around the tank to try and come up behind them. He took two deep breaths, and moved forward.

At that moment, a VC coming around the other way at a run ran head on into him, causing them both to stagger back two steps. Both he and the VC were surprised, delaying their reaction at seeing the enemy face to face. Vince recovered first, and ran up to the VC, striking him on the forehead with the butt of his rifle as the VC attempted to bring his own rifle up. The VC dropped in his

171

tracks, out cold. Vince stepped over the unconscious body, and quickly walked around the tank. As he came around the other side, he saw two other VC firing at the pinned down SPs in the field. He took careful aim, and fired a short burst, knocking one VC down, and causing the other to jump to his feet and turn toward him. Vince fired another burst at the same time the SPs fired at the VC. He died immediately from their combined fire.

Once he was sure there were no more living enemy, Vince yelled, "It's over, guys. I'm coming out."

He stepped out slowly, and began limping toward the SPs, who were rising from the field.

"I think there's still one live one on the other side," Vince said, as he reached the group.

"Sanchez, Johansen, go check it out," the Sergeant said. "You others, go check those bodies. Good work, Torelli. We owe you."

"Everyone OK?"

"Nevin lost part of his foot to that grenade, but other than that, everyone survived intact. Let's get back to the hangar. We're done here."

They walked back to the hangar, and Vince turned to the Sergeant, saying," I've got to find someone. Any way you can get me on the next chopper to the 93rd?"

"You wait here. I'll see what I can do."

He walked off toward a smaller building, disappearing inside. A few minutes later, he came back and told Vince, "A chopper's on its way. You're set to go. Listen, I want to thank you for your help. That was some good work out there. If there's anything else I can do for you, you just let me know. Well, we gotta go. There's a report of some VC by the aircraft park. You take care now, MP."

"You too, Sarge. Stay safe."

When the chopper arrived, several stretchers were loaded, and Vince climbed on board, settling in among the wounded. He looked around and saw that there were three Americans and two Vietnamese, all unconscious, with blood soaked bandages covering their wounds. He looked at one American, and saw that his face was covered with a large bandage, and that his arm was bandaged also. His uniform was torn, bloodstained and filthy, and Vince couldn't make out the unit patch on his shoulder in the dim light. As the chopper lifted off, he rested his head against the side, and dozed off.

A group of twenty-three VC made their way stealthily through the alleys and streets of Bien Hoa. They were all that was left of three companies whose original assignment was to attack the III Corps Compound. Their guide had been late to the pickup location which made them late to the attack, and the ARVN defenders were ready and waiting when the attack came.

The VC sent two companies in, holding one in reserve. During the first 7 minutes, 60 percent of the attacking VC were killed or wounded. A second attack by the survivors and the VC reserve company was decimated by the defenders, augmented by three attack helicopters from Bien Hoa. All the able-bodied survivors were now on the run in the city, attacking anything in their path.

The VC Sergeant supported his Captain as they made their way through town, half carrying the wounded officer.

"Let us rest, Sergeant," he said, coughing weakly.

The Sergeant gently sat him down, knowing he was doomed. The bullet that had struck his chest had punctured his right lung, severing several small arteries. Though the Captain didn't know it, he was slowly bleeding to death inside.

"We must not stay here too long, Dai Uy. The sun will be up before we reach the safety of our camp."

"Yes, Sergeant, I know. Five more minutes, then rouse the men. You will be in charge soon, Sergeant. Get the men to safety."

"Yes, sir. We will all go together."

Five minutes later, the Sergeant moved quietly among the men, shaking them awake. As they rose at the Sergeant's command, the sound of an approaching helicopter caused them to hug the walls a little closer. They were well aware of what a gunship could do if they were spotted. The helicopter flew without lights, but was marked on its belly by a large red cross on a white background. Three of the VC raised their rifles, and as the chopper passed overhead, fired on full automatic. They saw the chopper lurch, then resume its course, passing out of range in a matter of seconds.

"Next time, do not fire," the Sergeant said wearily, without anger. "You waste precious ammunition, and alert others to our presence. Now, let us go."

The Sergeant turned to assist the Captain, and found he had collapsed. His eyes were open and staring, the spark gone. His mouth was open, and blood trickled slowly out onto the ground from his wound. The Sergeant bent over him, searching his pockets, removing his personal identification and military papers, along with his pistol, sticking it in his own waistband. He gave the Captain's rifle and spare ammo to one of the VC who had lost his own weapon during the retreat. Last of all, he removed all rank insignia from the Captain's uniform. He then had two VC drag his body into the shadows of a nearby alley.

Leading the battered group, he turned southwest, back toward the jungle. In three hours, he and most of the others would be dead, killed by a Cobra gunship that spotted them at dawn, crossing a rice paddy.

Vince felt the chopper lurch, and woke with a start.

"You alright back there?" the pilot shouted.

"Yeah. What happened?"

"Somebody shot at us again. We took some hits, but don't seem to be in any trouble. We'll be landing in a couple of minutes."

When the chopper touched down, Vince climbed painfully out just as a team of orderlies, doctors, and nurses arrived to off load the wounded. He limped up to one of the nurses that was checking the wounded, and asked, "Are all the wounded brought in through here?"

"The ones that are sent to us are."

"If I wanted to find a friend who was sent here about an hour ago, how would I do that?"

The nurse frowned, and turning to Vince said, "Look, I haven't got time for this right now. We're full up with wounded, and more are coming in all the time. Go through that door," she said, pointing to a door at the corner of the building behind him. "Ask the Sergeant at the desk. He's got all the records. If anyone can help you, he can."

"Thanks, Ma'm," Vince said, as she turned away to tend to one of the wounded.

He limped to the door, knocked, then opened it and went in. He found himself facing a small desk, piled high with paperwork and folders. Behind the desk was a buck sergeant, sorting through the papers.

"Excuse me, Sergeant. I'm trying to find a friend of mine that was sent here an hour or so ago."

"What unit's he with?"

"557th MPs. Had a couple of chest wounds?"

"Yeah, I remember him. Two bullets. We don't get many MPs through here, especially one so badly wounded."

"So how is he? Can I see him?"

The Sergeant hesitated, cleared his throat, and began shuffling the papers on his desk, avoiding looking at Vince.

"I'm sorry, man. That would be impossible."

"Why? Look, I've got to find him. We been through too much together, and I got to let him know I'm here. You can't stop me now, Sarge, you just can't."

"It's not that I want to, soldier, it's just not possible. Your friend died on the operating table. I'm sorry."

"Oh, no," Vince groaned. A lump formed in his throat, making any further conversation impossible. He turned away, hiding the tears that welled up in his eyes, and walked out of the office into the night. Once outside he sat down on a bench next to the building, placing his rifle across his knees. Resting his forearms on the rifle, he hung his head and wept quietly. The grief he felt over losing his friend was like a vice squeezing his heart.

After a few minutes, he wiped his eyes, took a deep breath, and stood up. He went back inside the office, walked to the Sergeant's desk, and asked, "Any way I can get back to my company?"

"Nothin' movin right now. VC are attackin' all over the city and Long Binh. Besides, you need to be seen by a doctor yourself. Go next door, and tell 'em Sergeant Baldwin sent you over."

"I'm alright, Sarge. I just need a place to rest."

"Sure, the way you're limping around and the blood stains on your uniform tell me you're just fine. Now, go next door, and see the Doc. It ain't a request!"

Vince knew the Sergeant was right. He did need to see a doctor, and now that he knew Sanders was dead, he didn't really care what happened or where he went anymore. He left the office, and walked into the next room. A nurse saw him coming, looked at the dried blood on his uniform, and took him by the arm, leading him to a bench.

"Sit down here, soldier, and let me look at you."

Vince sat down wearily, and allowed the nurse to remove his shirt. She took off the bandage on his shoulder, and began bathing the raw wound with warm water.

Vince thought of Sanders, and wondered if he could help take care of the arrangements for getting his body home. He suddenly realized he didn't have any idea how he might help, or even what the procedures were, and besides, he didn't even know if Sanders had any family to claim the body.

"Excuse me, Ma'am. Can you tell me something?"

"Sure, soldier. What's up?"

"I lost a friend tonight, and I want to help make arrangements to get him home, or contact his family, or something. I think they should know what happened from someone who was with him. Do you know how I could do that?"

"Not really, but I can call your CO, and find out for you. What's your unit?"

"557th MPs, Long Binh."

"Oh, yeah. I remember him. I was working triage when he was brought in. Two chest wounds. I'm really sorry. He didn't have much of a chance. We got him to surgery right away, and started him on whole blood, but he was too badly wounded. He died within a few minutes."

She paused, swallowing the lump that formed in her throat.

"I'll check it out for you," she said, finishing bandaging his shoulder. "But for now, I'm going to admit you to the hospital. We need to have the doctor look at you, and keep an eye out for infection. You need antibiotics and lots of rest, and this is the only place you'll get it."

She filled out the admittance paperwork, then called an orderly.

"There'll be an orderly here in a minute to take you to a ward. I'll look you up tonight when I come back on duty, at 2300 hours, OK?"

"Sure, thanks, Ma'am. I really appreciate this."

An hour later, Vince was asleep on clean sheets, an IV dripping fluids into his arm to counteract the shock and dehydration caused by his wounds. Vince slept soundly for the next 12 hours.

T.J. lay heavily sedated on the operating table while the doctor removed the piece of shrapnel from his shoulder.

"Looks good in here. No damage to the bones or joint. Ah, here we are," he exclaimed, dropping the chunk of steel in a tray. "This one's lucky. He's going to be fine in a few weeks. Let's save this for him. Wash it off, nurse, and put it in a jar. I'll give it to him tomorrow."

The doctor finished suturing T.J.'s shoulder, then checked his arm.

"Nice work by whoever did this. We'll leave it alone for now. Alright, nurse, he's all yours. Keep him on antibiotics, and change those bandages every 12 hours. OK, bring in the next one."

The nurse wheeled T.J. to post-op where he could be monitored until the anesthetic wore off and then be transferred to a ward. T.J. slept the dreamless sleep of exhaustion, and an hour later he was taken to the same ward as Vince.

By 1600 hours that day, the attackers of Bien Hoa Air Base and Long Binh had been destroyed. Resistance on the air base had all but ended, and both ARVN and American infantry units were conducting house to house clearing operations in Bien Hoa City. Casualties among ARVN and American troops was light, considering the ferocity of the predawn attack. The VC, however, suffered over a thousand dead in the Bien Hoa area alone. Some units were so badly decimated that they ceased to exist as an effective fighting force. Other VC units, fleeing from the city, were relentlessly pursued on the ground and from the air, and systematically destroyed.

February 1968   1142 hours

Vince awoke slowly and groggily. His mouth was dry, and his tongue felt like it was covered with fuzz. At first, he didn't know where he was. He looked around the room, not recognizing his surroundings for a full half minute. He started to panic, looking for his M-16, before he remembered where he was. Once it became clear he was in the hospital, the events that led to his being there began to come back, bit by bit. He heard again the rocket explosion, felt the impact when he hit the pavement, saw faces of VC he shot, saw them fall, felt the pain of seeing Sanders hit.

He tried to sit up, but the pain in his shoulder and legs caused him to fall back. He lay there, his eyes squeezed shut to block the pain tears, until there was only a dull ache left. He opened his eyes, wiping them with the back of his hand. He lifted his head, and looked around for water to slake his thirst.

The door at the end of the ward opened, and the nurse he had talked to earlier came in. Stopping at each bed, she checked charts, talked briefly with those wounded that were awake, then moved on to the next. When she got to Vince's bunk, she pulled his chart.

"How are we feeling today?"

"Don't know about you, but I feel like shit." He replied.

"Well, nothing personal, private, but you look like shit, too! Can I get you anything? Water, juice, pain killers?"

"Oh, man, I'd give my right arm for some juice. How about a dozen or so pain pills, too?"

"You got it. Listen, I called your CO about you wanting to help with your friend's arrangements. I talked to your CO, and he asked me to call him back when you woke up. He said he would come by to visit with you. I'm going to get your juice and pills, then I'll make that call."

"OK, nurse."

The nurse brought Vince a large glass of orange juice and two pain pills, then left to call his CO, Lt. Griffin. Vince drank half the juice in three large gulps, then sipped the remainder over the next few minutes. He didn't take the pills yet, as he wanted to be awake and alert when the C.O. got there. He slowly and gingerly sat up in bed,

179

placed his pillow against the wall, then slid his body toward the wall, and leaned back using it as a back rest. He closed his eyes to rest from the effort it took his damaged and overtaxed muscles to do even that small task. Vince cleared his mind, and concentrated on willing the pain away. After a few minutes, it was a dull, nagging ache, a manageable level to deal with.

The door opened at the far end of the ward and Lt. Griffin walked in. He headed toward Vince, but stopped at the fourth bunk up from his. He spent a couple of minutes talking with the occupant, then patted him on the arm, and walked to Vince's bunk.

"Hey, son, how're you feelin'?"

"Sore, LT, but better."

"Glad to hear it. By the way, you been approved for a bronze star. Seems some Air Force Sgt. wrote you up for a medal because of what you and Sanders did at the airbase. According to him, you guys stopped an ambush single handedly, delayed and interrupted an attack by the VC, and showed exceptional courage and leadership during an attack on the hangar area. You guys accounted for 15 dead, all by yourselves. General Gustafson's coming himself later this afternoon to make the presentation, along with a purple heart. T.J. and Jackson are getting a silver star. Sanders gets a bronze star, too, as does Gilchrist."

"Where's T.J., LT? Is he OK? Have you seen him?"

"Whoa, Vince, slow down!! Yes, I have seen him, and he's a little beat up, like you, but he's gonna be fine. He's in that bunk over there." He said, pointing at the bunk he had stopped at before Vince's.

"Which one? The guy with his face all bandaged?"

"Yeah, that's T.J. He's doin' OK, Vince. Go over and visit him later if you can. He asked about you, too."

"What happened to him?"

"He, Jackson, and Gilchrist went with a couple of SPs to

180

check out a possible contact and got involved in a bad situation."

"Yeah, I know! I was there when the call came in."

"Well, they ended up stopping a major enemy attack. Killed over 30 VC, and delayed them so long that the airbase reaction teams were able to be well-prepared to deal with them. T.J. got messed up in a grenade explosion. Got shot in the arm, too. Jackson didn't get a scratch. The two SPs were slightly wounded. Gilchrist was hit hard, Vince. He died a couple of hours later. One of the SPs died, too."

"Jesus, that makes two." Vince said, more to himself than to Ski.

"What? What did you say?"

"Nothin', LT."

"Well, the nurse told me what you wanted. I know how you must feel, but there really isn't anything you can do. The Army will take care of everything. They'll notify his family, and an escort will meet the body back in the States. There'll be a full military funeral, full honors."

"You sure? Maybe I could write his family, tell 'em about him, and what he did here."

"I suppose so, but I'm kinda surprised you'd want to do that. I didn't realize you two were that close. Gilly seemed to keep more to himself than..."

"Wait a minute, LT. Did you say Gilchrist? I'm talking about Sanders."

"Sanders? What about him, Vince? I'm confused."

"He's the one I was asking about. I came here looking for him, and some Sgt. told me he died on the operating table. He's the one I wanted to help get home."

"Why, Vince? He's only going to Cam Ranh Bay."

"What!?"

"He's going to Cam Ranh Bay. You know, the 6th Convalescent Camp? He'll be there 3 or 4 weeks before he's well enough to travel home."

181

"You're kidding!! I thought he was dead. That dipshit Sgt. told me he died."

"Did he? What did you tell him?"

"I told him I was looking for an MP with chest wounds, and he said he died."

"So you didn't ask for Sanders by name?"

"Yeah. No. I mean, I don't think so." Vince thought for a second. "He thought I meant Gilchrist, didn't he?"

"I'd be willing to bet on it. Gilchrist died of two bullet wounds to the chest. Sanders was shot in the back."

"OK, OK, I get it. So where's Sanders? How's he doin'? Is he going to be OK?"

"Yeah, he'll be OK. It's gonna take a while, though. He got hit real hard. Doc tells me he should'a died. He didn't think Sanders would make it through the surgery, but he did. He's in intensive care, listed as critical, but the Doc says he'll recover. Good thing he's as strong as he is."

"Can I see him? Is he awake?" Vince said, the tears of relief welling up in his eyes.

Lt. Griffin put his hand on Vince's arm, squeezing gently.

"Maybe tomorrow, Vince. He needs his rest, just like you do."

The LT looked at his watch, then said, "Son, I gotta go now. You take it easy, get some rest. I'll be back tomorrow." He patted Vince's arm, and stood to leave.

"Thanks, LT. See you then."

Lt. Griffin stopped briefly at T.J.'s bunk on his way out. As he left, Vince lay back down on his bunk, and rolled over to face the wall. He began to weep softly in relief, thanking God that Sanders was alive. Vince felt as if a huge weight had been lifted from his shoulders. He smiled for the first time since the attack.

After several minutes, Vince wiped his eyes and again sat up. He called the nurse over, and asked if he could get up

182

and walk around.

"Sure. Probably do you a lot of good. How's that leg? Think you can walk on it?"

"I don't know. My whole body hurts."

"Here try these." She said, pulling a pair of crutches out from under the bed.

She helped Vince sit up and swing around so his feet were resting on the floor.

"You ready? Let's try getting you up."

She placed Vince's arm around her shoulders, and her arm around his waist, and lifted as Vince slowly stood up, groaning with the effort. Once he was on his feet, she adjusted the crutches to his height, then said, "Go for it, Soldier."

Vince spent the next 10 minutes moving slowly around the room, working the stiffness and soreness out of his muscles. He found he could get around OK if he took his time and didn't overdo it. He couldn't put much weight on his injured leg, but still could move around OK with the crutches. He made his way to T.J.'s bunk, and saw he was sleeping, so returned to his own bunk. He lay down, intending to rest a little, but was asleep immediately. He slept for the next 13 hours.

2 February 1968 0745 hrs.

Vince finished his second tray of food, then picked up his coffee, and sat back.

"You must be feeling better, Soldier." The nurse said as she took his tray.

That was the first food he had eaten in over 2 days. He hadn't realized how hungry he was until he took the first mouthful, then he ate ravenously. He had asked for and gotten a second tray, and ate that, too. He was on his third cup of coffee when he heard, "Hey, Torelli! You in here?"

"Yeah, T.J. Hold on, pal, I'm comin'."

Vince grabbed his crutches and stood up, then hobbled

over to T.J.s' bunk.

"Hey, man, how ya doing?" He asked.

"OK, Vince. I hear they're giving you a medal. Imagine that."

"Yeah, I know. I hear you're some kinda hero, too. Heard you guys stopped two battalions of VC all by yourself. Killed a couple hundred or so. Saved the airbase from total destruction."

"Yeah, except it was just me, alone."

Vince laughed. "That's probably what you'll end up telling everyone. The LT told me what you guys did. You know you're up for the Silver Star, don't you?"

"Yeah, he told me. Said you're gettin' a Bronze Star. Matter of fact, we got us a bunch of heroes. Sanders, Jackson, you, me, Gilchrist. Ain't we somethin'!"

"We're something, alright." He paused for a moment. He looked at T.J.'s bandaged face, and said, "How on earth did we end up here, T.J.?"

"Fate, my friend. Fortunes of war. Maybe we're just unlucky. Don't know, Vince, I really don't know. All I do know is I've had just about enough 'a this place."

"Me, too, T.J., me, too. Look, can you walk? I want to go see Sanders before he gets shipped out. If you can, you want to go with me?"

"Yeah, I'd like that. I need to get up and around, anyway. LT said he'd been hit real hard, almost died. I'm sure glad he's gonna make it."

"Me, too, man. Let's give it a try."

Vince and T.J. stood silently next to Sanders' bed, looking at the tubes and wires hooked up to him.

"Geez, Vince, he don't look too good."

"Look at all the stuff stuck in him, T.J. Tubes, needles, wires, all kinds 'a shit."

"I sure hope the doctor was right."

Sanders opened his eyes and muttered, "You guys done diagnosin' my condition? If so, how about gettin' me somethin' to drink?"

"Hey, Sanders." Vince said, breaking into a big grin, reaching out to take Sanders hand.

"Hey, Newbie," Sanders said, turning his head to look at them.

"You don't look so good. Whose the mummy with ya?"

"It's T.J., Sanders."

"Oh, yeah? What happened to you, T.J.?"

"Cut myself shavin'"

Vince cut in, saying, "Really, Sanders, how you doing? Can I get you anything?"

"I'm outta this war, Vince. Got my ticket home. Gonna make a stop over at Cam Ranh Bay for a little vacation, then back to Little Rock. You done good out there, Vince. Saved my ass, man."

Sanders coughed twice and groaned at the pain it caused him. His eyes fluttered, then closed.

"Sanders? Sanders, you OK?" Vince asked, squeezing his hand.

"Yeah, Vince, just tired."

Sanders voice was weak, barely louder than a whisper, his words broken, halting. "I got, gotta rest n-now. C-come b-back tomor..."

Sanders' head lolled to the side, and his breathing deepened as he fell deep asleep.

"Come on, T.J., let's go. He needs his rest."

Later that day, Vince returned to Sanders' bunk, and found he was still sleeping. He pulled a chair next to his bed, and sat down. Taking Sanders' hand, he said softly, "You rest, partner, get better," wiping his eyes with his other hand.

He started talking, telling Sanders about his family, his childhood, anything he could think of, talking steadily for the next hour and a half. While he talked, he fixed Sanders pillow, straightened his covers, placed a cool cloth on Sanders feverish forehead, and made sure he had a glass of

185

water within easy reach for when he woke up. Sanders slept the whole time, until Vince ran out of words, said goodnight and painfully made his way back to his own bunk.

Sanders was loaded into an ambulance two days later for the trip to the airbase. He was scheduled to be transported to the 6th Convalescent Camp at Cam Ranh Bay for further care and observation until he was well enough to go home. Vince and T.J. walked out with him as he was carried out and placed in the ambulance. Sanders called Vince over, just before they closed the doors. He handed him a small, folded piece of paper.

"Here, Vince, I expect you to use it." Vince saw that it was a Little Rock address.

"I'll miss you, Sanders. Who's gonna watch out for me once you're gone?" Vince said, a lump forming in his throat.

"You gotta watch out for yourself, now. You just remember what you learned, and you'll be OK."

He grabbed the front of Vince's shirt, and pulled him down so he was leaning over him.

"You're welcome at my house anytime, Vince." He whispered, staring into his eyes.

He let go as the driver closed the door. Sanders raised his hand, and said, "See ya, partner."

Vince raised his own hand, saying nothing. The lump in his throat made speech difficult, as the ambulance drove away.

11 March 1968 1355 hrs.
Vince was glad he'd been released to full duty again. He had had enough of light duty since his return to the company three weeks ago. Besides having to report to the 93rd Evac for physical therapy for his leg three times a week, he had been assigned clean-up details, filled sandbags, helped at the mess hall, and done office work. He

was eager to get back on the road.

For the last few days, he had been assigned to pick up the civilian workers in town in a deuce and a half, and take them to Long Binh. Vince would be on the road by 0400 hrs, making several stops throughout Bien Hoa to pick up groups of workers. He would drop them off at the checkpoint inside the main gate by 0500. He liked this duty because he was off until 1830, when he would drive the truck to the checkpoint, and take the workers back into the city. He was usually done in an hour and a half.

Man, he thought, *one more day, and back to regular duty.*

T.J. had returned to the 557th a week ago, and was assigned clerk duties in the COs office while his arm and shoulder completed healing. He was still experiencing some soreness and stiffness in his shoulder, but his arm was almost completely healed. He was pretty much a gofer, so he had easy duty with plenty of time to himself. He would meet Vince each day after noon chow, and they would spend an hour or so in the day room talking or writing letters. They both were a little quieter since that fateful night, more serious, and both did not joke or smile as much.

Vince was sitting in the day room writing a letter to Sanders. He had written him five times in the last few weeks, and had received one reply from Sanders' mother 2 weeks after Sanders had been transferred to Cam Ranh Bay, and one letter from Sanders three days ago. He sealed the envelope, then opened the letter from Sanders' Mother again. He had read it a dozen times, but hadn't grown tired of it.

> "Dear Mr. Torelli,
>
> My son, Lawrence, wrote me about you. He says he likes you and trusts you. You must be something because he doesn't warm to strangers easy. Lawrence told me what hap-

187

pened the night he was shot. He told me you saved his life. I just want to thank you for saving my boy.

Lawrence is all I got, Mr. Torelli. His daddy died before he was born. I got no other youngsters, so it's been me and him all our lives.

When Lawrence came to me and told me he enlisted in the Army, I was proud. He wanted to be a soldier ever since he been a little boy. He was always playing army with the other neighborhood boys, running and hiding. Carved himself a toy rifle from an old board. He'd play all day, everyday, same thing. I think he was always meant to be a soldier. It's honorable work, Mr. Torelli.

Lawrence told me there was lots of soldiers in your family too. Maybe that's why he liked you like he did.

He's in some hospital in Cam Ranh Bay. The doctors said he's doing fine and will be coming home next week. He'll be at Letterman Hospital in San Francisco for a while, then home to Little Rock. I'll be going to San Francisco to meet him and to take care of him.

Write to him, Mr. Torelli, cause I know he wants to hear from you. He don't have many friends anymore, so it's important to him.

Thank you again, Mr. Torelli, for saving my boy. You ever get to Little Rock, you will always be welcome in my house.

Ramona Sanders"

Vince folded the letter, put it back in the envelope, and placed it in the breast pocket of his utility shirt, just as T.J. walked in.

"Hey, hero, how ya doin'?"

"OK, T.J. How's the arm today?"

"Gettin' better. Guess I'll be on light duty for another week or so. I'm bored to death."

"It's your own damn fault. You could've gone home, you know."

"Yeah, but who's gonna look after you, now that Sanders ain't here? Seriously, though, I figure I had my share of bad luck. It's gotta get better from here on out. Besides, ain't much waitin' for me back home."

"Well, I think you're fuckin' nuts. If it was me, I'd a been outta here before the ink on my orders was dry. Listen, tomorrow's my last day picking up KPs. Want to come along?"

"Yeah, why not. I've got CQ duties until 0500, but I'll get Robinson to come in a little early. I'll meet ya at the motor pool at 0400, OK?"

"Sounds good. I gotta go get some stuff at the PX. Wanna come with me?"

"Yeah, sure. Let's go."

March 1968 0840 hrs.

Vince couldn't shake the nervousness he felt as he drove through the city. The signs of the VC attack were all around. Ruined buildings, rubble and mortar craters in the roadway, filled in temporarily with gravel. The people seemed unaffected, most of them never having lived in peacetime conditions. They were hardened to war, and felt no lasting effects from the Tet Offensive. They went about their business without a care in the world.

Vince wished he had a cold beer. It seemed he relied more these days on alcohol to calm him, to help him sleep. Most every night since his return to the company he would spend a couple of hours at the rebuilt EM Club, drinking, mostly beer, sometimes bourbon, until he was pleasantly drunk. Then he'd stumble to his bunk to sleep. He knew he was drinking too much, but the depression overtook him each evening as the sun went down and darkness crept over the land. He felt he needed the booze to help him stave off the uneasy feelings that came over him as the light faded.

He had changed. He was quieter and brooded more. He spent more time alone or with T.J., and less with the other guys. He would still talk with them when they came over to his table, but he never sought them out himself, preferring to sit alone. He did not mind his friends joining him, but seemed to seek out solitude. It was his way of healing his mind. Each day that passed brought him closer to his old self. Each night was a little easier to face.

Today he was riding with Wild Bill. They were assigned a checkpoint with two Quan Canhs and one Canh Sat, and were headed to their station a couple of hundred meters from the foot of the bridge over the Dong Nai River. Vince's mind wandered back to the day he first had seen the bridge with Sanders. He remembered the things they had talked about, the lessons he had learned. He silently thanked Sanders for his guidance and teachings, knowing he would never have survived that night in January if not for him.

A half hour later, they were set up at the checkpoint, stopping vehicles for inspection. Vince and Wild Bill had just checked a quarter ton with 2 GIs. Their orders had them going to the III Corps Compound, delivering some dispatches and six cases of beer. Over the next two hours, they stopped a dozen more American Vehicles, finding three GIs off limits in a jeep loaded with mess hall steaks headed for the black market. They made the arrest, then called for a truck to take the GIs and contraband back to the PMO at Long Binh.

Vince was sitting in the jeep with Wild Bill, resting, when he heard a motorcycle approaching. He looked up and saw a small Honda with two young men on it driving toward their checkpoint. One of the QCs walked out into the roadway, and began waving his arms over his head, trying to flag the motorcycle down. The bike began slowing as it approached the checkpoint, then, when it was 40 feet away, the driver downshifted, gunned the engine and accelerated at full throttle toward the QC. The QC began shouting at him to stop, but the driver swerved and continued accelerating. The QC drew his .45 as the motorcycle passed, and began firing wildly at the riders. At the sound of the shots, all the civilians in the area began diving to the ground, purely through reaction to the gunfire. The driver and rider hunched over, trying to make as small a target as possible, heading toward the bridge. The Canh Sat had drawn his .38, and began firing at the fleeing Honda, too.

Vince involuntarily hunched down as the M-60 on the back of his jeep began firing. He saw the heavy slugs tearing up the pavement ahead of the fleeing motorcycle. The slugs walked back toward the bike, then began impacting the machine. Pieces of metal and rubber from the rear tire were blasted off by the 7.62 slugs, flying in all directions. The motorcycle began swerving and wobbling wildly. The gunner adjusted his fire, and the back of the passenger's shirt erupted in a shower of blood as the bullets blasted through his body, and into the back of the driver's head. His head blew apart, spraying blood, bone, and brains everywhere. The motorcycle flipped on its side, throwing the driver's body to the side of the road, where it bounced twice and slid into the ditch. The passenger fell off backwards, bouncing and rolling for 30 feet, coming to rest in the middle of the road.

Vince looked back and saw the QC machine gunner grinning from ear to ear.

"Numbah one, eh MP? Quoc beaucoup good shot. I get both!! Numbah one!!"

Vince looked at Wild Bill, shook his head, and said,

"Yeah, pal, numbah one."

The two QCs and the Cahn Sat walked to the passenger's body, and one QC knelt down and began searching him. He pulled a handful of piasters from one of the pockets, counted them, then folded the bills in half, and put them in his own pocket. He continued searching the body, removing some papers. He pulled a wristwatch from the body's left wrist, and handed it to the other QC. Having finished his search, he grabbed the body by the feet, and dragged it to the side of the road by the driver's body. The Cahn Sat was now wearing the driver's watch, and was removing other items from his pockets, which he placed in his shirt pocket. When the search was done, all three stood around the bodies, smoking and talking, until an ARVN half ton pickup truck arrived. Two soldiers got out, picked up the bodies one by one, and unceremoniously tossed them in the back of the truck. They got back in the cab, and drove off quickly.

Two hours later, Vince and Wild Bill were sitting in the Lieutenant's office explaining why an ARVN QC used their M-60 to shoot down two people.

"Look, LT, it's their country, their people. We really don't have anything to say in what they do," Wild Bill said, his frustration showing.

"You're right, Hickok, but they ain't supposed to be in your jeep, using your weapons."

"We was just restin', Sir. Quoc, too. I didn't know he would use our '60."

"Well, ain't much we can do about it now. We were just lucky no civilians got hurt. You guys know the routine. NO VIET NATIONALS IN OUR JEEPS, unless they are specifically assigned to your unit, got it?"

Vince and Wild Bill answered together, "Yes, Sir."

"OK. We won't mention it again. The less said, the better. Now, you two get back to duty."

Later that night, Vince told T.J. about the shooting.

192

"The Gooks ever find out who they were, or why they didn't stop?" T.J. asked.

"Nah. They figured they were VC, but I'll bet they were just draft dodgers. May have been VC sympathizers, but I can't believe any hard core VC would be riding around on a Honda in broad daylight, without proper documents."

"Yeah, I'd go along with that."

"Man, T.J., that QC just opened up. Guess he didn't care about all the other people around. Sure was lucky no one else got hurt."

"Haven't you learned yet, Vince? These people don't give a shit about that. They have no regard for human life, man. It don't matter to them who lives or dies."

"I know that, T.J. It's just hard for me to understand."

"This country has been involved in one war or another for the last couple hundred years. Violent death is all around, always has been. It's as common as the sun risin' every day. It's a part of their lives. It's all they know."

"Yeah, that's all true, but that's not how we are, T.J. Are we to the point where violent death holds no significance for us? I don't think so. We, T.J., people like you and me, are the stabilizing cords that keep it all from unraveling."

"God, Vince, that's too much for me. I'd much rather just go have a beer."

"So would I," Vince said, grinning. "C'mon, T.J., you're buying the first round."

"Sure, if it will keep you from spoutin' all that philosophical crap."

"That remark is going to cost you TWO beers! Let's go."

PART III
SHORTIMERS

4 April, 1968   1745 hours

The last four weeks had been unusually quiet in the III Corps area. The VC losses during the Tet offensive had devastated their ranks, reducing their activity to small scale hit and run tactics and ambushes while they attempted to recruit and train new fighters. Bien Hoa and Long Binh had seen no enemy activity at all. No mortar rounds, no rockets, no convoy ambushes, no sniping. It gave Vince the time necessary to complete the healing process, both physical and mental.

He had started a regimen of exercise to strengthen his legs and body after his prolonged inactivity. He'd begun running three weeks ago, starting with a half mile, gradually working up to two miles a day. He had put on muscle, and felt better than he had in months. His physical wounds had completely healed.

He had been assigned to the night shift, city patrol, for the last week. He still was uneasy about being on duty at night, and avoided entering the airbase unless he absolutely had to. He and T.J. had been paired for two nights, and were scheduled to escort buses to the 90th until midnight. After chow, they were to assume town patrol. It had rained off and on until an hour earlier, when the overcast began breaking up, and a few stars could be seen through the rifts in the clouds. The rain had cooled the air, and a slight breeze was blowing.

"Let's take a run down Highway One to the bridge, T.J. See if anything's going on."

"OK. Anything in particular you lookin' for?"

"Nah, just bored. Drive on, my friend."

T.J. headed south through Bien Hoa, rounding a curve and passing Three Doors. He drove slowly, in no hurry.

Both he and Vince carefully checked out the alleys they passed, alert for snipers or an ambush. Several civil defense patrols were present, waving as they passed. Vince watched them closely, cradling his M-16 in his lap. He flipped the selector switch from "safe" to "auto", and had his finger on the trigger, ready to fire if he had to.

"Whatcha doin' Vince?" T.J. had noticed Vince readying his rifle.

"A wise man once told me 'don't trust anyone over here.' I've found other things he said were right on, so I'd be willing to bet that's good advice, too."

"Sanders?"

"Yeah, Sanders."

"Can't argue with that."

T.J. drove to the foot of the bridge over the Dong Nai, and parked by the bunker. They talked for a few minutes with the ARVN Lieutenant in charge of the bridge security detail. Lieutenant Song told them there had been very little activity in the Bien Hoa area and along the river, though the VC were becoming active again in the Loc Ninh vicinity and around the big base at Cu Chi. Hit and run ambushes along highway 13 were becoming almost a daily occurrence again. There were few strangers in Bien Hoa, and his intelligence information indicated the VC were rebuilding their units, but staying away from the larger American and ARVN installations and out of the cities while they underwent training and political indoctrination. Part of their training process was actual military action against the ARVN or allied forces. Survival depended on how quickly they learned.

Vince had talked several times with Song, and they had become firm friends. Vince felt he was honest and truly believed in the fight against communism. He had joined the South Vietnamese Marines when he was 16, five years earlier, and volunteered to become a Ranger, undergoing the rigorous training without complaint. Though he stood only 5'4" in his jungle boots, weighing 120 pounds, he was fearless, quick to act, and possessed a wiry strength that belied his small stature. His shock of bristling black hair, cut to an uniform 1" and sticking out all over his head, and his piercing black eyes mirrored his intense hatred of the communist enemy, and his penchant to shoot first and ask questions later.

After four years of dedicated service, having risen to the rank of Sergeant, he requested Officer Candidate School, and graduated a second lieutenant eight months ago. He became a platoon leader, and was assigned to the 2nd South Vietnamese Marine Battalion in Thu Duc. He had been wounded twice in the furious fighting during the Tet offensive, refusing medical attention each time. He was instrumental in leading a successful counterattack against the 1st Battalion, 273rd VC regiment that attacked the Thu Duc District Headquarters on February second. His Marines, augmented by ARVN and U.S. infantry and elements of the U.S. 11th Armored Cavalry poured devastating fire into the attacking VC, forcing them to withdraw. A second attack the next morning was met by a Marine counterattack, led by Song, that effectively broke up the attack for good.

Song was wounded for the second time in two days in that action. He had been assigned to the bridge security detail while he recovered. He was due to be released to full duty in two days, and was ready to return to his unit. He considered his mission in life to kill communists, and he was very good at it. He was merciless, and killed without hesitation, and made no distinction between the age or sex of the enemy. All communists were his enemy, and deserved to die.

After talking and joking with him for a half hour, Vince and T.J. drove off north on Hwy 1, planning on returning to the Long Binh POL to refuel, then hit the mess hall for coffee. As they approached the entrance to the city, a figure stepped from the mouth of Death Alley, waving his arms, calling out to them, "Lai de, lai de, MP, lai de", which meant "come here."

T.J. slammed on the brakes, skidding to a stop. Vince had his M-16 pointed at the figure as T.J. grabbed his rifle and got out of the jeep.

"Hands up, keep your hands up!" T.J. yelled.

They could see the person was a boy 11 or 12 years old. He, in turn, could see the two MPs with their rifles pointed at him, and stopped where he was, his hands above his head.

"GI, there," he said, excitedly, pointing down the alley. "He hurt beaucoup bad."

"Come here, lai de," Vince called, keeping him covered with his rifle.

The boy began walking toward him, saying, "You hurry, MP. Maybe he die soon."

"Stop there," Vince told him, as the boy got to the front of the jeep. He covered him while T.J. watched the mouth of the alley.

"GI inside. You come quick. He maybe die, come quick." The boy gestured toward the alley, taking a couple of steps in that direction.

"Call it in, T.J. I'm gonna check it out."

"Better wait for some help, Vince. That ain't a good idea!"

"I know, T.J., but I got to do something. I'd hate to think there's an American in there needing help, and we waited too long. Besides, I got a feeling the kid's on the level. I'll take him with me. You come after us, partner, just as soon as you can."

"I'm comin' now, Vince."

"No, man, you know the rules. We can't leave the jeep. I'll be OK. Call for help, then come give me a hand when it gets here."

Vince walked up to the boy, and pointed at the alley,

197

then grabbed a handful of the back of his shirt, and walked him to the entrance. Vince then put his arm around the boy's neck from behind, and pulled him back tight against his chest. Using him as a shield, Vince backed up against the near wall, and slowly worked his way into the alley, sweeping the opposite side with his M-16, ready to fire at the first sign of trouble. His heart was thumping against his chest, and he began to breathe rapidly. Sweat began running down his face as he again heard the explosions and gunfire during the airbase battle in the back of his mind.

T.J. watched him enter, then ran to the entrance and looked around the corner. He could see him moving down the alley, his back against the wall, holding the boy in front of him, covering the alley with his M-16. He watched until the darkness swallowed them up.

"Be careful, my friend," he whispered to himself, as he ran back to the jeep to call for help.

Vince swung his rifle back and forth as he moved down the alley. Each time the boy started to talk, he would clamp his hand over his mouth. Vince whispered "shhh" in his ear, and pointed down the alley. They had gone about 70 meters into the alley before Vince saw the blacker lump laying against wall about five meters ahead of them. Vince tightened his grip on the boy, slung his rifle over his shoulder, and pulled a small penlight from his pocket. He put it in his other hand, then drew his .45, and moved slowly toward the shape.

The penlight showed a figure in jungle boots and fatigues lying on his side, with his back to him. Vince could see the back of his shirt was stained with a dark substance, and as he approached, the light revealed it to be blood. The figure moaned softly, rolling onto his back. Vince saw he was an American, his face battered, swollen, and covered with blood. Vince let go of the boy, telling him to go get the other MPs. The boy ran back toward the entrance, and when Vince was sure he was gone, he knelt down next to the soldier.

"Hey, buddy, how're you doing?" Vince said, leaning over him, shining the light on his face.

He could see several deep cuts, and saw that his eyes were swollen almost shut. His upper lip was split, and he was missing some teeth. None of the injuries looked bad enough to be life threatening. His name tag read "Carlson", and his unit patch revealed he was with the 20th Engineer Battalion.

Vince carefully rolled Carlson onto his side, and slowly shined the penlight over his back. He could see several holes in Carlson's blood-soaked fatigue shirt from a small knife.

"Hang in there, buddy. Help's on the way."

Vince heard footsteps approaching, and quickly snapped off the light and unslung his M-16, covering the alley. The footsteps stopped, and a voice called out softly "Vince? It's me and Wild Bill. Where are you?"

"Over here, T.J." Vince replied standing up. "Give me a hand. This guy's hurt bad."

T .J. and Wild Bill hurried over to Vince, and crouched down, each facing opposite directions, their rifles at the ready.

"You guys cover me. I'll carry him out. You call for an ambulance, T.J.?"

"Yeah, when the kid came out, just as Hickock and Guillermo arrived. Julio's watchin' the jeeps."

"OK. Keep your eyes open. Let's go."

Vince pulled Carlson to a sitting position, bent down and put him over his shoulders. He stood up, and, flanked by T.J. and Wild Bill, moved quickly toward the alley entrance. Once out of the alley, he laid Carlson on the ground.

"T.J., keep an eye on the alley," he said, as he felt for a pulse. "Stay with me, Carlson. You'll be OK."

Three hours later, Vince was sitting in a hallway outside a treatment room at the 93rdEvac. He looked up as a doctor walked toward him, pulling off his rubber gloves.

"How is he, Doc?"

"He'll be OK. He's gonna lose his right eye, though. How'd you find him?"

Vince told him how he found him, and that while he was in surgery, he had called the PMO and learned Carlson had been listed as a deserter three weeks earlier. Carlson had hitched a ride into Bien Hoa two months ago, and disappeared. Rumor had it that he had a pregnant Vietnamese wife living in the city, and that he was teaching English at a small school to earn a meager living.

"What happened to him tonight? How'd he get injured?" the doctor asked, sitting down next to Vince.

"I don't know. The boy said the cowboys did it, but he didn't know why. My guess is that Carlson was probably wrapped up with the black market or drugs, and somebody didn't like the way he was doing business."

"Well, whoever it was nearly killed him. Beat him so bad he'll lose an eye, and his jaw will be wired for a couple of weeks. He'll need some dental work on those teeth, too. Only one of the five stab wounds was serious. Punctured his lung, but we got him patched up. He's going to be in the hospital for a few days recuperating. Is he going to LBJ, then?"

"Yeah, I imagine so, until a court-martial can be arranged on the desertion charge."

"I'll call the PMO when he's able to be moved. In the meantime, he belongs to me."

"OK, Doc. I kind of think he's been through enough, but I don't make the rules. I'll be back tomorrow to visit. I know what you're thinking," he said, holding up his hands, palms toward the doctor. "It's strictly an unofficial visit."

"OK, Torelli," the doctor said, reading Vince's name tag, "tomorrow it is."

200

5 April, 1968 1544 hours

Vince sat next to Carlson's bunk, listening to him tell his story. His face was swollen and heavily bandaged. His damaged eye was covered, and an IV slowly dripped into his arm. He had difficulty talking, his swollen mouth and wired jaw slurring his speech.

"So I left about midnight to go to the house of a friend who had some fresh milk for us. Got it on the black market earlier. I don't go out much during the day because, well, you know, I didn't want to get caught."

"By us or the Viets?" Vince asked, interrupting.

"The Viets don't care. Everyone around there knows where I was living. I only wear my fatigues when I have to go into the city, so they've figured out I'm a deserter. It was you guys I had to look out for. I knew I had been listed as a deserter. A buddy of mine from my company comes by to visit once in a while, and he told me. I know what I've gotten into, but I want to stay here, with my wife, and raise a family."

"Don't you have any family back home?"

"No. My mom died two years ago, and I got no brothers or sisters. I never knew my father. He left when I was two. I got an aunt in Chicago, but I haven't seen or heard from her in over ten years. I got nuthin' to go back to. I've got a new life here, a wife and a baby on the way. I belong here, now."

"That why you deserted, Brian? You know you can't stay here."

"Yeah, I know. I only got two months left on my tour, but the baby isn't due for about three and a half. I'd have to go home and leave Tui here, to have the baby alone. And there's no guarantee I'll ever get her and the baby to the States. This is my home now."

Carlson sighed, looked at Vince, and asked, "What's gonna happen to me now, Vince?"

"Well, when you're able you'll be transferred to LBJ to wait a court-martial. Chances are, they'll get you on AWOL charges rather than desertion."

"Why AWOL?"

"A desertion conviction means you'd spend years in a federal prison. You got to be gone a lot longer than two months for that. You'll probably get 30 days at LBJ, then either go back to your company, or be sent home with a dishonorable discharge. If you're lucky, you'll get a general discharge. It's not as good as honorable, but not nearly as bad a dishonorable. What ever happens, I don't think you'll be able to see your wife again for awhile."

"Oh, God." Carlson moaned, tears welling up in his eyes.

"Listen, Vince," he said, after regaining his composure. "You've treated me OK, and seem like a decent guy. Can I ask a favor?"

"Depends on what it is."

"Would you deliver a letter to my wife? Here's the address. Just ask for Tui."

"OK, I guess I can do that. I'll come by again tomorrow around four. You can give it to me then. I'll deliver it later, after I go on duty."

"Thanks, man. You don't know how much I appreciate this."

"I got to go now, Carlson. You need anything?"

"Not right now. Guess I'll be here for a few days, eh?"

"Yeah, five or six, at least. Look, I'll see you tomorrow."

Vince walked back to his hootch, and sat on his bunk, picking up the paperback he had bought a couple of days earlier at the PX. He opened the book and began to read, but soon his mind drifted back to Carlson. He wondered what it must be like knowing he would soon be separated from the only person he loved for a long time, maybe forever. Vince knew the ache and loneliness he felt being separated from his fiancée, and could only imagine how much worse it must be for Carlson. He sighed, shook the thoughts from his head, and began to read, losing himself in the book.

Later that night, Vince walked out of the alley, and got back into the passenger seat of the jeep, looking at his watch. He turned to T.J. and said, "It's already after eight, T.J. We better get going."

"You give it to her?"

"Yeah, poor thing. She couldn't stop thanking me, and crying. Look, let's go back to the company area for a minute. There's a couple of things I need to pick up."

"What have you got in mind, Vince?" T.J. asked, suspiciously, looking at him out of the corners of his eyes.

"Never mind, T.J. Just drive to Long Binh."

Twenty minutes later, T.J. parked in the company area, and Vince walked quickly to his hootch, avoiding the LT. He stopped at the foot of his bunk, opened his footlocker, and took out a box of crackers, package of cookies, and three tins of Kipper Snacks, placing them in a paper bag. He then walked to the mess hall, and told the sergeant he needed three oranges and three apples for one of the prostitutes at Three Doors. The sergeant grinned and winked at Vince, then went into the kitchen. He came out a minute later carrying a bag filled with the fruit.

"Here ya go, Vince. I hope she's worth it."

"Thanks, Sarge, she is."

Vince placed the bags in the back of the jeep, and got in the drivers seat. T.J. was nowhere to be seen, so he lit a cigarette and leaned back, closing his eyes and listening to the occasional radio traffic. It had been quiet all night, and the only radio traffic was from the MP units in the city talking to each other. A couple of minutes later, T.J. walked up, carrying a full cloth bag. He got in the passenger seat, placing the bag in the back with Vince's.

Vince started the jeep, putting it in gear. "What's in the bag, T.J.?"

"Nuthin' much. Just some stuff I wanna get rid of."

"Oh yeah? Like what?" Vince asked, grinning.

"It's nuthin, Vince. Can we go now?"

"OK, OK. Geez, I was just asking!"

Vince turned into the city, driving slowly. "I got to stop at Carlson's place for a minute, T.J.," Vince said, parking by the path to the house.

"How come?" T.J. asked, his turn to grin at Vince.

"OK, wise ass. I got some food for her, alright?"

"Alright! Alright! Are you gettin' soft in your old age?"

"No, that's not it. I'm just worried about her health, her being pregnant, and all."

They sat there in silence for a bit. Vince looked at T.J., and said, "So, you want me to take your bag in, or you gonna take it yourself?"

"I'll take it. Let's go."

Two days later Vince was visiting Carlson, telling him he had delivered the letter to his wife. He didn't mention the food he and T.J. had given her. The IV had been removed, and Carlson was more alert than before.

"I got another letter for her, Vince. Can you take it to her, please?"

"Sure, Brian. I'll take it tonight. I'm glad you're feeling better. I talked to the doc, and he says you might be out of here in another couple of days."

"Yeah," he said, quietly, "It only means I'm goin' to the stockade."

"I know. Just hang in there, Brian. Maybe it'll work out. I'll help any way I can."

"Thanks, Vince, but there ain't much you can do. Besides, you've done enough just gettin' my letter to Tui. What am I going to do, Vince? I don't want to lose Tui and the baby. I want to be here when my son or daughter is born."

"I know, Brian. I wish there was more I could do."

"I do, too, Vince. Look, I appreciate whatever you can

do, but don't get your ass in a wringer over this, OK?"

"Sure, Brian. Listen, give me the letter. I'll deliver it tonight.

"How'd she look? Was she feelin' alright?" he asked, handing the letter to Vince.

"She's doing fine, Brian. Health is good, baby's starting to kick. You got nothing to worry about."

"That's good to hear. God, I wish I could see her again, be with her," Carlson said, his voice cracking.

"Listen, Brian, I got a couple of hours before I've got to go to work. Want me to stay awhile? We could play some cards, or talk, or whatever. I brought this, too," Vince said, retrieving a small paper bag he had put on the floor when he arrived. "You like oranges? I got a couple grapefruit, too."

"Yeah, Vince. That would be great. The food here really stinks," Carlson said, smiling.

Later that night, Vince and T.J. were parked near Cambo Alley, watching the people and traffic going by.

"Hey, T.J. Would it be so bad if Carlson hadn't gotten caught? I mean, he's got a new life here with Tui and the baby. He's got no one back in the world, you know. His only family is here, now."

"Tell ya the truth, Vince? I kinda wish we could help him more, know what I mean?"

"Yeah, T.J., I do. You know, if I could, I think I would."

"Don't be sayin' that around the wrong people, Vince."

"It's just talk, T.J. What do you say, want to go get some coffee?"

"Sure. Airbase or Long Binh?"

"Let's give the Airbase a try again, OK?"

"On our way," T.J. said, starting the jeep's engine.

9 April, 1968   1940 hrs.

"I can only stay a few minutes, Brian. I got a letter here for you from Tui. She sure misses you. I took her another bag of food, too."

"Thanks, Vince. I miss her, too, man. I sure wish there was someway we could be together again. I'd give anything to get outta here. If I ever did, I'd just disappear, take my wife and go, no one would ever see me again."

"What would you do, man? How would you live?"

"I'd find a way. Farm, teach, something. We'd be ok."

"You should try getting Tui to the States. You'd both be better off there."

"I've tried. All they'll tell me is to fill out the paperwork when I get back to the States. Could take a year, then they could deny my request."

"I can get you the paperwork, help fill it out. If you need a character reference, I'll give you one."

"Thanks, Vince. Yeah, maybe that's the way to go. Tell you what, bring 'em by tomorrow night after chow, and I'll start the process. You better get goin'. Here's the letter. See you tomorrow, Vince."

Vince dropped off Carlson's letter and another bag of food, then waited while Tui read the letter and wrote a short response. She sealed it in an envelope, and gave it to Vince, amid non-stop tears and thank you's.

Vince and T.J drove onto the Airbase later that night, and made their way to the mess hall for breakfast. As they got their food and sat at a table, an explosion outside rattled the windows, followed by two more, each a little further away. At the first explosion, Vince and T.J. dove under the table, banging into each other.

"God damn, T.J. that scared the shit out of me!!"

"Me, too, man."

Four more mortar rounds exploded in the distance, as Vince and T.J. crawled out from under the table and sat down. They grinned sheepishly at each other, bearing the stares of the airmen who had remained seated during the brief attack.

"Guess I'm still a little jittery." Vince said, wiping sudden sweat off his forehead.

They ate their food in silence, and left, returning to the city to finish out the night.

After cleaning their weapons at the end of the shift, they went to the mess hall for coffee. T.J. later went to the day room to play pool, and Vince went to his hootch. He lay on his bunk in his underwear, thinking about Carlson, wondering how he could help him, realizing he couldn't. His thoughts turned to his fiancée, as he drifted off to sleep. He saw her face, her smile. He could hear her laugh, and once again felt her head resting on his shoulder. With those thoughts in his head, he fell asleep, waking that afternoon fully rested. He quickly showered and shaved, then filled the small canvas bag, and went to the company area office, and hitched a ride to the hospital with one of the MP patrols.

As he walked into Carlson's ward, the duty nurse smiled, and said, "Back again? What did you bring him this time?"

"Just some fruit, Nurse Jamison. Want some?"

"No thanks. He can use it more than me. Don't stay too long, OK?"

"Sure. I'll only be a few minutes. Got guard mount in less than an hour, anyway."

Vince walked over to Carlson's bunk, and placed the bag on the floor. "Hey, Brian. How you doin'?"

"OK, Vince. What'd you bring me?"

"Same stuff, Brian. Open it later, OK? After I've left."

"Sure, Vince," Carlson said, a puzzled look on his face. "What's up?"

"Look, Brian, I can only stay a couple of minutes. I gotta get back for duty soon, so I came to say goodbye."

"What? Why, Vince? I'm not going anywhere for awhile. Are you leaving Long Binh?"

"No, Brian. Just listen, OK? Don't ask too many questions, 'cause this is hard for me, and if it takes too long, I might change my mind." Vince took a deep breath, letting it out slowly.

"I've been doing a lot of thinking the last few days, Brian, and I've made up my mind about something, come to a decision. Remember when we were talking the other day? You said you had no one back in the world waiting for you, and your family and life was now here. Who would it benefit to send you back to the States, or put you in jail? You? The Army? I realized it would do no one any good, so I made a decision, and just want to say good luck, and have a nice life."

Vince stood up and held out his hand. Carlson reached out and grasped it, and they shook hands slowly.

"Good bye, Brian."

"Bye, Vince," Carlson said.

Vince turned and walked away without looking back. Carlson watched him until he was gone, a puzzled look on his face, wondering what that was all about. Shaking his head, he leaned over and picked up the bag. Looking inside, he saw a set of jungle fatigues and a pair of boots. He quickly hid the bag in under the covers, and lay back down, smiling to himself. He now understood.

10 April, 1968 2010 hrs.

Vince, T.J. and Sorenson were pulling convoy duty, escorting 35 double flatbed trucks to Newport where they would be loaded with supplies from the ships in the harbor. They were one of 3 gun jeeps assigned to escort duty, along with a V-100. They met the empty trucks at 1830 hours at the staging area, then escorted them to the Newport docks. It took almost three hours to load the trucks, mostly with beer, soap and candy for the PX. Vince, T.J. and Sorenson sat in their jeep drinking cokes and talking, waiting for the loading to be completed.

"So I get in-country three months ago, and everybody's tellin' me about all the shit that happens around here, and I ain't seen nuthin! I can hardly wait, man. Ol' Charlie messes with me, he's askin' for trouble." Sorenson said, pushing his glasses back up on his nose.

Vince and T.J. looked at each other, and Vince slowly shook his head as T.J. grinned back at him. Sorenson stood 5'7", and weighed somewhere in the area of 230 pounds. He already had a receding hairline at 20, and looked like he desperately needed to get some sun. His pale skin seemed pasty and unhealthy, and his overall appearance was one of softness. He wore black-framed glasses that kept slipping down his nose.

"What?" Sorenson asked, seeing the look pass between them. "What's up, you guys? Did I say something wrong?"

"Look, Sorenson, you don't know what you're sayin'," T.J. replied. "Be careful what you wish for, man. You might be real sorry if it comes true."

"Hey, T.J., I heard you and Corporal Torelli got in some shit during Tet. I wish I could'a been here. What happened to you? I heard you guys really kicked some ass. How'd you guys get wounded? You kill any of the little bastards?"

"Whoa, slow down. Stop asking so many questions, Sorenson, and pay attention to what's going on around us," Vince snapped. "Enough, now. You keep your eyes and ears open, and your mouth shut, OK?"

"Yeah, sure, Corporal. Hope I didn't say nuthin' to offend you. I'll be quiet now, just like you said. Yep, you'll hear no more from me. No sir-ree, not another word. Total silence."

"T.J., take a walk with me. Sorenson, you stay with the jeep. C'mon, T.J." Vince said, walking slowly toward the docks.

T.J. walked along with Vince in silence for a short while. "Kinda tough on him, weren't you?"

"Yeah, I suppose so. It's just that he kept asking all those stupid questions, and saying those stupid things. He was driving me nuts!"

"He's an FNG, Vince. He don't know any better yet."

"Yeah, I know. Let's hope he doesn't find out the hard way."

"Like us, huh, Vince?"

"Yeah, like us."

They walked to the water's edge, and sat on the dock, their legs dangling over the river. Neither had anything to say, both being lost in their private thoughts, remembering the night at the air base. Vince lit a cigarette, taking a deep drag, and shuddered.

A half hour later, they were on their way back toward Long Binh on Hwy 316. All the trucks were loaded with goods destined for the PX at the air base, III Corps Compound, and Long Binh. Vince's jeep was the last vehicle in the convoy, following about 40 meters back from the last truck. T.J. had the headlights off, using the taillights of the truck in front of him as a guide. They had gone about 8 miles, moving along at 20 miles per hour when the first RPG hit the third truck in line, exploding just behind the cab. Fortunately for the driver, the truck was loaded with cases of beer, and the RPG penetrated several cases before exploding, sending beer and shreds of cans in all directions. The beer effectively insulated the driver from the explosion, though it startled him so much that he jerked the wheel to his left, running the truck off the road into the field.

Several AKs opened up from the brush 30 meters away, the 7.62 mm bullets spraying the next truck in line. One round went through the passenger door, striking the driver in the right leg just below the knee. The shock and pain caused him to grab his leg with both hands, and slam on the brakes with his left foot, stalling the engine. The truck slid to the right while the trailers slid to the left, jackknifing, and blocking the roadway, bringing the rest of the convoy to a stop.

"Get on the gun, Sorenson," Vince yelled, grabbing his M-16.

T.J. pulled around the stalled convoy, and raced up to the damaged trucks, screeching to a halt a few meters away.

"There, Vince, over there," he yelled, pointing at the muzzle flashes from the field.

Vince fired a half a magazine toward them, and at the same time Sorenson opened up with the M-60. An MP in the other jeep fired a grenade, and the mini gun on the V-100 began returning fire. A ribbon of red tracers reached out to the jungle, pulverizing the vegetation.

Sorensons' first burst struck the ground 30 feet into the field. He raised the muzzle, and fired another short burst. This time the rounds struck 10 feet in front of the jungle. He adjusted his aim and fired a sustained burst into the jungle, moving the muzzle back and forth rapidly, spraying bullets all over the area. Vince and T.J. had taken cover behind their jeep. The other MPs continued to fire blindly into the jungle. There was no incoming fire, and Vince yelled, "Cease fire, cease fire." The shooting gradually stopped, and all was quiet.

"Anyone call it in?" Vince asked.

"Yeah, I did," Chavez said, standing up.

"Anyone hurt?"

"I think one of the drivers is. I'll check it out."

The entire firefight had lasted less than 45 seconds, though it had seemed like 45 minutes to Vince. The wounded driver was tended to and made comfortable, then taken to the 93rd Evac by the other MP jeep. A squad of ARVN Rangers from Thu Duc was en route to sweep the area, but were not expected for at least 20 minutes. None of the trucks had been disabled, and the drivers were able to quickly clear the jam and get the convoy back on road. An MP from the other jeep took over driving the wounded man's truck, and the convoy went on its way.

The ARVN Rangers swept the ambush site, and found only shell casings and a bloody sandal. They followed a well-marked trail several hundred meters into the jungle, but turned back when nothing and no one was found.

Later that morning at the mess hall, Sorenson couldn't stop talking about the ambush. He would tell the story over and over to anyone who would listen. He would not be able to sleep until well past noon.

11 April, 1968   1630 hrs.

Vince walked into Carlson's ward, and saw that his bunk was empty. He stood there for a few moments, staring at the empty bunk, then turned to leave. As he walked out, he saw the nurse approaching.

"Hello, Corporal." she said.

"Hi, nurse. How was Carlson feeling before they transferred him?"

"You didn't hear? No, I guess you couldn't have. Carlson took off."

"What? What did you say?"

"He took off. Gone, split, adios."

"How?"

"Who knows? Sometime last night, he just pulled out the IV, and walked out."

"Did he have any clothes or uniform?"

"Nope. Just his light blue hospital pajamas. CID people were here an hour ago asking the same questions."

"Anything else you can tell me?" Vince asked her.

"No. That's all I know. I've got to make my rounds now. Look, for what it's worth, I think it was real nice the way you treated him. Maybe this is for the better. See ya, Corporal," she said, as she started walking through the ward.

Vince grinned at her back, then turned and walked out the door.

1812 hrs.

As he stood at attention, Vince could hardly wait for guard mount to end so he could get into Bien Hoa. 35 minutes later, T.J. parked by the path to Carlson's house, and Vince walked to the front door. He could see the door was standing open, and walked in. He walked through the small, 3 room house, and found it was empty. As he walked back into the main room, he saw an envelope lying on the floor. Vince walked over and picked it up, noticing his name was printed on it. "I don't remember that being there when I came in," he said to himself.

Vince opened the envelope, and took out a single sheet of paper, covered with neatly printed words. It was dated the day before. He began to read.

"Vince:

I want to thank you for your kindness to my wife and to me. It's a debt I never will be able to fully repay. I had to do this, Vince. I just know if I didn't, I'd never see Tui again, and never see my baby. I'd go to LBJ, then be shipped home without her.

I told you in the hospital this is my home now. The only person I care about is here. This is where I belong, and where I plan to stay. I know what I'm doing, Vince. I've taken Tui and left the city. You won't be able to find me, so don't bother trying. I'll be ok.

Stay safe, my friend. I will never forget your kindness. Who knows, our paths may cross again someday.

God Bless You,

Brian"

Vince refolded the letter, and put it back in the envelope.
"He say where he went?"

Vince jumped, startled, and spun around to face the speaker.

"Jesus, you scared the shit out of me. Who the hell are you?"

"Sgt. Robert Canale, CID. I know who you are, and I'm looking for your buddy. He is a deserter, you know. What I haven't figured out yet is what your involvement in this is."

"Well, I certainly am impressed."

"Oh, a smart ass, too, eh? Well, you better watch your mouth, soldier. We're lookin' real closely at your involvement in this."

"Look all you want, Mr. CID. I've got no involvement in this."

"That right, asshole? My information has it you got real chummy with this low life. He give you any clue as to where he snuck off to?"

"Tell me something, Sgt. Do they pick you guys based solely on your personalities?"

"Huh? Whatta you mean?"

"Never mind, you answered my question. If there's nothing else, I've got to get going."

Vince walked out the door, and back to the jeep. He heard the Sergeant call out after him, "We'll be watchin' you, Torelli. We're not through with you."

"Let's go, T.J.," he said, as he got in the passenger seat.

"What did the CID bozo want?"

"He's trying to find Carlson. I got a feeling he won't have much luck."

"You know something I don't?"

"Here." Vince said, handing him the letter.

T.J. read the short message, then handed it back to

214

Vince.

"Well, I hope he knows what he's doing."

"He does, T.J. I just hope he's ok. Let's go."

As T.J. started the engine, a face appeared at the window of the house across the street. It was an American, and as T.J. and Vince drove off, he raised his hand in an unseen wave goodbye.

13 April 1968   1645 hrs.

Their Huey was airborne at 1000 feet, heading back to Long Binh. It had been a long, hot, boring day. There had been more patients than usual, thanks to a particularly virulent strain of flu that had shown up a few weeks earlier. It had hit the children hardest, due to their borderline malnourished condition. It took almost two additional hours to complete the MedCap, and now Vince was happy to be heading back to the company. He was hot, thirsty, tired, and was looking forward to a cold shower and a hot meal. He hoped this would be his last MedCap, since he had less than two months left before he rotated back to the States.

Vince felt the helicopter change course suddenly and drop down toward the jungle. He looked out the door, and saw that they were flying in a southwesterly direction about 300 feet above the trees.

"What's going on, T.J.? Why'd we change direction?"

"Don't know, Vince. I'll check on it." T.J. moved up behind the pilot's seat, and started talking with him. Vince couldn't hear what they were saying, but he had a bad feeling in the pit of his stomach. T.J. returned to his seat, and leaned toward Vince and the doctor.

"A platoon of grunts ran into an ambush while checking out a settlement along the Dong Mon river a few miles from us. They've one dead and three wounded, and were calling for a medevac. Since we've got a doctor on board, the pilot volunteered us for the extraction."

"Great. Remind me to thank him later," Vince said. "Where are we going?"

"It's a government settlement called Ben Sang. Lots of rice paddies near by, plantations, that sort of stuff. The grunts got hit approaching the vil. A couple of the wounded are supposed to be in bad shape. They're set up a couple hundred meters east of the settlement. They've secured an LZ, and set up a perimeter."

"How hot is the LZ?"

"Luke warm. Some sniper fire, now and then. We'll be there in a couple of minutes. Lock and load, pal," T.J. said, chambering a round in his M-16.

"Jesus, T.J. We're getting too short for this shit," Vince said, as he loaded a round in his rifle, looking out the door as they cleared the jungle.

They were flying over a large rubber plantation. They crossed a paved road, Highway 15, and Vince could see rice paddies, and a small river in the distance. Across the river was a large settlement. The pilot turned to follow the river in an easterly direction, and Vince could see yellow smoke drifting up from a clearing in the brush and elephant grass south of the river.

As they slowly circled the clearing, he could see the platoon had set up a perimeter facing the settlement. In the center were the wounded, attended by a couple of soldiers. The pilot slowed to a hover at the far side of the clearing, and quickly set the chopper down. The doctor jumped out and ran the short distance to the wounded, and immediately began treating the most seriously hurt. Vince, T.J. and Flannery followed, crouching by the doctor, watching the perimeter.

"Load him," the doctor said, pointing to a private with a bandaged leg. "Him, too," indicating a soldier with an arm wound.

Flannery helped them up, and half supporting the GI with the leg wound, walked quickly to the chopper. The doctor lifted the bandage on the last wounded GI's chest, saw the pink bubbles, and yelled at T.J. "Get me a piece of plastic, quick."

T.J. pulled a plastic baggie from his shirt pocket, emptied out the cookies he kept inside, and handed it to the doctor. He slapped it over the chest wound, grabbed T.J.'s hand, and pressed it down onto the plastic.

"Press hard. Don't let up. He's got a sucking chest wound, and it has to be sealed."

The doctor grabbed a sterile dressing and role of gauze, placed the dressing over the plastic, then wrapped the gauze tightly around the wounded soldier's chest, sealing the wound.

"OK, get him on board."

Two of the soldiers picked him up and quickly carried him to the helicopter.

Vince could hear sporadic rifle fire from the perimeter. He thought back to that night on the air base, and remembered the fear he felt. A familiar knot began to build in his stomach.

"Shake it off, Torelli," he said to himself, taking several deep breaths. Suddenly he heard the heavier chatter of a machine gun, and saw green tracers erupting from the brush to his right. He flung himself flat, hugging the ground, as the heavy slugs ripped the air above his head.

"Shit, T.J., you see him?"

"To the right, Vince, 50 meters. They're a couple of meters back in the brush."

Another burst of fire caused them to duck, but Vince could see where it was coming from. He swung around and began firing into the brush toward the hidden machine gun. T.J. joined him a few seconds later. The next burst from the hidden gun reached out to the chopper, and Vince could hear the slugs ripping through the helicopter's thin skin. The pilot immediately increased power and lifted off, heading away from the gun's fire.

217

Great, Vince thought, *guess we're walking back.*

Small arms fire had erupted all along the perimeter now. Vince and T.J. hugged the ground as the fire increased, several bullets kicking up the dirt around them. They fired back, shooting at the muzzle flashes and smoke.

One of the GIs began firing grenades into the brush with a grenade launcher, trying to knock out the machine gun, with no success. The gun continued firing, reaching out to the dug in soldiers. Vince heard a cry of pain, then someone calling for a corpsman. Vince fired again in the direction of the machine gun, then crawled six feet to his left, and fired again. Just then, two Huey gun ships roared low over the clearing, gaining altitude at the far end, turning and beginning a second run. The first fired two salvos of rockets into the hidden VC as it flew overhead. The second followed close behind, both door gunners pouring M-60 fire into the brush. Both gun ships turned and flew low over the brush, their machine guns tearing up the bushes and grass, the red tracers arcing to the ground. After this pass, they rose into the air and hovered, checking for enemy fire. There was none, and the GIs were moving out toward the brush to sweep the area.

Vince sat up and watched as the gun ships flew off toward Bien Hoa. He loaded a fresh magazine into his M-16, then lit a cigarette. "What now, T.J.?" he asked, settling down into a more comfortable position.

"Well, guess we get to ride back with the grunts. We'll find out soon enough. Here comes the Sergeant."

"You two, come with me," the Sergeant said, turning on his heel, and heading back toward the perimeter.

Vince and T.J. followed him to the edge of the clearing where the Sergeant knelt down. They knelt next to him, looking through a break in the brush toward the settlement.

"You two take cover here, and keep an eye on the vil. Watch for any VC entering or leaving. I'll be back in awhile." He stood up and ran toward the clearing.

"Ain't this somethin', Vince?" T.J. whispered. "Still doin' grunt work!"

They could hear rifle fire off to their right, and men shouting, an explosion, then silence for a couple of minutes before another series of shots would erupt. It had begun to rain, the large drops quickly soaking Vince's fatigues. The noise from the rain spattering the brush and grass drowned out all other sounds. Vince hunched down a little more, carefully watching the village.

T.J. tapped Vince on the shoulder, and when he turned toward him, put a finger to his lips, then pointed to their right. Vince looked where T.J. was pointing, and saw two black clad figures crouching in the clearing just outside the brush line about 25 meters away. As he watched, two more, carrying rifles, emerged and crouched next to the first two. They began gesturing toward the settlement, apparently discussing their route, though Vince could not hear them. The VC rose to their feet and began slowly making their way along the brush line toward Vince and T.J.'s position, looking behind them often.

Vince raised his M-16, as did T.J., sighting on the approaching enemy. As they came closer, several of the American infantrymen emerged from the brush 15 meters behind them. Spotting the VC, they opened fire just as Vince and T.J. did, catching them in a deadly crossfire. Two fell immediately, dead as they hit the ground. The other two turned toward the settlement, and began running crouched over to make themselves as small as possible. One, limping badly, fell after a few steps. The last continued, unscathed, in spite of the volume of fire from the American soldiers. Vince sighted carefully on the running figure, flipping the selector switch to semi-auto. Just before he could fire, the running VC clutched his side, and staggered. The VC stopped, turned toward the pursuing Gis, and raised the rife he was carrying. Before he could pull the trigger, he was struck by several bullets, spun around, and fell on his face.

The firing stopped, and Vince and T.J. rose to their feet. They walked out of the brush as the other GIs came toward them, and walked carefully toward the two VC, covering them all the time. Vince could see that both were dead. Other squad members were checking the other two. Vince lit a cigarette, cupping it in his hands to protect it from the lessening rain. He walked closer, and saw that the last body appeared to be a young boy. He knelt down by the corpse, lying face down, and gently turned it over. He was shocked when he saw the dead VC was a girl, no more than 15 years old. She was still clutching the AK 47 in one hand. He just stared at the body, not moving for a full minute.

"Never seen a dead VC before, MP?"

Vince looked up at the infantry Sergeant, and said, "Seen enough to suit me. Just never saw any female VC, up to now."

"Get used to it. This area lost a lot of their hard core VC during Tet, and the girls are being used more and more to fill out their fighting ranks. We found two more in the brush back by the LZ."

Vince looked back at the girl, shaking his head, and muttered, "Man what a war."

"Hey, Sarge, we got a live one over here," one of the grunts called from out in the field.

"Gotta go, MP. You did OK, you and your buddy. Anytime you want to tag along with us, just look me up."

The Sergeant walked off into the field, leaving Vince to himself. He looked around and saw T.J. sitting with three of the grunts a short distance away, talking quietly. He looked at Vince, winked, then returned to his conversation. Vince stood up and slung his M-16 over his shoulder, lit another cigarette, and walked over to T.J.

"What now, T.J.?"

"Well, there's a company of grunts on the way. They'll have to sweep the vil later today, so when they do that, we will be going back to Long Binh by jeep. We're out of it, now."

"Good. This isn't what I had in mind when I got here, T.J. I'm getting pretty tired of this shit."

"Yeah, I know how you feel. I thought I wouldn't be doin' grunt work no more, but here I am, still humping the boonies."

An hour later, they were being driven back to Long Binh by one of the privates. The driver was excitedly talking of the battle, but Vince and T.J. were quiet, keeping their thoughts to themselves. They looked at each other as the driver rattled on. Vince just looked away, watching the countryside go by.

22 April, 1968   2110 hours

The four rockets slammed into Long Binh in less than three minutes. Two struck open areas, doing no damage other than blowing fountains of dirt and bits of vegetation into the air. One landed next to a barracks in the Engineer Battalion, blowing a hole in the sandbags and the wall, wounding two PFCs slightly. The fourth blew up the POL near the eastern perimeter, causing a huge secondary explosion that sent a tremendous fireball several hundred feet in the air. It would be three hours before the fires could be controlled, and several thousand gallons of diesel fuel, two storage tanks, a pump house, and three tanker trucks were destroyed. The fuel station was out of service for only two days.

Vince and T.J. were driving down Hwy 15 toward Three Doors. They were trying to find an AWOL GI who was supposed to be staying there, according to an informant of Vince's. The informant was a 12 year old orphan boy who lived on the streets, supporting himself by theft and informing to the Americans. In return for information,

Vince would give him food, candy, clothes, and other things from the PX he could trade on the black market.

Earlier today, he told Vince about an AWOL GI staying at Three Doors. Vince was able to confirm the AWOLs name through the PMO, then had T.J. drive them there.

"Should we wait for the QCs?" T.J. asked, parking two doors away.

"Nah. It'll take them forever to get here. Let's just check it out ourselves."

Vince walked to the front door, arriving just as it opened up, and two American GIs walked out, bumping into him.

"Well, good evening, gentlemen," Vince said, grabbing each by an arm, and spinning them around. "Assume the position."

The two placed their hands against the building, and spread their feet.

"Aw, shit," the black corporal said.

"Search the other one, T.J." Vince said, as he started to pat the corporal down. Feeling a lump in his back pocket, Vince reached in and pulled out a plastic baggie half full of marijuana.

"Planning a party, Corporal?" he asked, stuffing the baggie in his shirt pocket.

As he patted down his legs, he felt another lump in the blousing of his left pant leg. Loosening the blouse, several small plastic bindles fell out. Vince picked them up, seeing they were filled with a white powder.

"Heroin or Meth?" he asked the soldier.

"You figure it out. You found it, asshole."

"Nice talk. You kiss your mother with that mouth? It doesn't really matter. Whatever it is, it means a lot of bad time at LBJ."

"What do you mean?"

"Any time you spend in custody at Long Binh Jail is bad time. It doesn't come off your duty time here. Anything on your guy, T.J.?"

"Just one joint."

"Let's get 'em to the PMO, and book 'em."

Vince handcuffed the two together, took their I.D. cards, and put them in the back of the jeep. They took them to the PMO on Long Binh, completed the booking, then drove them the few blocks to LBJ. As they headed back toward Bien Hoa, T.J. asked Vince if he wanted to try again to find the AWOL.

"I doubt he's still going to be there. We'll get him another time. Let's go to the airbase for chow."

"On our way, Vince."

1 May, 1968 1330 hrs.

It had been raining all day. Vince sat in the jeep on the checkpoint across from the Bien Hung theater, wrapped in his poncho, trying to stay dry with little success.

"Man, T.J., whoever designed these ponchos obviously never had to wear them in the rain."

"Well, they do keep some of the rain off. Not much, but some."

Traffic was heavy, and they had been busy all morning checking the American vehicles.

They did not have any Quan Cahns or Cahn Sats with them, so they weren't stopping any Vietnamese vehicles. American traffic had been slow for the last hour with few vehicles driving by, giving them an opportunity to sit and rest. Foot traffic to the theater had picked up earlier, as there was a children's puppet show that started at one.

Vince looked across the road to the theater. Two young Vietnamese men were leaning up against the wall near the front door, smoking, looking around. Vince thought it odd that they would be hanging out there, and turned to T.J.

"If we had some Quan Canhs with us, I bet they'd be interested in talking to those two," he said, pointing at them.

223

"Could be deserters, or draft dodgers," T.J. replied, looking at the two young men.

"I hope that's all they are. Here comes a deuce and a half. Let's flag 'em down.

As they were checking the driver's I.D. and travel papers, one of the Vietnamese men looked at his watch, said something to the other, and walked away, stopping at a small cafe a block away. The other walked around the side of the theater, returning with a small canvas bag. He walked into the theater, remained inside for a minute, then left without the bag. He walked to the café, and joined the first man, who had ordered cups of the thick coffee heavily laced with cream and sugar.

Vince handed the drivers' papers back to him and sent him on his way, everything being in order. He joined T.J. in the jeep, lighting a cigarette. It had stopped raining, and Vince took off his poncho, rolling it up and stuffing it under the seat.

"Where'd our friends go?" he asked, nodding toward the theater.

"Beats me. Didn't see 'em leave."

"I didn't like the looks of those two. They're up to something."

"What?"

"I don't know, but they didn't look right to me."

"C'mon, Vince. You're getting awful suspicious in your..."

An explosion close by cut off any further conversation. Vince and T.J. dove to the ground, covering their heads with their hands. Vince looked up after the noise subsided, and saw smoke pouring out the door of the theater. As he got to his feet, grabbing his M-16 from the jeep, the first people began staggering from the building, dazed and crying. Others came out bloodied, carrying children, crying hysterically.

"Jesus, T.J. Let's go," he said, running across the road.

224

They forced their way past the people and children streaming out the front door, stopping to help up an old woman who had fallen. As they entered the theater, they saw that the last few rows of seats had been blown out by the force of the explosion. Smoke hung thick in the air, and several people were crying and moaning on the floor. Bodies were everywhere, and Vince began to slowly make his way into the room, checking several as he went.

The first body he saw was a young boy about seven years old. He stopped and knelt over him, checking for a pulse. Vince saw his arm had been blown off just above the elbow, and by the amount of blood around him, knew he was dead. He moved on to the next child, another young boy who was also dead. The next body was that of a women, burned and twisted by the blast. Vince could see several other children's bodies laying around, not moving. Blood was everywhere, making the floor slippery, and he could smell the coppery scent as he walked through it.

As he moved further into the theater, a faint moan reached his ears. He looked toward the sound, and saw a young girl, blood coming from her nose and ears, soaking the front of her blouse. She was crying softly, moaning from pain, semi-conscious. Vince knelt over her, checking her injuries. He could see a ragged wound to her chest bleeding freely when he pulled her blouse open. He pulled a dressing from his belt, opened it and pressed it to the wound to try and stop the blood. She moaned again as he pressed down. He said, softly, "Sorry, sweetheart," then gently picked her up and carried her outside.

He could hear the sirens of the approaching ambulances, and saw several American and Vietnamese soldiers helping the injured in front of the theater. He knelt down and laid the limp body on the ground. Taking a bandage from his first aid kit, he started to wrap it around her chest, when he suddenly realized she was no longer breathing. She had died in his arms as he carried her out. He slumped back on his heels, and muttered "Oh, God, no." He covered his eyes with his hands, as a single tear welled up and ran down his cheek.

T.J. saw his friends' grief, and walked over to him. He sat next to him, and placed his arm around his shoulders. Looking at the little girl's body, he softly said, "It don't mean nuthin', man. It don't mean nuthin'."

Vince wiped his eyes with the back of his hand. "Why, T.J.? Why the kids?"

T.J. did not answer. He could not think of anything to say.

"I hate this fucking place, T.J. God, how I hate it here. What a fucking waste."

Vince suddenly stood up and began looking around the crowd that had formed in front of the theater. Standing near the back were the two men he had seen before the explosion.

"Come on, T.J. I want to have a talk with those two," he said, pointing at them.

He started walking rapidly toward them, with T.J. a few feet behind him.

The two VC were watching their handiwork as the dead and injured were carried from the theater. They belonged to the local VC cadre, and had been given this mission to prove to the people that they were not safe under the present military regime. Their purpose was to create as much destruction as they could to show that the Americans and South Vietnamese could not protect them. They decided to put a bomb in the theater for the impact the dead children would make. Their superiors would be pleased when they reported back to them later tonight.

As they watched the medics and rescue workers, they saw the tall American MP walking toward them, a deep scowl on his face. They looked at each other and by mutual understanding, turned and started to walk away. Vince saw the two men start to walk away. He ran the last few steps, catching up to them. Grabbing one by the back of his shirt, he threw him back toward T.J., following a few steps behind.

"Hold on to him, T.J. I'm going after the other one."

The second VC, seeing Vince grab his accomplice, began to run, dodging around the people walking along the street. Vince tossed T.J. his M-16, and ran after the VC. After a block, the VC looked behind him and saw the tall MP chasing him, only 10 meters behind. Increasing his speed, he dodged into an alley, widening the gap once he was away from the crowded street. As he came to a corner, he again looked behind and saw the MP was still following, though the distance between them had increased to 15 meters.

He turned into the next alley, picking up a heavy board as he ran. He turned the next corner, and stopped, flattening himself against the wall. Breathing heavily, he raised the board and waited. He heard the MPs' running footsteps approaching and tensed, ready to strike the second the MP rounded the corner. Suddenly, the footsteps stopped, and the MPs helmet liner slowly inched itself past the corner. The VC swung the board, connecting solidly with the helmet, knocking it back into the alley. The VC smiled triumphantly and stepped around the corner, raising the board to finish the job. Other than the helmet liner lying in the dirt, the alley was empty. His triumph changed to confusion as he looked around for the MPs' body. He took three steps into the alley, passing a doorway which slowly opened as he went by.

Vince came out the door behind the VC, and placed the muzzle of his .45 to the back of his head.

"You run, you little shit, and I'll blow your fucking head off."

After taking off his helmet liner and holding it out in front of him, he had moved it past the corner head high, as if he was trying to peer around it. The force of the blow from the board cracked the fiberglass helmet, knocking it from his hand. Stumbling backwards, he bumped into a door which opened from his weight. He stepped back into the room, closing the door just as the VC came around the corner looking for him.

The VC froze in his tracks, feeling the barrel against the back of his head. He suddenly dropped to his knees, swiveled around and struck Vince in the knee with the board. Vince fell to the ground, and as the VC got up, raising the board above his head to hit Vince again, Vince pulled the trigger of his .45, shooting him in the thigh. The heavy slug broke the thigh bone, blowing chunks of flesh and bits of bone out the back of his leg. The VC collapsed, dropping the board and grabbing his leg, screaming in pain.

T.J. rounded the corner just after hearing the shot, his M-16 ready. He ran up to the VC, and covered him with the rifle.

"You OK, Vince?" he asked, looking at his friend.

"Yeah, I think so. My knee hurts like hell, though. He caught me a good one with that board."

"Can you walk?"

"Yeah, I think so. Give me a minute."

Vince sat up and began rubbing his knee, wincing with pain. T.J. slung his rifle over his shoulder, took out a bandage, and tied it tightly around the VCs' leg above the wound to stop the bleeding.

"Nice shot, Vince. This little bastard's not gonna be runnin' from anyone for a long time."

Still rubbing his knee, Vince said, "Yeah, but I was aiming for his chest."

He stood up and found he could walk, though his knee hurt when he did. He walked in a circle, testing it, then said, "Let's get out of here, T.J. Can you handle him?"

"Yeah. I don't think he's gonna give me too much

trouble. C'mon, VC, we go now."

He grabbed the back of the VC's shirt, and began dragging him through the alley, toward the street.

"By the way, I turned the other one over to the Cahn Sats. When I told him we thought he was one of the ones who set the bomb, they started slapping him around, screamin' at him. I don't know what they were sayin', but whatever it was, he looked terrified and started talking a mile a minute. One of the Cahn Sats told me he said the other one was the one who had the bomb, not him. That's when I figured I better try to find you in case you needed some help. Silly me!"

As Vince limped into the street, two Vietnamese QCs ran up and took charge of their prisoner. Vince and T.J. walked back to their jeep, and sat down. Vince lit a cigarette, inhaling deeply.

"How many dead?" he asked, not looking at T.J.

"14. Mostly children, some women. 31 injured. A couple of those will probably die from their injuries."

"God. How can they do that, T.J.? This isn't part of the war. Those people died for nothing. They weren't soldiers. They didn't even take sides. They just happened to be in the wrong place at the wrong time. What a shitty war, man."

Vince hung his head in his hands, and sighed.

"I just don't get it, T.J. Why?" He looked up at his friend, his anguish etched on his face.

"It don't mean nuthin', Vince" T.J., said, grabbing his arm. "It ain't our war, man. We'll be outa here in a few weeks, then the hell with this country and everyone in it. It ain't our problem. We just do what we have to do, and get the hell out in one piece. That's all we gotta do, Vince, just keep thinkin' that. Just put this behind you, man, OK?"

"Sometimes that isn't so easy to do, T.J. I won't ever forget this, don't think I can."

"I know. Neither will I, but we gotta do the best we can,

Vince, just gotta go on."

"Let's get out of here, T.J. This place is making me sick."

T.J. started the jeep, and drove off, heading out of the city.

The next day, both the VC underwent intense and prolonged interrogated by ARVN CID Agents. As a result, two houses in Bien Hoa were raided, and arms, ammunition, medical supplies and documents were recovered. Four more hard corps VC were captured, though three were wounded during the raid. One died of his wounds later that day.

From the captured documents, the ARVN and American intelligence officers were able to locate the place and time the local VC Commanders were holding a planning meeting on Rua Island in the Dong Nai River, west of Bien Hoa. A SEAL team was inserted several hours prior to the meeting, taking cover where they could see the meeting place, a small abandoned village, without being seen themselves. Their orders were to observe only, avoiding contact. When the meeting was in full swing, they were to draw back to the western shore of the island, and radio "the coop is full" to the airbase, where a flight of Phantoms awaited. The Phantoms were loaded with a full compliment of bombs, including napalm, destined for the island.

At 0547 hrs. six days after the bombing of the theater, the message was received, and the four Phantoms blasted off the runway. The mission was a complete success.

13 May, 1968 0425 hrs.

Vince and Sorenson had been training a new MP, Hardman, for the last 10 days. He was just about ready to be released for full duty. This night, they were working a town patrol gun jeep, cruising the city. It had been so quiet in the city lately that the nights seemed to drag on forever. Even the Cherry Bar and Three Doors had been deserted earlier in the evening, the girls sitting out front along the road trying to entice some business inside.

Vince was tired, fighting fatigue, trying to stay alert as he talked to Hardman. As they drove north on Highway 15, Vince yawned deeply. As he looked back to the road, he saw a dark lump just off the asphalt about 30 meters ahead. He was instantly wide awake.

"Slow down, Hardman. Kill the lights."

As they got closer, the lump became a body. Hardman stopped the jeep 10 meters from the body, to Vince's approval, shutting off the engine, and reaching for his M-16. Sorenson had the M-60 covering the buildings as Vince and Hardman cautiously approached the body.

"Hardman," Vince whispered, "Don't touch anything when we get there. Let me do the checking. You just watch and learn on this one."

Vince waved Hardman back a few feet, then approached the body. Walking around it, he looked for signs of life and for anything unusual. He saw a puddle of blood under the head, soaking into the dirt.

The body was that of an ARVN soldier, and there were no signs of life. Vince rolled him over, then searched his pockets for any papers or I.D.

"Call the PMO, Sorenson. Tell them to notify the Quan Cahns. This is one of theirs. Hardman, come take a look."

Hardman walked up and saw the single bullet wound in the forehead.

"Who did this, Sergeant?"

"Could've been the VC, but more likely it's from a robbery. This fool was probably out visiting one of the whores nearby, and got jumped by some Cowboys when he left. See the bruises and cuts on his face? He must've fought them. There's cuts on his knuckles, and one of the punks shot him. His pockets have been turned inside out. If it was VC that did this, he probably would have been

231

mutilated, too. Hasn't been dead too long. The body's still warm, and the blood hasn't dried yet. Poor son of a bitch. Just out for a piece of ass, and ends up dead. Well, looks like we're here till the QCs arrive. Let's go back to the jeep."

Once the QCs arrived, they briefed them on what they found, then left, going back to Long Binh and the POL to refuel, then back to the Company Area to go off duty. Vince watched as Hardman cleaned the M-60. He was impressed with this kid. He knew how to disassemble the big gun quickly and easily. He looked for rust or corrosion in all the right places, and was meticulous in cleaning and oiling it. He obviously had paid attention in AIT during the weapons training. He didn't ask too many questions, but the ones he did ask were important. He kept alert and noticed everything going on around him. Vince felt he would make a good MP, and had confidence in his ability to react properly when faced with dangerous or critical situations. They were scheduled to work bus escort from the airbase that night, and Vince thought he would put him on the gun. Sorenson would drive, and Vince would ride shotgun. Vince yawned and said, "Hurry it up, Hardman. I want to get some breakfast and get to bed. I'm beat."

"Be done in a minute, Sarge."

Vince still hadn't gotten use to that title. He had received his promotion orders just two weeks ago, and officially received his stripes just 11 days earlier. The three stripes on his sleeve were still new, and though he was proud he had been promoted, he was self-conscious about being called by his new rank. He enjoyed the added responsibility, and took his squad leader duties seriously. He made sure the others in his squad did things right, and would not allow them to take shortcuts. He knew that being lazy could be fatal, and didn't want that on his conscious. He was always fair in his treatment of the squad, but he did expect them to do things right. He personally inspected each MPs' gear and weapon before guard mount, making sure it was clean and operating properly.

The squad knew why he was that way, as he was somewhat of a legend in the Company. Everybody had heard the tale of the Tet attack and what Vince had been through, though the story changed some every time it was told.

After Hardman was done, Vince inspected the gun, found it to be satisfactory, and turned it in to the arms room. They went to the mess hall for some breakfast, meeting T.J. inside.

"How'd it go last night?" T.J. asked.

He had been on guard duty at the PMO bunkers at Di An, then had desk duty the rest of the night. It had been extremely quiet, and he had been bored sitting behind the desk. He had fought the sleep trying to creep up on him, and was thankful when the night ended. Tonight, he would be back on town patrol with Clark in a two man jeep.

"Real quiet. Found another dead ARVN by Cambo Alley. Looks like the Cowboys are getting bolder. Other than that, nothing was going on. We're on bus escort tonight, so this will give Hardman a chance to learn how that's done. I'm putting him on the gun tonight."

"How's he doin'," T.J. asked, glancing over at Hardman, who was pretending to be interested in his breakfast.

"He might just make it. He's doing fine, and I expect he'll be done with his training in another month or so," Vince said, winking at T.J.

Hardman looked up, startled, and said, "A month? I thought I was due to be released in a couple of days?"

"You were. What do you think, T.J.? Should we release him so soon?" Vince said, unable to keep from grinning at

233

the expression on Hardman's face.

"Aw, c'mon, guys. You're screwing with me, aren't you?" Hardman said to Vince, relaxing now that he knew they were just teasing.

"Yeah, we are. You're doing fine. I would think another two days will do it. We've got a couple shifts of bus escorts, and that ought to take care of it. I'll see the LT after that, and most likely recommend you be released for duty."

Vince stood up, picked up his tray and said, "I'm beat. Time for bed. See you tonight, newbie."

He walked away, followed by T.J. They dropped off their trays and dishes, then walked to their hootch.

"Is he really doin' good, Vince?" T.J. asked.

"Yeah. He'll make a good MP. By the way, got another letter from Sanders yesterday."

"Oh yeah? How's he doin'?"

"Great. Back to a hundred percent. He's applied to the police department. Takes the test next week. He still wants us to come see him when we rotate back to the world."

"Man, he was lucky. I thought for sure he wasn't gonna make it back to the States. Now he's fine? Totally recovered? Ain't that somethin'."

"He's a strong guy, T.J. I knew he'd be OK. His mom says 'hi', too. She's real proud of him. He said she's got his ribbons and medals in a case on the wall, along with his picture in uniform."

He thought for a minute, then said, "Maybe I will go see him when I get back."

They walked into their hootch, talking quietly about their day. When he got to his area, Vince sat on his bunk wearily.

"I'm calling it a day, T.J. I'm beat."

"Me, too. Sleep well, Vince."

15 May, 1968 2045 hrs.

It was just about dark as they left the airbase. Vince's gun jeep was in the lead, with a second gun jeep between the first and second buses, and T.J. in the third jeep following the fourth and last bus. The buses were filled with 175 new arrivals, their plane having landed a little over an hour ago. As they drove through Plantation, Vince told Hardman to be alert as Sorenson turned off the headlights to make them less visible. It was a cloudless evening, the moon was rising, and visibility was good.

They turned south, toward Hwy 1, and headed through the rice paddies. They had gone no more than a quarter mile when green tracers reached out from the brush along a creek bank to their left 60 meters from the road. Two B-40 rockets followed almost immediately. The first went high, passing over the buses to explode in the paddy on the opposite side of the road. The second struck the road embankment next to the first bus, sending gravel, dirt and shrapnel tearing into the side of the bus.

The first volley of slugs from the Chicom machine gun passed between Vince's jeep and the bus behind them, then began to impact the bus, tearing up the front tire and punching holes low in the side of the bus. Vince yelled for Sorenson to speed up, then turned to yell at Hardman to return fire. Before he could say anything, Hardman had begun firing the gun toward the area of the attack. T.J.'s jeep had also started firing, and the convoy had sped up. The lead bus was riding on the shredded remains of the left front tire, but the driver stomped on the gas, and kept up with Vince's jeep.

Vince grabbed the grenade launcher, and fired toward the brush without aiming. The grenade exploded 30 meters behind the brush line. He quickly loaded another round, and fired, adjusting his aim. This one exploded at the exact point the tracers were coming from, causing the firing to stop.

Rifle fire had started from two or three points along the brush line, and Hardman raked the brush with the M-60. Bullets clanged off the side of the jeep, causing Vince to flinch involuntarily. Hardman cried out in pain, but continued to fire. In a few more seconds, they had passed beyond the range of the ambush and after they had gone another mile, Vince pulled over to check on casualties. Hardman was sitting down in the back of the jeep, grimacing in pain.

"You guys OK?" Vince asked, getting out of the jeep.

"I think I've been shot, Sarge," Hardman said, leaning to his right to relieve the pain.

"Where, man?" Vince asked, looking him over, not seeing any visible wounds.

"In the ass. Hurts like hell," Hardman moaned, leaning forward to lessen the pressure.

Vince could see blood soaking through his pants on the left side of his butt. He gently probed the area, finding Hardman's left buttock had been creased by a bullet.

"It's just a scratch. Sit on it, and the bleeding will stop. You'll get a purple heart for this. Maybe we'll pin it on your ass, where you got hit, OK?"

"This isn't funny, guys. Man. I never thought I'd get hit. You sure it'll be alright?" he said, trying to lean back to see the wound.

"Yeah, you'll be fine. Probably get a week off, then back to duty."

Vince walked along the line of buses, checking in each to see if there were any more wounded. There were four wounded soldiers in the first bus, only one of them serious, and one in the third bus that was standing when the ambush erupted and the driver stomped on the gas, causing him to fall backwards and hit his head on a seat railing, knocking him unconscious.

As he checked the last bus, three MP jeeps came racing up, along with two ambulances. The one serious injury was transferred to one of the ambulances, which sped away. The other injured, including Hardman, were put in the second ambulance for a slower ride to the 93rd Evac a few miles away. The driver of the first bus changed the tire with the assistance of some of the passengers while the MPs stood guard, then the convoy continued to the 90th Replacement.

After dropping off the buses, Vince went to the 93rd Evac to check on Hardman while the other MPs went to the PMO to file their reports and brief the ARVN strike team leader on the incident. The ARVNs would be heading out at first light to try to find the VC responsible for the attack, but Vince knew this was a useless gesture, as the VC would be gone hours before the team arrived, taking all their weapons and any dead or injured with them. The best the ARVNs could hope for would be to find shell casings, and maybe some blood if any had been wounded.

Vince learned that Hardman would be released in a couple of hours since his wound was superficial. He had been placed on 1 day bed rest and a week of light duty to allow it to heal enough so he could be released for full duty.

After midnight chow, Vince and Sorenson drove to the 93rd to pick up Hardman and take him back to the Company. He had received five stitches in his left buttock, a tetanus shot, and several changes of dressings to apply over the next week. After dropping Hardman off, Vince and Sorenson finished the night on gate guard duty at the 90th Replacement.

24 May, 1968   1930 hrs.

Vince, T.J., Sorenson, Clark and MacIvers met with the QCs and CSs in front of the Combined Police Center in Bien Hoa. There was a raid planned on Three Doors for 2030 hrs. by the Vietnamese, and the MPs were going along to take custody of any Americans found inside the whorehouse. The ARVN CID had received information through their interrogation of a suspected VC sympathizer, that one of the local drug kingpins would be visiting his favorite prostitute that night. He was wanted by the Vietnamese authorities for drug trafficking, theft of government property, and several murders, some he had ordered and some he had committed personally. The MPs met with six Cahn Sats and eight Quan Cahns in the briefing room, and after the briefing were told by the local Police Chief they would only be going along for show, anyway, since this was a "joint" operation and they had to be included. He made it clear that they were not to get involved or interfere in any way.

"You will remain at your jeep and not enter any civilian dwelling without permission from the raid commander, Police Captain Ngoc. Is that clear, Sergeant?"

"Absolutely, Sir."

"Good. Now, go."

He turned and said something to the Captain, nodding in Vince's direction, then walked out of the room. Captain Ngoc spoke in rapid Vietnamese to the other raid members, who immediately got up and rushed out to their vehicles. Vince and T.J. followed them outside to their own jeep. Vince had no intentions of interfering or being any more involved than he absolutely had to, with only three weeks left until he rotated back to the States.

They drove up Hwy 15 following the QCs and CSs to Three Doors. T.J. stopped behind the last Vietnamese jeep about a half block from the entrance.

"Think this is far enough away to satisfy them, Vince?" T.J. asked.

"I sure as hell hope so. You know this raid wouldn't be happening if the dealer had kept up with his payoffs to the Chief, don't you?"

"Yeah. Pretty corrupt society, ain't it? I wonder what's

238

gonna happen to all those guys when this war ends? What're they gonna do when the great American dollar ain't around anymore?"

"They'll get by, T.J. They always do. Look, here they go," he said, pointing at the raiding party.

They watched as the raiding party rushed the front doors, taking the sentry outside by surprise. Two of the QCs knocked him to the ground, then grabbed him and dragged him away, covering his mouth to keep him from warning the occupants inside. The others crashed the door, knocking it off its hinges. They ran inside, yelling in Vietnamese.

"Think they'll get him, T.J.?"

"Yeah. If not alive, then dead."

"They're staging this operation because he ain't been payin' off the Chief?"

"That's what I hear."

More shouts came from inside, some screams from the prostitutes, then a series of shots rang out. Vince and T.J. ducked down, drawing their sidearms. More shouts and the sound of breaking furniture punctuated the night as two partially dressed American soldiers stumbled out the ruined front door, turning toward the jeeps and the MPs.

"Over here, guys," Vince yelled.

The Americans ran to them, crouching down when they got to the jeeps.

"What's going on in there?" Vince asked the nearest soldier.

He was bleeding from a gash on his cheek, and his eye was starting to swell closed. He wiped away the blood with the back of his hand.

"Goddamn it! Fuckin' gook got me good. The little bastard comes runnin' in, sees me layin' on the bed, and just up and clubs me with his pistol. Yells at me to get out. I beat it outa there just as he starts shootin' at someone in the next room."

"Yeah" the second GI said. He had a nasty lump on the left side of his head at the hair line.

"He just ran through my room, then stops at the door, and starts shooting at someone. The QC behind him butt strokes me as I ran by him, heading for the front door."

"Who're they shootin' at?" T.J. asked, keeping a close eye on the front door.

"Beats me. There was some pudgy little gook in the next room. Looked like a business man, dressed in a suit. He came in about 8:15, and ole Mamasan treated him like royalty. I think maybe he was some sort of big shot around here. Had a couple of guys with him that acted like body guards. I didn't wait around to see any more."

"You guys OK?" Vince said, looking at their injuries.

"Yeah, I guess so."

"Clark, you get their ID, take them to the dispensary, then come back here. Where you guys from?"

"Seventh Battalion, Eighth Artillery."

"Here in Bien Hoa? Good, you're close by. Get going, and stay away from town for awhile."

"Thanks, Sarge. We owe ya one."

"Forget it. Now go."

Clark and MacIvers drove off and Vince and T.J. moved closer, as there had not been any more shots for awhile. They watched as several of the QCs and CSs came out, pushing and dragging three Vietnamese men into the street. One of the men, the oldest, was bleeding from several cuts on his face and head. The Cahn Sat Police Captain yelled at him and shoved him, causing him to stumble into another Cahn Sat, who immediately slapped him on the side of the head. The Captain then punched him in the kidney, causing him cry out and fall to his knees, clutching his back. Both the policemen began yelling at him, obviously asking him questions. He shook his head side to side, yelling back at them.

The Captain grabbed him by the hair, pulled his head

back, and, leaning over him face to face, again asked a question. The man suddenly spit in the Captains' face, at which the Captain released the mans hair, drew his .38 revolver, and struck him three times across the head and face, opening more cuts and knocking him unconscious. He holstered the pistol, turned away and said something to the other CSs. Two walked over, and each grabbed an arm, dragging the unconscious man to their car, placing him in the back seat. They then got in the car, and drove away.

"Guess that wasn't the answer he was looking for, eh, T.J.?" Vince whispered.

"Not very smart, that's for sure."

One of the QCs came out leading three of the prostitutes. Placing them in his jeep, he, too, drove off. The rest of the QCs and CSs all got in their vehicles, and drove away, leaving the MPs alone out front.

"Guess we're done, eh, Vince?"

"Guess so. Vietnamese justice in action," he replied, shaking his head. "I wonder if that's the guy they were looking for."

"Beats me. I hope so, or that poor bastard's in for a very rough night. Let's go back to work. Maybe we can check the Cherry Bar. There's been a lot of GIs there off limits lately," T.J. suggested, as they walked back to the jeep.

"Alright. Hey, remember what Sanders did there when I was in training?"

"The guy with the gun? Yeah. Sanders sure had guts."

"More than guts, T.J. He could read people like a book. And he knew how best to handle them. Did I tell you he passed all the written tests for the police department? I got a letter from him yesterday. He'll make a good cop."

T.J. started the engine, and made a u-turn, driving south down the road toward the bar.

"I thought he was going to die in there that night, Vince. You know, he told me later he knew that GI wouldn't shoot him. I asked how he knew, and he said he just knew. He said he could see it in his eyes, and told me to always look 'em in the eyes. The eyes would tell everything you needed to know."

"He was right, T.J."

"Sanders was the best, Vince. He really knew his stuff. I think you're right. He will make a good cop."

"I sure miss him, T.J."

"Me, too, Vince."

T.J. stopped the jeep a couple of doors down from the Cherry Bar.

"Here we are. Shall we go in?"

"Lead on, my friend."

29 May, 1968   2045 hrs.

They picked up the loaded convoy at Newport, and headed out of the dock area to Hwy 316, heading north toward Long Binh. The convoy was composed of 35 five-ton semi trucks from the 261st Transportation Company, loaded with ammunition destined for Long Binh. The first 20 were carrying everything from small arms ammo to 105 howitzer shells. The last 15 were loaded with napalm canisters, which would be transferred to the airbase later in the week.

Vince was in the lead gun jeep, with Sorenson on the gun and Hardman driving. There were three other gun jeeps assigned to the escort, plus a V-100 pacing the trucks at the middle of the convoy. Since the cargo was so important, two Huey gunships had been assigned to shadow the convoy a couple hundred meters off each flank, as an added deterrent to any VC that may be setting up an ambush.

It had rained for several hours earlier in the day, but had stopped a couple of hours ago, allowing the highway to dry up. The sky was still overcast and threatening, with a low ceiling, and the chopper pilots were watching the weather closely in case they had to make a run back to Bien Hoa.

As the convoy moved up the highway, the two choppers flew up and down its length, sometimes as much as a half mile to the side, staying at 500 feet of altitude. The pilots were especially watchful, since two months earlier the VC had ambushed a smaller ARVN ammo convoy, destroying several trucks and almost half the ordnance the convoy was carrying. Four ARVNs were killed and several others wounded from the huge explosions that followed the attack. The ambush was launched by a squad of VC just north of the Newport bridge. The first volley of B-40 rockets struck several trucks, setting them on fire, and detonating the ordnance they carried. Those secondary explosions in turn ignited other trucks cargo, causing them to explode, too. The highway was closed for several hours while the fires burned out and the debris removed.

Vince was well aware of that attack, as were all the MPs on escort duty that night. He knew that if an ambush came, there would be little hope of survival. The amount of explosives they were carrying made death a certainty if any of the trucks were hit. He felt better that the gun ships were flying back and forth, covering a lot of ground, and making their presence known. Hopefully, they would discourage any VC in the area, driving them under cover. Vince watched the choppers, barely visible in the dusk. They would be with the convoy until they crossed the Dong Nai River, then would break off and return to the airbase for the night.

As Vince watched the gunship flying off to the left, a stream of green tracers reached up from the field, appearing to cross in front of the helicopter. The unfortunate ship flew right through the stream of bullets, taking several hits. Thick, black smoke began pouring out the engine cowling, and the gunship began flying erratically, losing power and altitude. The pilot radioed Vince, as the

243

convoy commander, that he was setting the ship down several hundred meters off the highway. He had spotted a clearing a quarter mile ahead large enough to land in, and was going down before he lost all power. Neither he nor any of his crew were injured, and he requested they come get them out before the VC could show up.

Vince picked up the radio microphone. Pressing the transmit button, he said "Side Arch four, this is Side Arch One, over," calling T.J. at the rear of the convoy.

"This is Four. You got problems up there?"

"Yeah, T.J. One of the escort choppers was just shot down. I need you up here, now."

"On our way, Sarge."

Within a minute, T.J.'s jeep came driving up alongside Vince's. Pacing him, T.J. asked what he needed.

"You take Sorenson with you, and go secure the chopper. The four of you are now on guard duty. I'll let the PMO know you're out there, and someone will be out to relieve you in a few hours. The crew will bring your jeep back to the convoy. Be careful out there, T.J. The gooks may still be around and be looking to find the chopper."

"Ok, Vince. Back to grunt work, eh? C'mon, Sorenson, join the party, and let's get goin'."

Vince watched them drive off the highway into the field. He watched until they disappeared into the thick brush 50 meters out.

"Be careful, T.J." he whispered to himself.

Ramsey drove carefully through the brush, dodging thick clumps. The ground was muddy, and the jeep slogged through with difficulty. Every couple of minutes, the chopper pilot would fire a flare into the air to help guide them to their position. It took them about 15 minutes to make their way to the clearing. It was fully dark by the time they got there, and T.J. didn't see the pilots as they drove up to the chopper.

As the jeep stopped, the two pilots came out of the

brush to the right. The copilot was armed with an M-16, while the pilot had a .45. The door gunner was still on the chopper, manning his M-60.

"Sure glad to see you guys. For a while there, I thought we were going down hard. We were lucky to find this clearing when we did. Took a couple slugs in the engine. They hit the convoy?"

"No. Seems like they only went after you guys. You are to take the jeep. We're gonna stay here and secure your bird. Head that way," T.J. said, pointing back along the way they came. "Follow our tracks to the highway, then head north, and catch up to the convoy. Barton, get the gun and ammo off the jeep. We may need it."

They took all their weapons and ammo, their poncho liners, flak vests and helmets, and moved off to the chopper, while the two chopper pilots and the crew chief and door gunner climbed in the jeep. The pilot started the engine, and, just before driving off, said, "See ya, and thanks, guys. We flyboys get real nervous bein' on the ground. Be safe, men."

"OK, guys. Let's set up a perimeter. It's gonna be a long, cold night. Two holes, one over there, one here, two of us per hole. Ramsey and Barton in this one, me and Sorenson in the other. We'll take the M-60; you guys keep the grenade launcher. I want one of you to stay awake at all times. The other can catch a nap. I'll take the first four hours in our hole, then wake Sorenson up. You guys decide whose got first watch. C'mon, Sorenson, we got a hole to dig."

Digging in the muddy ground was easy enough, but the sides kept sliding in, and they had to pack the edges to keep it from collapsing. It took them 40 minutes to get the hole big enough for the both of them. T.J. set up the M-60 to cover the brush line 30 meters away, put on his flak vest, then slipped the poncho over his head. Putting his helmet on, he slid down in the hole, sinking slightly in the

245

mud. Two hours later, it started to rain again, slowly filling the hole with water.

Thanks, Vince. This is a great assignment, he thought, as he sank deeper into the mud.

He could just barely make out Barton in the other hole, looking out toward the brush. Sorenson was snoring softly, sound asleep. How anyone could sleep under these conditions was beyond T.J. He never did sleep that well out in the bush, and knew he wouldn't sleep tonight.

Damn rain. They could be on us before we know it. Can't hear shit in this stuff. He tried to shift his position, and found he had sunk so far into the clinging mud that he was stuck.

"Shit. Ain't this somethin'," he muttered, as he began digging out around himself with his hands, flinging handfuls of mud out of the hole.

After a couple of minutes, he was able to get his butt loose, and stand up. He was soaked through, and covered with mud from the waist down. He pulled his legs loose, and stepped up out of the hole. Grabbing his rifle, he walked slowly in a circle to work out the kinks. He saw Barton wave at him as he walked by. He stood in the darker shadow of the chopper to relieve himself, then leaned up against the side, partially sheltered from the driving rain. He looked at the sky, and could see the clouds starting to break up.

T.J. stood there, looking up for a awhile, thinking of the 17 months he had spent here. He felt lucky to have survived, and was happy he had a friend like Vince. He was looking forward to leaving 'Nam, but was sad, too, because he knew he would miss the best friend he had ever had. He never had a friend like Vince before. Thinking about it, he thought maybe it was because of what they had been through together, and how much they had relied on each other over the last year.

"Guess I'll just have to go visit him now and then," he muttered softly to himself.

Just as he was getting ready to step out of the shadow to walk back to his hole, a slight movement caught the corner of his eye. He froze, then turned his head slightly, looking toward the area where he had spotted the movement, watching patiently. After a half a minute, he saw a shape moving slowly just at the brush line, circling their position. A second shape followed, then a third and a fourth. T.J. looked over at Barton's hole, and saw he was looking away from the shadowy figures, unaware of their presence. He picked up his M-16, slowly snapped off the safety, and sighted down the barrel at the figures.

Tracking them, he held his fire, knowing they could not see him. T.J. waited, watching and tracking the shapes. They stopped and crouched down, causing T.J. to lose sight of them. One shape started creeping into the clearing, walking slowly, crouched over, toward the helicopter. T.J. had him dead in his sights, and had begun tightening his finger on the trigger when Sorenson sneezed loudly. The VC froze, dropping to the ground. He waited for a minute, and hearing no more, got up and quickly made his way back to the brush, disappearing from view. T.J. waited a full five minutes before moving away from the chopper. He walked back to his hole, and nudged Sorenson with his foot, shaking him awake.

"Sorenson, wake up, wake up."

"I'm awake, T.J. What's the matter?"

"We had some visitors. Out there in the brush."

Sorenson sat up, grabbing his rifle and his helmet.

"They're gone now, I think. You scared 'em away."

"I did? How'd I do that?"

"When you sneezed. I think they knew we were here, but couldn't tell exactly where we set up, with the darkness and the rain. One was sneakin' in toward the chopper, tryin' to find us when you startled him. He must have got scared. I'm sure they're gone now, but we all better stay alert, in case they come back. This chopper may be too big

247

a prize for them to pass up."

"OK. I'll go tell Barton and Ramsey. I need to stretch, anyway."

T.J. climbed into the hole, and sat in the mud, trying to get comfortable. Sorenson joined him a few minutes later. They kept watch the rest of the night without incident. The rain continued to fall steadily, soaking them through. The water in T.J.'s hole was almost four inches deep, and he had sunk into the mud again.

By five A.M., the rain had slackened off, and by first light, the clouds had broken up, showing patches of clear sky. A few minutes later, a squad of grunts entered the clearing. A Lieutenant looked around, and, spotting T.J., walked over to his hole.

"Morning, Corporal. Have a nice night?"

"Just great, LT. Rained all goddamn night, had a visit by the local VC, got stuck in the mud twice, missed our dinner, and didn't sleep a wink. Just your average night in the 'Nam."

"Visitors, huh? What happened?"

T.J. told him about their visit, and said, "Musta been new at it, cause they ran away when Sorenson sneezed. The chopper's OK. We're tired, cold, and hungry. You guys got a vehicle nearby we can hitch a ride with?"

"Yeah. 300 meters that way is a deuce and a half. It'll take you back to Long Binh. Good job, guys. We'll take it from here. Get going."

"Yessir," T.J. said, saluting. He turned and shouted, "Ramsey, Barton. Pack it up. Let's get outta here."

An hour and a half later, he was back in the company area, heading for the shower, glad the night was over.

4 June, 1968, 0110 hrs.

Vince finished his food, bused his dishes, and headed back out to the company area. Renfro met him at their jeep a few minutes later, and they headed toward the POL to refuel. Renfro drove slowly, talking all the way.

"I got three weeks left, Vince, then back to the world. I can hardly wait. Only two more weeks on the street, then company duty until I clear my paperwork."

"I'm happy for you, Renfro. Pull up to the pump, and I'll fill it up."

Renfro parked by the pump, shutting off the engine. Vince placed the nozzle in the tank, and began filling it. He turned to Renfro, leaning up against the jeep, and said, "I'll be going home myself in a few more days."

A faint "foomp" reached his ears as he finished talking. Recognizing the sound of a mortar round being launched, he yelled "incoming", and began running away from the POL. Renfro took off running, too, a few feet behind Vince.

They had run no more than 20 meters when the round exploded behind them, destroying a small diesel storage tank 50 meters back, setting the fuel on fire. Gobs of flaming fuel splashed all around them as they ran, trying to get as far away as they could. The second round exploded next to their jeep, destroying it and setting the gasoline in the tank on fire. The third round landed ten seconds later, 15 meters closer to them. The fourth and last round exploded 20 meters behind Renfro, the force of the blast knocking him and Vince to the ground.

Renfro hit the ground and lay still. Vince rolled over and sat up, dazed, and looked around, trying to gather his wits about him. When his head stopped spinning, he crawled over to Renfro, who was still unconscious. He checked him over, finding several bloody spots on the back of his shirt and legs. Pulling his shirt up, he could see several shrapnel wounds, none of which looked to be life threatening. Renfro began moaning, moving his arms, trying to push himself up as consciousness returned.

"Lie still, Jack. You've been hit."

"Vince? What happened?"

"We got caught in a mortar attack. You got some shrapnel in you. Nothing too bad, though. Might get you home a couple of weeks early. You just lie still. Help will be here in a few minutes. I'm gonna go check on the jeep. Don't worry," he said, when Renfro grabbed his sleeve as he started to stand up, "I'll be right over there. You're going to be fine."

He pulled Renfro's hand off his sleeve, squeezed it gently, then stood up, swaying slightly until the dizziness passed. As he walked back toward the jeep, he could see it was a total wreck, burned and blasted from the shelling. The heat from the fire was intense, and he was unable to go any closer. He walked back to Renfro, as the sirens of the fire trucks got louder and closer, and sat on the ground. Renfro rose up, leaning on his elbows.

"You know you're bleeding, Sarge?" he asked, pointing at his leg.

Vince looked down and saw his pants leg below the right knee was wet with blood.

"I'll be damned," Vince said.

He pulled up his pant leg, and saw a two inch gash that was still bleeding. He probed the wound with his finger and found it was a clean cut. Vince pulled out a dressing, and pressed it tightly over the wound to stop the bleeding, as the fire crew arrived and began fighting the flaming fuel.

A gun jeep from the 615 MPs arrived, stopping near Vince.

"That you, Torelli?" one of the MPs asked, seeing him sitting on the ground.

"Yeah, Weezer. Call an ambulance, would you?"

"Got one comin'. You OK?"

"I'm alright. Renfro needs it more than me. Anyone else hurt?"

"Nope. The Post took about 8 or 9 rounds, but this was the only damage."

The sirens' wail was becoming louder, causing Weezer to

look over his shoulder.

"Here comes the ambulance. I'm gonna go check on the damage. Take it easy, just lie still, OK?" he said to Renfro, as he turned to walk away.

Turning to Renfro, Vince put his hand on his shoulder, and said, "How're you doing, Renfro?"

"OK, Vince. Hurts. Got me a purple heart, though."

"Yes, you did. Probably get to go home now, too. This ought to get you out a little early."

"I hope so. I've had enough of this shit, Vince. I'm too Goddam short to be dodging mortar rounds."

"I know, man. I'm getting mighty short myself."

"You really think I can go home now, Vince?"

"Yeah, you're on your way. Wish I could go with you."

The ambulance took them to the 93rd Evac. Renfro was taken into surgery to have the shrapnel removed, while Vince received nine stitches in one of the treatment rooms. The doctor gave him a slip for five days light duty. As Vince left, he crumpled it up and threw it in the waste basket, muttering "I don't need this shit."

He waited for his ride outside, sitting on a bench, smoking a cigarette. The shock of being wounded again hit him two minutes later, and he started trembling uncontrollably, the sweat pouring down his face. He took several deep breaths, getting his emotions under control.

"Two more weeks. I almost get my ass blown off with two more weeks left."

Thinking for a moment, he turned and went back inside, and took the doctor's slip from the waste basket.

7 June, 1968 1440 hrs.

Dear Vince,
I hope this letter finds you in good health and spirits. I been busy since I last wrote to you. I got my high school diploma. Took

the GED test and passed first time! Pretty good, huh? I put in an application with the police department, and they called me. They want me to come take their physical test after next month. I know I can pass it, but I'm scared of taking the physical agility. I been working out, getting stronger and stronger, but I'm not sure I can do the running stuff. My wind still isn't up to where it used to be. I got a couple of weeks left before the test, so I'm going to run every day. My momma says hi, and wants to know when you are coming to visit us. Says she already told you all this in her letter last month. That's OK, cause I wanted to tell you myself, too. I hope you can come when you get home. If I remember right, you only got about 3 weeks left, right? If so, you got to be extra careful now. Don't do nothing stupid, Vince. Don't get careless or lazy. I seen lots of guys forget where they were when they got that short. Some of them got hurt because they got careless. Don't let that happen to you.

I got a girlfriend now, too. Her name is Rachel. I met her at church a few weeks ago. You would like her, and I know she would like you. She's pretty as can be, like your lady. I hope you get the chance to meet her some day. I hope this gets to you before you come home, because momma and I would like to hear from you. Write me and let me know when you are going home. Who knows, you might see me on your porch one of these days. See you. Stay safe.

Your friend, Sanders

Vince smiled to himself as he re-read the letter. It pleased him that Sanders had a new girlfriend, and was doing so well. He had no doubt he would pass the physical agility with flying colors, and soon would be hired by the Little Rock Police Department. Shaking his head, he folded the letter, and put it in his breast pocket as he walked back to his hootch.

He lay on his bunk and took out the letter from his mother, saving the two from his fiancee for last. He read how his parents had just come back from a week at the cabin near Clearlake, that his Dad's back was bothering him again, and that he may have to take a week off work to rest it.

His Aunt Betty in New York was planning a big family get together next summer, and they were planning to go. His brother was going, and she hoped he would go, too. It had been too long since they had gone anywhere as a family. His grandma was doing fine. She went to Reno last month, and won again, this time it was $2,000.

Vince smiled, remembering how his grandmother would take the bus to Reno once a month, and how it seemed she always came back a winner. His mother closed the short letter with her usual warnings to be careful, and that she loved him, and was counting the days until he came home. He knew the pain she felt, and his brother had written how she cried when she thought no one was around. He knew how she worried and missed him, and he always tried to keep his letters cheerful. He never wrote of what really happened from day to day, and to this day, his mother still didn't know what had happened that January night six months ago. She had been told by the army that he had been wounded, but not the whole story. Vince had written his brother, telling him, and asked he let his dad know. He asked him not to tell their mom, because she

253

would just worry all the more. He wrote her himself, and told her he had been wounded, but it wasn't serious, and that he would soon be good as new. He had not written anyone about his second wound when the POL was hit, and his fiancée knew even less than his mother. She had been told of his wounds during Tet by his mother, and he had only mentioned it briefly when replying to her worried questions, reassuring her it was only a minor wound, nothing to worry about.

He refolded the letter, and put it with the others in his footlocker. He then took out the two from his fiancée, and read each twice before turning in for the night. As always happened after reading her letters, he found it difficult to sleep, laying awake for several hours, thinking, before dropping off just as the sun was coming up.

9 June, 1968   0845 hrs

Vince had been assigned to handle the orientation of a new arrival by the name of Beeson, and had drawn town patrol to orient him to the area on his first day off post. They spent the day driving around, Vince showing him the area, the airbase, plantation, Ho Nai Village, the bridge over the Dong Nai, and the other major locations in and around the city.

He took Beeson to the Combined Police Center in Bien Hoa, and introduced him to the Cahn Sat Chief of Police, then to the PMO in Di An. They ate lunch at the little roadside cafe Vince liked in Buu Long, then went back to the company area so Beeson could get his paperwork completed. He needed to sign some papers to have an allotment taken out of his pay each month to be sent directly to his wife in Fargo, North Dakota. He had gotten married one month before shipping out to 'Nam.

While in the clerks' office, the LT told Vince that he, Beeson and Tully would be assigned a gun jeep, along with T.J. and Sorenson in a second gun jeep, to escort two flatbed trucks to the Thai base at Bear Cat, about 30 miles southeast of Long Binh. The base was in need of a re-supply of ammunition, in particular artillery and mortar shells, and some fresh vegetables and rice. Three days earlier, two tanker trucks containing diesel fuel, and two with potable water had tried to enter the base unescorted, coming down from Xuan Loc. They had gotten within one mile of the perimeter before the VC ambushed them, damaging three of the four trucks. One of the water trucks was disabled and left alongside the road. The other three were able to limp into the base, after a fast response team from Bear Cat arrived to escort them in, though half the fuel and all the water was lost, due to the damage to the tankers. They were extremely lucky the damaged fuel trucks did not catch fire.

A second attempt the next day was more successful. A fuel truck and two more water trucks made it in without any problems. The Thai troops had increased their patrols, due to the increased enemy activity in their area. They had been shelled almost nightly for the last three weeks, and had found lots of signs of increased activity outside the base. A couple of the patrols had triggered booby traps during the last week, causing three deaths and eight wounded, four seriously. Vince was told a Huey gunship was being sent to the base at the same time, and would provide added security by shadowing their small convoy.

Vince was familiar with the roads, as he had been to Bear Cat several times. He did not like the route, the last couple of miles being a dirt track about a lane and a half wide leading through some areas that were classic ambush sites. He wasn't happy about this assignment, but didn't say any anything. He just figured the LT had his reasons for sending him, and that they were good reasons.

As if he had read Vince's mind, the LT said, "I know you've only got a week left, Sergeant, but there's really no one else except T.J. that has your experience and savvy. This is more important than anyone knows. Bear Cat could be in real trouble if they are attacked in force. They don't have enough ammo, they're short on water and food, and there's not enough fuel for their vehicles. It would take a couple of hours for a relief force to reach them, and that could be all the time the VC needs. There's a Thai Captain and Lieutenant that will be hitching a ride with you guys tomorrow. They will be riding in T.J.s' jeep, so you guys don't need to be here until 0900 hrs. You get to sleep in tomorrow. Once the convoy has been turned over to the Thais, you guys come back. I'll give you the rest of your time here off."

Vince saluted and said, "Yessir, LT. Is that all, Sir?"

"Yeah, except be careful, Vince. Charlie knows we're comin'."

"Always, Sir."

"Dismissed, Torelli."

Vince saluted again, turned and walked out. Getting in the jeep, he picked up the radio and called T.J., asking him to meet him by the entrance to the airbase so he could tell him of their assignment tomorrow. T.J. was less than thrilled, reminding Vince they had a week left in country, and wondering if the LT realized that.

"We shouldn't be doin' this stuff, Vince. We should be windin' down, gettin' ready to go home, not pullin' this convoy shit. Especially since we are goin' into a known hot area. Man, I don't like this at all!"

"I know, T.J., but it's our job. This is it. No more after tomorrow. We start clearing our paperwork for home. Man, I thought this would never come."

The radio crackled to life, detailing Vince to a traffic accident involving an American jeep and a civilian Lambretta just outside Di An.

"See ya back at the company, T.J. Duty calls."

Turning to Beeson, he said, "Forward, my man."

256

Beeson put the jeep in gear, and drove off. T.J. sat there for a minute, then shook his head, muttering, "I got a bad feeling about this."

10 June, 1968   1055 hrs.

Vince was leading the small convoy slowly along the dirt road a mile and a half outside Bear Cat. They had word that an escort was leaving the base to meet them to provide more security during the last mile. Vince could see several vehicles stopped in the road up ahead, and as they got closer, he could see they belonged at the Thai base.

Several Thai soldiers were clustered around a deuce and a half at the end of the Thai column. Vince stopped the jeep 30 meters from the truck, with the rest of the convoy stopping behind him, spaced 20 meters apart. Vince could see the front tire of the truck was flat, and the soldiers were diligently working at changing it. While he watched, T.J. pulled up next to him.

"The captain here," he said, nodding toward the Thai officer sitting next to him, "wants to know why we stopped."

Vince turned to the Captain and said, "Truck's blocking the road, Sir. Flat tire. They should have it changed in a about ten or 15 minutes."

"I don't like sitting here, Sergeant," the Captain said, looking nervously around. He spoke near perfect English. "We need to get these supplies into camp. Can we go around it?"

"Not a good idea, Sir," Vince replied. "I think we'll be Ok until they get the truck moving, and the road is obviously safe, since they came out to meet us without any problem."

"We are, how do you say, a sitting goose out here. We should go to the camp, now."

"Again, Sir, with all due respect, we shouldn't get off the road. Intelligence has this area crawling with VC. A couple of patrols ran into booby traps last week, and the camp has been shelled almost every night. I kinda have to think it would be better to just wait. I doubt they're in the area, with the chopper overhead and this strong an escort group.

"See," he said, pointing to the road ahead, "a perimeter has been set up, and they are alert. Nothing can get close to us now, and if they haven't hit us yet, they aren't going to. We know the road isn't mined, but we don't know about the fields. We need to stay on the road."

The Captain looked at Vince with a sneer. "If you haven't the courage, Sergeant, you can stay here. I am going to lead the convoy in. We will go around the truck, and drive triumphantly into the base, while you sit here worrying. Now, are you going with me?"

"I don't think so, Captain. It's dangerous, and it's unnecessary. Since I am in charge of the Americans, we are waiting until the truck is drivable. If you and your LT want to go on ahead, you can." Turning to T.J., he said, "Let him have your jeep, T.J. You guys dismount and wait with us."

"Sounds good to me, Vince. C'mon, Sorenson, you heard the Sergeant."

They got out of the jeep, and walked a few meters away, stopping to watch the Captain's next step.

The Captain turned to face Vince, and said, "Fine, Sergeant, but your superiors will hear of this insult."

Turning to the Lieutenant, he rattled off a rapid string of Thai. The Lieutenant snapped to attention, saluted, then got in the drivers' seat. He started the jeep, then looked to the Captain for instructions.

"I will see you at the camp. Do not be too long," the Captain said to Vince.

He spoke again to the Lieutenant, who immediately put the jeep in gear, and started slowly forward. He turned off the road and drove along the shoulder around the disabled truck. Continuing past a small pick up and two jeeps, the Lieutenant started to turn back onto the roadway.

Earlier that morning, just before dawn, an explosives team from the VC company that had been harassing the Thai camp had planted a 105mm shell on the shoulder of the road. The shell had been found unexploded after an ambush the VC had staged a week earlier. Supporting artillery fire from Bear Cat had driven the VC off before they were able to do too much damage to the Thai patrol.

The VC had used this ambush site too many times, and the artillery had been pre- registered for just such a situation. So swift was the fire support from the Thai base that the VC suffered three killed and five wounded from the first two shells.

After the fight, the VC returned briefly to recover their dead, and, while removing the bodies, came upon the unexploded shell. Never one to miss an opportunity, they took the shell with them to their base camp, where their explosives expert rigged a pressure fuse to it. The team then took the shell back to the road, and buried it just off the roadway, rigging the fuse so that any vehicle driving by would trigger it. The shell was powerful enough that the resulting explosion would destroy the vehicle, and most likely kill anyone inside it.

When the escort came out to meet Vince's convoy, the lead vehicle set off the fuse, but it failed to detonate the shell. The jeep rolled directly over it as the Lieutenant tried to drive back onto the road, releasing the stuck fuse.

The resulting explosion tore the jeep in half, blowing the engine compartment back over the rest of the vehicle. The driver took the full force of the blast. The search team was unable to find anything left of him larger than a few inches. The Captain was blown out the right side of the jeep, missing his left leg at mid thigh, and his right leg from the knee down. Shrapnel peppered his body, and he died within 30 seconds of hitting the ground.

Shrapnel from the shell and the destroyed vehicle peppered the first parked jeep and wounded two Thai soldiers. The rest flung themselves to the ground, not knowing what had caused the explosion, fearing it was an another ambush. When there were no more explosions, and no gunfire, they cautiously got to their feet, realizing it had been a booby trap, and walked over to the destroyed jeep, finding the Captain's body nearby.

Vince just stood over the body, and stared, shaking his head slowly from side to side.

"Stupid, goddamn idiot. Another useless death," he muttered to himself.

Turning to T.J., he said, "Call it in, T.J. Let's get this road cleared, and get outa here."

He turned and walked back to his jeep, lit a cigarette, then sat in the passenger seat to await the search team and ambulance.

June 13, 1969   1630 hrs.

Vince had finished clearing supply, and had picked up his medical records from the dispensary. He had spent most of the previous evening in the EM Club where he and T.J. were given a going home party. He had drunk too much beer and eaten too much barbeque, and had to rush outside twice to throw up, returning to the party each time the retching stopped to drink and eat again. The party ended up in his hootch after the club closed, with several MPs bringing six packs of beer. They partied until after 0300 hrs, when everyone left for their bunks. T.J. staggered off to his bunk, while Vince walked down to the latrine where he washed his face, took a leak, then walked back to his hootch somewhat unsteadily.

As Vince passed the first bunk inside the back door, he stopped. Swaying drunkenly, he looked at a figure lying there, reading a book. Blinking his eyes to focus them, he saw the book was "Journey to the Center of the Earth" by

Jules Verne. He smiled, remembering the last time he saw someone reading that book. As he turned to walk away, he heard a familiar voice say, "Hey, Newbie."

He stopped, startled, and turned back to the bunk.

"Sanders? That you?"

The figure lowered the book, but his face was in shadow, and Vince was unable to get a look at his features.

"Well, Vince, looks like you made it. You be goin' home in a couple days. I tole you you'd be OK if you listened to me. You done good, Vince. It's over now. You can go home and forget all this, start over."

"I can't ever forget, Sanders. Every night before I go to sleep, I remember. I dream of that night all the time. Sometimes I wake up scared and sweating, and sometimes I can't get to sleep at all. Will it ever get any better?" Vince's eyes welled with tears as he hung his head, his shoulders slumping.

"It will get better, my friend. You got to be strong, now. You got to go on with your life. Time will ease your pain, Vince. Before you know it, the sharp edges will be gone, dulled by life back in the world, by being with your family and that girl of yours. Trust me, Torelli, I ain't never lied to you before, and I ain't gonna lie to you now."

"I know, Sanders. I owe you my life, you know. I don't think I would've made it outta here alive but for you. Every day, I hear you talking to me, teaching me, helping me get through. I remember everything you ever said, Sanders, and it kept me alive. I'm so tired. I'm tired of this place, I'm tired of this war, and I'm tired of being scared every day."

"You don't need to be scared no more, Vince. Your time is up. Go rest now. It's gonna be a nice day tomorrow. You goin' home."

"OK, Sanders."

Vince turned and started to walk away, when he suddenly stopped and turned back.

261

"Hey, Thanks, San..." he started to say, then realized he was staring at an empty bunk. Blinking his eyes rapidly, he looked around the nearly empty hootch, seeing the sleeping men, then back at the empty bunk. Shaking his head, he staggered to his bunk, sat down and took off his boots. He lay down on his back, and fell asleep almost instantly.

T.J. sat up in his bunk next to Vince's, and looked over at him.

"Who you talkin' to, Vince? Vince?" he whispered.

Hearing the soft snores from Vince's bunk, he shrugged his shoulders, looked over at the empty bunk Vince had been standing in front of, then lay back down to sleep.

June 15, 1968 1445 hrs.

Vince stood outside the terminal building at the airbase, looking at the runway shimmering in the heat. He looked off to the east and remembered that night a half a year ago. He heard the explosions, the gunshots. He felt the pain of his wounds again, the grief for lost friends.

He looked up in the sky, and saw a plane approaching in the distance. Watching closely, the plane grew larger as it approached the runway, wheels down. He saw it touch down and roll to a stop on the taxiway opposite the terminal.

T.J. joined him at the fence. Throwing his arm over Vince's shoulders, he pointed and said, "That's ours, Vince. You ready?"

"I've been ready for a year, T.J. I just can't believe I'll be getting on that plane, and leaving this shithole in a little bit."

"I know, Vince. I can't believe it, either."

He turned to Vince, and lowered his voice.

"I ain't never had a friend like you before, Vince. Maybe it's because of the war and what we been through over the last year, but that ain't the whole reason. I knew the first

262

time I met you at the 90th that we was like kin. We think alike, we like the same stuff, we feel the same about stuff, and I knew you was someone I could count on in times of trouble. I want you to know I'll never forget you. You will always be my friend."

"Thanks, T.J. That means a lot to me. You've been about the best friend I ever had. Between you and Sanders, you guys taught me how to survive this place. I owe you more than you can ever know, and I, too, won't ever forget you. Your friendship is important to me, and I am glad we met. You ever need me, T.J., anytime, anywhere, you just call. I'll be there, my friend," Vince said, gently squeezing T.J.'s arm.

Vince looked out at the plane, its door standing open, a line of soldiers walking toward it.

"It's time, T.J.," he said, looking at his friend. "Let's get the hell outa here."

They grinned at each other, and started walking to the plane. As Vince reached the stairs, he turned and looked back. He held up his hand, his middle finger extended to the sky, then turned, grinning, and walked up the stairs into the plane. He did not look out the window until the plane had been in flight for over an hour.

GLOSSARY OF TERMS

AK-47 – Assault rifle used by the enemy

ARVN - Army, Republic of Vietnam

AWOL – Absent without leave

BLOOPER, BLOOP GUN – Nickname for the M-79 grenade launcher

BOONDOCKS, BOONIES, BUSH – Terms used for the jungle or any remote area away from a base camp or city

CHARLIE – Viet Cong – derived from the military phonetic alphabet for VC (Victor Charlie)

CHICOM – Chinese communist – usually referring to weapons

CID – Criminal Investigations Division

CLAYMORE – Fan shaped anti-personnel land mine

COBRA – AH-1G attack helicopter

COWBOY – Vietnamese criminal gang member

CO – Commanding Officer

CPP – Combined Police Point – police station shared by American and ARVN MPs, and Vietnamese National Police

CS – Cahn Sat - South Vietnamese National Police – also called "White Mice" due to the white uniform shirts they wore

DAI-UY – (Di Wee) – Captain

DEROS – Date Eligible for Return from Overseas – date of the end of a persons' tour of duty

DEUCE AND A HALF – Two and a half ton truck

DI DI MAU – Vietnamese phrase for "get out of here" or "go away"

EM CLUB – Enlisted Mens Club

FNG – "Fuckin' New Guy" – term for a newly arrived person in Vietnam or to a new unit

GI – Nickname for soldier – derived from the fact that everything in the army is government issued and belongs to the government

GUN JEEP – Jeep equipped with a machine gun

GUN SHIP – Armed helicopter

GRUNT – Nickname for an infantry soldier

HE – High explosive

HUEY – Popular name for the UH series helicopter

HOOTCH – Nickname for living quarters

HQ – Headquarters

INCOMIING – Receiving enemy rocket, artillery, or mortar fire

LAMBRETTA – Small gas powered cart used for transporting people or cargo by Vietnamese civilians

LBJ – Long Binh Jail – actually Long Binh Stockade – military stockade at Long Binh Post – last word changed as a pun of President Lyndon Baines Johnson

LIFER – Career soldier

LP – Listening post – located forward of defensive perimeter

LRRP – Long Range Reconniassance Patrol

LT – Lieutenant

LZ – Landing Zone

M-16 – Colt AR-15 magazine fed rifle – fires semi-auto or full auto - .223 caliber

M-60 – Belt fed machine gun – 7.62 mm caliber

M-79 – 40 mm grenade launcher

MACV – Military Assistance Command, Vietnam

MEDCAP – Medical Civil Action Program

MEDEVAC – Medical evacuation by helicopter

MP – Military Police

NEWBIE – Nicer term for an FNG

NVA – North Vietnamese Army

PBR – Patrol Boat, River

PMO – Provost Marshals' Office – Military Police Station

QC – Quan Cahn – South Vietnamese Military Police

RPG – Rocket propelled grenade

RVN – Republic of Vietnam – South Vietnam

SAPPER – Enemy infiltrators
SEAL – Navy special warfare forces (SEa Air Land)
SHORT, SHORT-TIMER – Person with little time left in Vietnam
SLICK – Unarmed helicopter
TET – Vietnamese Lunar New Year Holiday period
V-100 – Armed security vehicle typically used by Military Police for convoy escort
VC – Viet Cong

ABOUT THE AUTHOR

John Schembra was born Jan. 3, 1948 and raised in the San Francisco Bay Area.

He retired Feb. 2001 from a small northern California police department as a Sergeant after almost 30 years service.

Prior to becoming a police officer, he was a Military Policeman assigned for a year to the 557th MP Co., Long Binh, Bien Hoa, South Vietnam, where he had several "adventures" that provided the basis for his first novel, *MP*.

He has earned a B.A in Administration of Justice and an M.A in Public Administration. He spent his retirement time writing as well as teaching other police officers emergency vehicle operation/pursuit driving through the Contra Costa County Sheriff's Office and Police Academy. He also instructs officers in the driving simulators, is a train the trainer for emergency vehicle/pursuit/ simulator instructors, and has been recognized as a Subject Matter Expert by the State of California in emergency vehicle operations/pursuit driving.

He has had several trade articles published in law enforcement magazines such as *Law and Order*, *Police Officer's Quarterly*, and *The Backup*. He is also a member of the Police Writers Association, a very supportive writers' group for anyone affiliated with any type of law enforcement organization.

In his spare time (what little there is) John enjoys reading, fishing, and most of all, spending time with his family.

You can keep track of John's work on his author website:

http://www.writers-exchange.com/John-Schembrea.html

OTHER BOOKS IN THIS GENRE YOU MIGHT ENJOY

95 BRAVO
By Larry Deibert

It is 1970, and the United States is still deeply bogged down in the quagmire known as Vietnam.

Greg Taylor, a rural bred Pennsylvanian, finds himself becoming yet another cog in the massive military machine known as the US Army.

My novel follows him from the dehumanizing nine weeks of basic training, through his six month stint as a Military Policeman at Aberdeen Proving Grounds, Maryland, and then to his ten plus month tour of duty in Vietnam and ends when he first visits the Vietnam Memorial in Washington, D.C., in 1985.

He has several hair-raising adventures at APG, before he receives his orders for Vietnam, and once he is there, in a relatively secure area, finds that the war can claim victims anywhere in the country, even in so called safe areas.

After one near-death experience, he meets a young army nurse, one that he had a crush on several years before, and though fraternization between officers and enlisted personnel is strictly taboo, they find a way to continue their love affair and look forward to the day they will be back in the states as man and wife.

This novel gives the reader an overview of the Military Police mission, and also shows the frustrations shared by the men and women who served there.

You can learn more about this novel on the book page:
http://www.writers-exchange.com/95-Bravo.html

Made in the USA
Lexington, KY
18 September 2013